From This Day Forward

Anne Louise Bannon

HH
Healcroft House, Publishers
Altadena, California

ISBN: 978-1-948616-35-5

Library of Congress Control Number: 2023918327

Contents

Acknowledgements

I will confess, most of this particular book sprang forth from my fevered brain without having to do a lot of research and the like. That being said, Diana Mathur helped with the skiing scenes – thank you, Diana.

Thanks always go to my two favorite editors, Carol Louise Wilde and Meredith Taylor. I'd be dead in the water without you, whether you're offering comments or simply support. Both are critical.

Then there is my Repair Cafe Pasadena/Altadena community. Thank you guys for your creativity, general support, and pulling my head into a space that isn't dominated by my latest work in progress.

Finally, there are the two people without whom, I cannot write. Michael Holland, beloved husband and cheerleader. Corrie Ann Klarner, wonderful daughter and the perfect sounding board.

To my own little family, Michael and Corrie

Prologue

To Breanna, 4/27/02

    Topic of the Day: What else???
My dearest, sweetest Breanna -
In just over fourteen hours from now, you and I will finally be jumping the broom. I can't believe it. I know it's going to be one really long day, but I can't sleep, I'm so excited.

I was so happy when Mom, your mom, and Aunt Mae gave us that picture album tonight. I did tell you that Grandma Wycherly and Stella gave Mom and Dad one on the night before their wedding, right?

You know, the funny thing is, all I can think about right now is not ours or Mom and Dad's wedding, but a few days the week before, when Mom officially adopted me. It was the first part of us becoming legally a family. As Dad said, it was a day that changed nothing and changed everything at the same time.

It wasn't like we didn't know it was coming. The lawyer had called sometime in January - I don't remember when. Hell, I had turned thirteen only a couple weeks before the adoption. We had a court date the Wednesday before the wedding for the hearing. I knew the judge was going to call me to the stand, and I was really nervous. Both Mom and

Dad told me not to worry. All I had to do was be respectful, but honest. I kinda knew how to do that.

Mom and Dad got me from school just before noon that day. My teacher, Mrs. Fleming, seemed relieved. Well, I was pretty antsy that week and pretty much on the ceiling that day. Our case was the last on the docket, but that meant we needed to be at the courthouse by two that afternoon. I changed into a suit and Mom got picture after picture of Dad and me, as he taught me how to tie my tie. Mom had on a nice navy-blue dress and her aquamarine necklace and earrings. She always wears the aquamarines when it's special, and you can bet she'll be wearing them tomorrow.

At the courthouse, the judge was a lady. Okay, we were still phrasing it that way. She was nice. I later heard there had been a favor involved in getting us an adoption even though Mom and Dad weren't technically married at that point.

The judge first asked me how I felt about Mom adopting me. Like that was hard. I was totally down with it and said so.

"We're going to be a real family now," I said.

"Because you have a mom and a dad?"

I laughed. "No! I had a real family with my first mom and my grandma. It's just making Dad, my second mom, and me a real family, you know? I mean, we didn't start out that way, and now we are one. It's cool."

The judge laughed (please, do not ask me what her name was - I do not remember). But then she asked why my parents weren't changing my last name.

"It's because it's my first mom's name," I told her. "That's important, too. My second mom isn't less a mom because she's the second one. That's just when she came into my life.

My first mom is important and so is my second mom. And it's, like, really cool that none of us has the same last name."

"I see," the judge said. "And you're taking both your parents' names as your middle names?"

"I never had a middle name before," I said. "Now, I've got two. That's, like, amazingly righteous, isn't it?"

The judge laughed. "I believe so."

I don't remember what else she asked me, but she seemed happy. In any case, she approved the adoption. There wasn't much cheering. Only Mom and Dad were in the hearing room with our attorney because it was a court hearing. We got a picture of us with the judge. And the rest of the family was waiting for us with flowers and balloons at a restaurant closer to our place. Aunt Mae and Uncle Neil were there, with all the cousins, except Lissy. She wasn't born yet. Sy and Stella were there and Grandma and Grandpa Wycherly.

Mom and I exchanged presents. It's weird that I don't remember what she gave me. But I do remember what I picked out for her. It was a gold necklace with one of those gold charms that said, "World's Best Mom."

Yeah, I'd kind of set the next part up with Darby when I showed him the necklace the week before. It was based on the shit he gave me, but I'm really glad we did.

"I've got the best mom ever!" I told Mom.

The O'Malley kids protested.

"Nuh-uh!" they screamed in one voice. "We've got the best mom!"

Aunt Mae totally blushed, but she really loved it. You know, she kinda needed it.

It's like I keep telling you. Whatever barriers Mom and Dad have had to put up to keep us safe, they have invited you in. You are now part of us. I know how scary that is. Hell, I've been living with it since I was twelve. But it's kept me close to Mom and Dad, and I hope will keep us close, as well.

Invitation

C ome share our joy...

You are cordially invited to be with us as our daughter, Lisa Jane Wycherly, is joined with Sid Edward Hackbirn in Holy Matrimony to be celebrated at a noon mass on March 1, 1986... Mr. and Mrs. William T. Wycherly.

March 1, 1986

I looked at the readout on the digital clock next to the guest room bed at my sister's house. 3:06 a.m. Sighing helplessly, I flopped back onto the bed. It was getting better. I'd been checking the clock at regular intervals almost since I'd landed there around midnight or so.

I had kind of figured it was going to be a little hard to sleep that night, one of the reasons I was so glad we'd gotten back to my sister's place so late the night before. I hadn't realized it was going to be impossible. I tried desperately not to think about why. I squeezed my eyes shut and pushed my mind back to the weeks and months before. The sound of poker chips landing in the center of a table caught my attention. It had been two weeks before…

(Friday, February 21)

My dear friend Esther Nguyen was hosting the party in her duplex. I sat next to my sister, Mae, with Esther, Kathy Deiner, Angelique Carter, Sarah Williams, and Sister Maria Campos. Mae had warned the others that playing poker with me could be a losing proposition. However, the stack of chips I had in front of me was modest at best. Maria seemed to be cashing in that night.

"You gonna bet?" Esther demanded as Maria gazed, unseeing, at her cards.

The two tiny dogs owned by Esther's roommate, and, okay, boyfriend, Frank Lonnergan, sat at Kathy's feet, whining for a snack. Coco and Reilly had already tried suckering Mae and me and didn't get very far.

"Give me a minute." Maria is rounded with dark black hair and was wearing civvies that night.

My eyes narrowed slightly. If Maria was putting that much thought into her bet, her cards were probably okay, but not great.

"One pair, two pair, three of a kind, straight, flush, full house," Sarah chanted almost under her breath. She had never played poker before. Mae and I had taught her the chant so that she could remember what beat what. Unfortunately, that also made her much harder to read. Sarah's brown hair fell into her long face. She was also almost six months pregnant at that point. "One pair, two pair..."

"Who invited her?" Esther growled. She's medium height with a round face and black hair cut short. Her fortunes, so to speak, were at a low ebb at that point, and if she was staying in the game, it had little to do with what was in her hand.

"You did," said Kathy, a tall Black woman with closely cropped black hair and rich, dark chocolate skin. "Don't be so touchy."

"You got nothing to worry about," Esther grumbled. "You're not on budget. I still got to support Frank."

If Mae, Angelique, and Maria didn't know that Frank and Esther had become a couple, it was because they weren't that close to them. Frank and Esther had moved from just being friends into full couple hood some months before. But since they seldom said so, almost no one knew they had.

"Jesse said he'd back you," Kathy replied. Jesse is Kathy's husband. She blinked and pressed her lips together, which meant she didn't have much in her hand.

"If he won't, Sid will," I said. I could say things like that because Sid and I had merged our assets over a year before. "He's already backing Mae and Maria."

"I'll bet three," said Maria. Definitely holding something that was okay, but not great.

"Three," Sarah mumbled. She usually added to the pot whether she had anything or not. It was annoying, really, but I did have to cut her some slack.

Mae sighed. "Three, huh?" She didn't have squat. She looked at me. "Are you sure you can afford this?"

I laughed. "Of course. I never gamble more than I can afford to lose. Let's see. We're at three thousand, right?"

Mae groaned and promptly folded. "I told you not to tell me how much we're playing for."

"I'll see your three." I tossed in the chips. "And raise it five." I figured that would be enough to get Maria and Kathy to fold, and with Sarah adding to the pot, no matter what, I'd be good. "Kathy?"

Kathy laid her cards down. "I'm out. Your bet, Esther."

Esther cursed and folded.

"How much are we playing for?" Mae asked suspiciously. Truth be told, she had reason for her suspicion.

"I'll never tell." I winked at Kathy.

"I don't want to know!" Mae yelped. She was about five months pregnant, herself.

"Are you sure about that?" Angelique teased. She'd folded during the first round of betting.

We were playing penny ante, but we were letting Mae think we were playing for a whole lot more.

"Five, huh?" Maria glared at her cards. She went for it. "I'm in. Sarah?"

"Oh, gee. Alright." Sarah threw in the red chip, but I knew she would.

"Why don't you want to know, Mae?" Maria asked.

"It's Sid's fault," Mae said. "Show 'em, Lisa."

"Eight high straight." I grinned, laying my cards on the table.

Maria sighed. "Beats me."

"One pair, two pair, three of a kind..." Sarah showed her hand. "Did I lose?"

"Yes, Sarah," Esther growled.

I pulled in the chips. "Your deal, Maria. Ante up."

I tossed the white chip into the middle of the table.

"It's Sid's fault I don't want to know," Mae said again as Maria shuffled. "We went to Las Vegas at the beginning of the month to celebrate Neil's birthday." Neil is Mae's husband. "Anyway, I don't remember which casino we were at, but Sid was playing roulette and I went over to see how he was doing. So, he hands me his chips and tells me he's tired of playing this penny ante stuff." Okay, Sid probably had used a naughtier term. "And that I should play some for him. So, I did, and I won. I gave Sid back his chips and a few extra, then cashed in mine and nearly fainted. I'd been playing with a hundred- and five-hundred-dollar chips. The way he'd been talking, I thought I was playing with dollar chips at most. I came away with almost six-thousand dollars. That's why I don't want to know what we're playing for. Sid may be backing me, but if I think I'm dropping hundreds of dollars, I'll be a nervous wreck."

"So, we're playing five-card draw, jacks or better," Maria announced, dealing with a suspiciously deft hand. "Sarah, do you have a pair of jacks or better?"

"Um. One pair, two pair... No."

"I'll open for one," Angelique said. She has full, dark brown hair, and a model's figure, and had probably not much more than a pair of jacks in her hand.

"I'm in," said Mae. It was possibly optimistic. I could usually count on Mae to stay in until we'd gotten our second set of cards.

I had a pair of queens, which wasn't great, but worth staying in for. The others stayed in as well.

"This is really interesting," Sarah said while the rest of us bet. "I hope Dan doesn't mind."

"How many cards do you want?" Maria asked.

"Um. Oh. I think I want one." Sarah tossed the card she didn't want, then pulled in the one Maria dealt her. "Dan was so upset when we took Kathy to that male strip show."

"Why did you tell him?" Esther snarled, still not happy about what was in her hand.

Angelique took three cards. She had little more than a pair of jacks. Mae took two, which showed some optimism. I guessed that she was trying to fill out a straight. She liked doing that.

"You took Kathy to a strip joint?" Maria grinned. "I would have loved to have seen that. How many cards do you want, Lisa?"

"Two."

Maria dealt them. "Dang. I wish I was part of this group then. Esther?"

"Three. It's no fun taking Lisa. She don't get that embarrassed." Esther probably had a pair of something worthwhile.

"Sid took me a year ago," I explained. "I got past that. The rest was easy."

Esther rolled her eyes. "Besides, it's no big deal. You don't see anything more than when I caught Frank in his briefs."

"I wouldn't know," I said, chuckling. "Sid wears silk boxer shorts."

Angelique smirked, because she knew what kind of underwear Sid wears. "And how do you know Sid wears silk boxer shorts?"

I grinned. "I do his laundry sometimes."

Okay, I also saw Sid pretty much every morning in his skivvies. The reality was that if I was still a virgin, it was only because Sid and I had not had full sexual intercourse yet. But the heavy petting we'd been engaging in made that more of a technicality than a reality. I couldn't help blushing.

"Angelique," Sarah sighed. "That's not very nice."

Angelique shrugged. "Hey, it's no big deal."

I grinned. "Really, Sarah. Sid's past does not bother me. Mostly because it's in the past."

Angelique laughed. "And you will reap the benefit of his past antics."

Okay. Sid had been pretty, well... Loose. He believed in free love. That had been how he was raised, and until our relationship had gone in a more, shall we say, traditional mode, he'd seen no reason not to sleep around. Yes, I'm religious, and yes, I do believe that sex works better within a committed, exclusive relationship. Sid had agreed to that, so I was willing to go along with a looser definition of what constituted marriage. But the real reason there hadn't been full intercourse had little to do with our respective values. As much as I loved the women around that table that night, I really wasn't up to explaining why we were only into seriously heavy petting and not the real thing.

I looked at my cards. "I'll call. Besides, you don't have to see Sid in his undies to know that he wouldn't wear briefs. They would spoil the line of his pants."

The others laughed.

"You only have two more weeks," Angelique said with an evil grin. Of all the women there, she had a better idea of what my wedding night was going to be like than any of them. Well, she had been one of Sid's more preferred girlfriends, back when both were prone to sleeping around.

"I'm raising three," said Maria. Hm. She had something. "You getting nervous, Lisa?"

"About what?" I smiled. I was holding triple queens. Definitely worth staying in for, especially after that last pot.

"About wedding night," Esther said, rolling her eyes.

"That, I'm looking forward to," I said and laughed. "You know, I am so glad you guys finally got around to this party."

Kathy shook her head. "After that disaster of a shower."

"I'm so sorry about that!" Sarah groaned. "I can't believe I fell for Janet and Sylvia's plan."

I smiled at her softly. "Sarah, it wasn't your fault. You were trying to be nice. I hadn't told you how much I hate showers, nor that Sid is fixed. So, how were you going to know there aren't going to be any babies?"

Sarah rolled her eyes. "Okay, maybe about Sid's surgery. But still. I could have at least asked you if you wanted a shower."

Kathy snorted. "Why those two keep assuming everyone wants the same things they do." She shook her head. "Sarah, it's not your fault. They can be pretty convincing. Still. I can only hope that Lisa telling them what for made an impression."

I shrugged. "We may never know. I'm practically the last to get married."

"You seemed to enjoy the youth group shower," Maria said with a laugh.

"What I want to know," Esther said. "Is where you got that thing you gave her, Maria?"

"I confiscated it from an eighth grader," Maria said. She was the principal of the parish school.

"Oh, that!" I blushed even as I caught my breath. "Sid told me what it was for. Maria, did you know?"

"Of course." Maria shrugged. "How do you think I knew to confiscate it? I call. Sarah, whatcha got?"

"I'm not sure." Sarah put her cards on the table. "I think it's either a straight or a flush."

"Ten-high straight flush!" Esther groaned. "And she only drew one card. Who invited her?"

"Does this mean I win?" Sarah asked.

The rest of us groaned.

4:16 a.m. I tossed again. My Grandma Caulfield snored gently in the bed across the room from me. Mama and Daddy were in the other guest room on the ground floor of Mae and Neil's house. In the corner of the room I was in, a long white dress made of lace with a silk underdress hung. I'd made it months before for this very day. I didn't want to think about that. I pushed my mind to earlier, to the second week of January.

(Wednesday, January 8)

Why Sid and I had been sent to Tijuana had both of us wondering. After all, the super-secret organization that we work for, Operation Quickline, is strictly domestic. If we needed or wanted to leave the country, it usually took a few days to a week to get it approved. But the orders were clear. There was a pickup of some importance that needed to be made in the small city across the Mexican border.

Well, no surprise. It wasn't that simple. We had dressed down. Sid is usually a stickler for business dress during working hours, but in this case, we'd needed to look like tourists. So, he was wearing an Aran Isles sweater over a sport shirt and his incredibly tight jeans. I had on a cotton sweater over an oxford shirt and less tight jeans. We both had our armored running shoes on that had all sorts of interesting tools and weapons hidden in the soles, but we didn't have to resort to them, so that's irrelevant. We'd also taken my truck because Sid's Beemer was getting its usual tune-up that day.

The shop was filled with chess sets made of varying colors of onyx and looked reasonably innocuous. I was grateful that the pickup did not involve one of the full chess sets, but merely an onyx rook. I was even more grateful for the rook when we realized that we'd been made almost the second we'd left the shop.

The reality of the spy biz is that people try to follow you, and if you're expecting it, it's easy to spot. This tail was weird, though. For one thing, he (or she, we couldn't really tell) was particularly persistent. We got to my Datsun four by four pick up without trouble, still the tail was there. As we pulled out from the parking lot, we quickly realized a Chevy Impala was not only following us but sticking close and not trying to back off.

"What on earth?" I asked as we waited in the back up to get across the border.

Sid shrugged. "I have no idea. Why don't we see what happens when we get back inside the U.S.?"

As if that helped. The Impala seemed even more determined to follow my bumper, even as I pressed the accelerator and hurried up Interstate 5.

"I can't shake him!" I groaned as we sped through San Diego County. I glanced at Sid. "We could go off-road."

He sighed. "Looks like our best chance."

We had to wait until we got to Orange County. We switched freeways, then drove into the Saddleback Hills after getting off the freeway. The Impala hung close. I eventually pulled through a fence into the scrub, drove a bit, then stopped and switched the truck to four-wheel drive. Sid noted the coordinates on the compass that dangled from my rear-view mirror and wrote them down as we changed directions. The Impala got stuck right at the end of the road, but Sid and I both agreed that getting far enough away that we couldn't be seen was the preferred option.

It would have been the perfect solution except that my engine died just beyond the first set of hills.

"What's the matter?" Sid asked, his voice tight with tension.

I rolled my eyes. "We're out of gas."

"What?"

"Four-wheeling is hard on the mileage, Sid."

He cursed and opened the glove compartment. "Alright. We'd better radio for help."

As if that was going to help. The sun's bottom edge was already touching the horizon, not to mention the bank of clouds moving in from the ocean to the west. We got no answer from the radio. I gathered what bits of wood I could find to build a fire. Sid sighed deeply.

He is so handsome. His hair is dark and wavy, his eyes bright blue, and he has the sweetest dimple in his chin. His beard was already coming in - he usually shaves twice a day because of it. And while he's not a large man, barely three inches taller than me and I'm average, he still has enough grace and style to outshine much larger men. He is, however, a total urbanite. Outdoor skills? Those are my specialty. Still, he made the effort.

The only problem was when he picked up a stick and I heard the deadly rattle. Thank God, Sid froze. I whipped my snub-nosed pistol out of the holster in the back of my pants and nailed both snakes before Sid realized what was going on. He stepped back, just a touch shaken.

"Okay," he sighed. "That was close."

"No kidding." I walked over and picked up the dead reptiles. "Lucky for us, they must have been hibernating. On the other hand, we've got dinner."

"Really?" Sid looked at me. I couldn't quite tell if he was appalled or interested.

I grinned. "Sure. Rattlers are great eating. Come on, Sid. You eat escargot and calamari."

He sighed. "But they are easier to deal with as escargot and calamari rather than snails and squid."

"Picky, picky, picky."

Sid can be pretty picky about what he eats, but he has an adventurous streak, and I knew it. So, I'm fairly sure he knew I was just teasing him. [Yeah, I got that. Still wasn't sure about the snake, though. - SEH] He helped build the fire, although I was in charge of dressing the snakes. They roasted up nicely, and Sid admitted that they were surprisingly tasty. Thank God, I had some salt, pepper, and garlic powder rolling around in the back of my truck.

After we ate, we tried the radio again and got an answer. The problem was that between the approaching bad weather and the dark, we were going to have to wait to be rescued. That made sense. We would have been impossible to spot in the dark, not to mention the rain headed our way. We'd already asked our good friends Jesse and Kathy to pick up our son, Nick, at school. The man on the radio said that he'd get Kathy and Jesse the message that we were alright, but Nick should spend the night with them. It wasn't the best option. Nick really got worried when Sid and I had to leave him. But there was little else we could do. I gathered several decent-sized rocks and anchored them around the wheels of my truck and prayed there wouldn't be any flash flooding. As the first drops fell, I slid the carpeted floor pieces in the truck's shell onto the lips of the side cabinets to make one level space. Sid got in first, then pulled me in after him.

He got his contact lens kit out of my purse – he usually keeps one in his suit jacket because he sometimes gets stuff in his eyes. Only since he wasn't wearing a jacket, he'd asked me to carry it. He's very nearsighted and while he has the soft lenses that he can sleep in, he can't do it very often and it's better if he takes them out at night.

"Do you still have those blankets in that compartment?" he asked.

"Of course." I opened the space in the side cabinet. "Here you go."

"Great." Sid pulled open the lid to the opposite cabinet. "And I've just remembered we have something else. A nice little sauvignon blanc that didn't get opened during our ski trip after Christmas."

I looked at him, frowning. "We didn't have a corkscrew."

Sid chuckled. "I know. But I made a point of remedying that when we got back." He opened the window to the truck's cab and reached through to the glove compartment in the dashboard and opened it. "Alas, we have no glasses, but I think we can make do."

I couldn't help laughing. "Only you could make a disaster a romantic encounter."

"Only you could make a disaster livable." He smiled softly at me, then reached over and kissed my lips. "And after we've had our little drink, I think I want dessert."

My breath caught. He wasn't talking about food or wine. The one nice thing about being in the middle of nowhere was that there was no one to complain about how noisy we got.

The next morning, a helicopter from the Marine base to the south set down near us and the guy on board left us with several cans of gasoline and directions to the freeway. Not that I entirely needed the directions. Sid and I got back to our house in Beverly Hills before noon. Kathy and Jesse had left a message that they'd gotten Nick to school that day.

We had an hour or so after showering to look at the onyx chess piece before we had to get Nick from school. Sure enough, the bottom of the piece had a tiny flap that opened and inside was a canister of thirty-five-millimeter film. Sid cursed.

"This is unprocessed," he complained. "It's how I used to send stuff out when I was in 'Nam."

"So, what do we do with it?"

He shook his head. "Call Henry, I guess."

Henry James is our immediate supervisor and a good friend. In fact, he was one of Sid's groomsmen for our wedding coming up. The weird thing was, when Sid called him, he wasn't the least bit surprised. However, we had to wait until the next day to see him. In the meantime, Jesse, who had been recently recruited into our side business (which is how we usually referred to Quickline) and is a photographer, developed the film in the canister we'd been given. The documents on the film had something to do with nuclear missiles, but what, we weren't sure.

When we got to Henry's office in the Federal building in Westwood - Henry is a public information officer for the FBI in addition to supervising our line and a couple of other top-secret programs - Henry looked at the prints and nodded. He's a tall man with a bright red face. His office was the standard, although next to his desk was a large map of the United States that hung on the wall. I was a little shocked when he tugged at the bottom of the map, and it rolled into the bar mounted on the wall over it. Underneath was a similar map, with four brightly colored lines connecting several cities.

"That's a map of Quickline," Sid said. He looked at me, then Henry with a puzzled frown. "So, why are we looking at it now?"

"You'll find out soon enough." Henry looked at the map and adjusted a couple of numbered pins. "The genius of the system is that no stop is more than two hours away from another stop, so that our couriers can make a pickup or drop within an eight-hour time frame and otherwise lead normal lives. It's like I told Sid last summer. We have several operatives who have spouses and children who have no clue how they support their families." He looked at us and grinned. "We're going to be making a few changes in the system, so you two will want to watch this. Most of what we get goes to the number ten stop on all the lines."

"New York City." Sid nodded. "I remember from when I was doing running."

"Why not Washington, D.C.?" I asked.

"Langley, actually," Henry said, then rolled his eyes. "Our Company contacts don't want us going directly to their HQ."

The Company was how we referred to the CIA, when we weren't using ruder terms. [Central Incompetent Assholes being the nicest. - SEH]

"However," Henry continued. "This is more relevant to Division Twelve Theta's mission, and they're close to the Yellow Four stop in Great Falls, Montana."

I'd never heard of Twelve-T before, but that didn't mean anything. The divisions are the smaller shadow organizations within the FBI and CIA, organizations so secret mostly only their members know they exist. Quickline is Fifty-Three-Q. That doesn't mean there are fifty-three or more different organizations. The numbering schemes made no sense to me, and I was beginning to suspect that it was random. [And then some, as we later found out. - SEH]

Henry used his finger to map out a route on the map. "You'll need to have Red Dawn process these onto a microdot, then you can package it however you like. But send him over to Blue Three, then it can be pushed to the Blue Four stop, then Yellow Four, who will deliver it to the Twelve-T contact."

Sid and I nodded. That part of the process was familiar because that's mostly what we did. We'd get a package usually from someone on one of the other lines, then send it on to the next address on the package. Okay, we also did the occasional investigation, and other chores, too.

5:01 a.m. At least, we were in striking distance of dawn. I laid back and closed my eyes. I had spent most of the last couple months before worrying about details including the guest list, menus, dresses, wedding favors (was I really the only person in the world who liked Jordan almonds?), music for the reception, music for the mass, who needed to be where when (and in some cases wishing said relative wouldn't be there). What I had not had time for was dealing with my very real ambivalence about being married. It wasn't Sid. I would have been perfectly happy with the commitment we had and just living together, except for my religious beliefs. Marriage is a Sacrament in the Catholic Church, and I wanted that for us, even though Sid is an atheist. Sid respected that, which is why we were doing the church thing. The rest of it, well, Sid and I had wanted to celebrate our love for each other with our families and friends. Mama had wanted a full matrimonial blow-out, and she wasn't the only one.

I didn't want to think about that, however, and the sound of women chattering in the living room of Sarah Williams' apartment filled my brain.

(Thursday, February 13)

The living room in the older building was sparsely furnished, but chairs were scattered in a circle around the couch. Sarah's husband Dan, who is also the youth minister at our church, had been banned, and I was grateful for that. Dan is militantly anti-alcohol, and while I don't drink much, I do like a glass of wine occasionally and at that point, sorely needed one.

Janet Weinstock and Sylvia Perez had convinced Sarah that it would totally hurt my feelings if there wasn't a wedding shower for me, and a surprise one at that. Janet and Sylvia had forgotten that at the last surprise party in my honor, a year before, I'd gotten kidnapped by members of a Colombian drug cartel. The worst of it was I'd forgotten to remind both Janet and Sylvia that I absolutely did not want a wedding shower. There had been a blowup at Irene

Sanchez's baby shower about three and a half months before, and I'd foolishly thought that would have gotten through to them. So had Kathy and Esther. That Janet and Sylvia decided to surprise Kathy and Esther, as well as me, should have been a big hint that a shower would not be welcome. Sarah told us she wanted to have a quick dinner meeting that Thursday night.

I hate showers in general. I am not a very domesticated woman. Yes, I sew and knit, but that's as domesticated as I get. When Sid first hired me as his associate in the spy biz, he'd needed to keep me under twenty-four-hour surveillance, so I'd moved into his house. I stayed because he had (and still has) a housekeeper. I hate housework and cooking. If the ever-wonderful Conchetta Ramirez isn't around to cook for us, Sid does the cooking because he likes it and is a much better cook than me.

So, naturally, Janet and Sylvia had to make this shower a kitchen shower.

"You love to eat so much," Sylvia said.

I smiled and poured a full glass of wine. She had a point. Me? I was still shaking from the surprise. A buffet of mini tacos and mini burritos had been set out on the dining room table, along with a couple of salads and some chips and overly lemony guacamole. The spiciest thing on the table was a small dish of pickled jalapenos, which was something.

Janet laughed as I dished several of the peppers onto my plate. "You'd better be careful with those, Lisa. They're really hot."

I looked over at Esther, who shrugged. The jalapenos were warm, but not the tonsil searing experience Esther and I enjoyed.

"Thanks, Janet," I said.

The table had been decorated with cutesy and saccharine potholders. Esther picked up a round one and annoyed the heck out of Janet by trying to make it fly like a Frisbee. Kathy caught the potholder and put it back on the table. She was not in a good mood, either. I kept smiling as if I was fine. I have to be pretty good at hiding my stress. It's how I stay alive sometimes. It didn't help.

Esther grabbed another potholder to toss.

"Pull!" I muttered.

Esther tossed and Kathy watched as my eyes followed the flying potholder until it hit its apex.

"Pow!" I hissed.

Kathy chuckled. "I'm glad your purse is in the other room."

"I don't want to put bullet holes in Sarah's ceiling."

Kathy looked at me. "Are you going to be okay?"

"Yeah." I took another sip of wine. "It's not their fault, Kathy. They really don't know me that well, and I don't make it easy for them."

"I know." Kathy sighed.

She knew why I didn't make it easy to know me. She had the same problem. When her husband, Jesse, had been recruited into the side business that previous fall, Kathy had become part of it, too.

As soon as everyone had some food, Janet handed out sheets of paper for our first game - unscrambling kitchen words. I debated crushing my sheet into a ball, but went along with it. Esther made dirty words out of her list, and I wished I'd thought of that. To make things worse, several of the words referred to appliances that hadn't been part of a modern kitchen since before most of us were born. I mean, really. What's a dripolater? Kathy won the game and got a teacup.

"Now, we'll play Kitchen Bingo," Janet announced.

"I'm not playing that," Esther said loudly.

Half the room looked shocked and disappointed. The other half looked relieved. [Let me guess which half you were on. - SEH] I got up and got another glass of wine.

"Um, Janet, why don't we just open gifts now?" I asked, coming back into the living room. "I've got to be up early tomorrow for work."

"Oh. Alright."

I smiled, even though I was not looking forward to opening gifts, either. "Sarah, can I borrow a pair of scissors, please?"

"Of course." Sarah grabbed a pair from Dan's desk at the back of the room and handed them to me.

It's an old joke that the number of ribbons a bride breaks at her wedding shower will be the number of children she'll have. I'd had a feeling that Janet and Sylvia had nicked the ribbons on the packages to make them break more easily. I did not want to deal with breaking ribbons.

"Don't you want to know how many children you're going to have?" Sylvia giggled.

Something snapped inside me. "I already know how many children I'm going to have." My voice shook a little as I glared at Sylvia and Janet. "I have one, and he is all I'm going to have."

"And he's not even yours," someone said, supposedly in sympathy.

The women drew back uncomfortably and even scared as I scoured the room for the person who'd said that.

"I may not be the woman who gave birth to him, but Nick is just as much my son as if I were," I snarled, blinking back tears. I turned on Janet and Sylvia. "And there aren't going to be any more. Sid and I can't have kids."

Janet trembled. "Why didn't you say anything?"

"Because I don't want people feeling sorry for me and not talking about babies around me and treating me with kid gloves." I sniffed. "That just makes it worse." I swallowed and got a good sip of wine. "Now. I'm cutting the ribbons off, and that will be the end of it." I took a deep breath. "I'm sorry about the fuss."

"That's alright, Lisa," said Erin MacArthur. "Every bride is allowed a good breakdown."

Sadly, I got in another one. I tried to appreciate the gifts. But the reality is that I get as bored watching Sid wander through Williams Sonoma as he does watching me in a fabric store. I opened a box filled with round mesh screens with handles on them in three sizes and frowned, then smiled and thanked Susie Talbot for them. Irene Sanchez began chuckling.

The next box was really heavy. Inside was an orange enameled Dutch oven.

"Huh," I said. "My mom used to have one of these."

Both Erin and Irene started laughing.

"You don't know what that is, do you?" Erin said, giggling.

"It's a Dutch oven," I said, blushing. "I see them in the stores sometimes."

Kathy shook her head. "That's a premium Dutch oven. Enameled cast iron by Le Creuset."

"How thoughtful of you, Diana." I smiled at the woman who'd given it to me. "Sid will love it."

"You don't cook much, do you?" Irene asked.

I tried to smile. "I can follow a recipe as well as the next person." The women all looked at me. I sighed. "But, no, I don't cook very much. I don't want to hurt anybody's feelings. These are wonderful gifts and I'm sure Sid will love them. I'm just not much of a cook." The tears started flowing again. "Or anything else you guys expect me to be."

Kathy put her arms around my shoulders. "It's alright, Lisa."

Erin slid over next to me on my other side. "Of course, it's alright, Lisa. You're much more interesting this way."

Sarah and Irene also got it. Suzy was on the fringes. The rest of the room, I had my doubts about. Certainly, Janet and Sylvia couldn't figure me out. We finished unwrapping presents, while I told everyone how happy they'd make Sid, which it turned out they did. [That was one nice haul. - SEH] There were gourmet cookbooks, including one with gorgeous photographs featuring recipes from Italy. Erin had packaged it with a tall cake pan with a latch on the side. She'd also bookmarked the recipe for a timbalo that the pan went with.

The party ended soon after. Janet made sure that I got all the potholders that had been used as decorations, then left.

"You doing okay?" Esther asked, as she, Erin, Irene, Kathy, and I helped Sarah clean up.

I shrugged. "All the reasons why I didn't want to get married." I sighed. "I guess I still don't."

Sarah looked worried. "Are you and Sid fighting?"

"Not any more than usual." I blinked my eyes. "It's not him at all. It's being married. You know, the expectation that I'll be doing the cooking. That I'll change my name. That I don't like hot sauce." I frowned at the stack of potholders. "How many of those are there?"

"I counted twenty-five," Esther said.

I half-smiled. "That's a box of shells."

Kathy got it, but the others didn't. The next morning, Kathy and I took the potholders to the firing range. Each of us had a twelve-gauge shotgun and a box of ammo. We took turns throwing the potholders in the air for each other, and by the time we had blasted every last potholder to smithereens, we still had half a box of shells left. I hadn't had so much fun shooting in years.

5:25 a.m., just a few minutes shy of regular wake up time. I didn't have to be up for another couple hours and would have happily slept in. But there was no point in trying to sleep that morning. I sat up and swung my legs over to the edge of the bed. Sid would never have believed it, but I wasn't hungry. [You're right. That almost never happens. – SEH] I started wondering what Sid was doing. Probably getting ready to go running. He's usually up around five and nudging me awake by five-thirty. I am not a morning person, and he is. We usually run together with Nick and my dog Motley every morning except on Sundays. Sundays, I sleep in. He still runs.

Truth be told, I probably like complaining about running more than I, in fact, hate it, but it is not my favorite activity. It is necessary, which is why I end up doing it every morning. That morning, I found the running suit that Sid had packed in my overnight bag and put it and my regular running shoes on. I slid the last bit of cash from my wallet into my pants. Grandma continued to snore. I slipped outside the room and in the semi-darkness, made my way out to the front of the house. I stretched in the driveway of Mae and Neil's house in North Pasadena. The air was just a touch nippy, and I happily sucked it into my lungs. I headed east down the street a block or two, then headed north two more blocks, then east again. I only heard it in my head, but there was a phone ringing…

(Monday, February 24)

Sid and I were in our office that Monday, the last week before the wedding. It was my day to answer the phones, and when the call came through from Dr. Kline's office, I didn't have to put her on hold. I put the call on the speakerphone.

"Dr. Kline," Sid said. "Good to hear from you."

We were both holding our breath.

"The test came back negative. You're clean," said her soothing voice. "I told you last October."

"We still didn't know," Sid said.

"We do now." Dr. Kline chuckled. "It's like I told you, Sid. Seven months seemed to be the longest. On the other hand, all the data and everything else I've seen strongly suggests that the virus shows up in the bloodstream before six months. It's been almost a year since your last possible exposure. You do not have the AIDS virus."

Sid closed his eyes. "Thank you."

"You may now fornicate in peace," Dr. Kline said. "But please make sure you are covered."

"That won't be an issue, Doctor." Sid smiled at me. "I seem to be settling into the old married man thing."

She laughed. "Oh, that's right. Well, do both yourself and Lisa a favor and stay out of trouble."

"That is my plan."

Sid said goodbye and switched off the phone.

"Yes!" I yelped. "I told you. I told you we were clear!"

"I don't care." Sid held his hands up. "It was not worth the risk of infecting you."

I tried not to roll my eyes and didn't quite succeed. "You know what this means. Full sexual intercourse."

"Yeah." Sid grinned, then winced and sighed. "There is one problem. I want to deflower you without having to worry about recharging, and when are we going to have the time?"

"What do you mean?" Yeah, I was upset. I'd been waiting for this for months.

It was part of the compromise. Sid had given up sleeping around for my sake, no matter how willingly. I was allowing for a looser definition of marriage on my end. I mean, why not? Sid and I had already promised our lifetime commitment and fidelity to each other almost a year before. We were, for all intents and purposes, already married, with our assets mingled, raising our son, sharing our toiletries. If we weren't having full sex, it was because Sid did not want to risk infecting me after he'd found out he'd been potentially exposed to the AIDS virus.

Sid held up his forefinger. "We have barely an hour and a half before we need to leave to pick up Nick from school and get your parents and grandmother from the airport and bring them to your sister's place." He added the middle finger to the gesture. "Tomorrow, in the mid-morning, we pick up Stella and Sy from the airport, then spend all day shuttling them around to check out your nephew's training, plus whatever celebratory hilarity ensues from there, and we both know there will be plenty. Three, having Stella around is going to be a problem, because even if she doesn't come barging through any closed doors, she will knock until we answer, and that is not conducive to a pleasant first experience."

I couldn't help sulking. "And we've got the adoption hearing on Wednesday and the party after that, lunch with the parents on Thursday, plus your bachelor party that night. Maybe Friday morning."

Sid's eyebrow rose. "After a bachelor party?"

"Oh. Right." I sighed. "Sid, this is ridiculous. Why don't we just wait? It's only a few more days, and we can keep on with what we've been doing."

Sid laughed. "You mean, I actually get to deliver you to the altar pure and unstained?"

I shivered, thinking about what we'd been up to. "Maybe not so pure and unstained. Let's face it, Sid. If I'm still a virgin, it's merely on the technicality of no penetration."

Thanks to Sid's terror of exposing me to any of his bodily fluids beyond saliva (and it had been way too late for that one when we'd realized that he might have been exposed to the AIDS virus), there had been plenty of oral sex for me. Other creative measures for him.

He grinned at me. I could see him thinking about not having to wear his jeans to bed anymore. I bit my lip, then pushed him into my desk chair.

"What?" he asked.

"We've got at least an hour," I said. "We can celebrate a little bit."

"And what do you have in mind?" He groaned as I demonstrated. "Honey, do you know what you're doing?" He groaned again in ecstasy. "Crud, you do! Good gravy, you do!"

[Again, not what I actually said. – SEH]

I eventually headed south and down to Colorado Boulevard, then headed west along what I eventually realized was the route for the Rose Parade, thanks to the red stripe down the middle of the street. As I ran past the campus of the local community college, I checked my watch. Only a few more hours to go, which wasn't all that reassuring. I looked around at the stately buildings, then ran on, my brain filling with another event shortly after we'd returned from Tijuana.

(Monday, January 13)

It was a little odd that it was my pager that went off, rather than both Sid's and mine. We looked at each other and shrugged, and I returned the call, putting it on the speakerphone.

"I was told to ask for Big Red/Little Red," said the nervous voice on the other end of the line.

"What's your caller code?" I asked. Sid's eyebrow lifted.

The caller gave the right code. Still... "I've got some merchandise for you."

"Okay," I said. "Where are you?"

"Los Angeles."

"Where in Los Angeles?"

"I'd better not say."

I sighed. "Fine. When and where do you want to meet?"

"Can we do it tonight? And do you have a place?"

"Sure." I gave him the address of a place in Westwood. "Be there by eight-thirty. I'll be at the end of the bar. Ask for the person spring cleaning her fishbowl."

"I'd rather not talk to you."

I looked at Sid. He shrugged. "What's the code rating on this?"

"Rating?"

"Didn't you get you get a code and priority rating on this?"

"I just touched down from overseas. You got some way I can spot you?"

"Um. Sure. I'll be wearing a light blue velvet jacket with a wire ring brooch and sitting at the end of the bar under the TV."

"I'll drop it by eight-forty-five."

"Okay."

Sid and I shook our heads but went with it. Okay, we verified the call with the Dragon, the head of Quickline, and it was legit. We left Nick at home on his own. Well, he was just about to turn thirteen. That was old enough. He still wasn't thrilled about us leaving.

Just in case, Sid and I both went to the drop and did it wearing our transmitters. The TV in the bar had a soccer game on, I think. I slid onto a stool at the end, under the TV set. Sid had gone in ahead of me and was seated in a booth at the other end of the room. I heard a quiet cough in my ear and, likewise, coughed. The transmitters were up and functioning.

I ordered a glass of white wine, but as I did, I spotted three youngish women leaving the bar and walking over to Sid.

"Well, look who's here," said a deep, throaty voice in my ear. The woman I had to believe it belonged to was tall, model thin, and boasted full blond hair.

"Hello, Jenna." Sid's voice was just a hair cool but welcoming enough. "Oh, and Leslie and Cora. Nice to see you ladies. How are you?"

"Damn good," Jenna said.

Cora giggled. "Sheez, Sid. It's been eons. We've heard some nasty rumors."

"Such as?" Sid asked.

Leslie had a slight lisp. "Such as you've dropped out of the singles' scene."

Sid chuckled. "I'm afraid I have."

"You're kidding!" Leslie's voice all but screeched.

"Sid, are you serious?" Jenna asked. "Have you really dropped out?"

"Oh, yes." Sid's eyes caught mine, and he winked.

"But what happened?" Cora asked.

"I think you ladies know." Sid laughed.

Jenna groaned. "Oh, no. Not her."

Sid chuckled. "Absolutely her. In fact, I'm meeting her in a bit. You want to stick around and say hi?"

Jenna groaned again. "Really, Sid? Why would we want to stick around and say hi to your little ice cube?"

Sid's voice got on the tight side in spite of the jovial tone he used. "Lisa is no ice cube."

I checked my watch. It was eight-fifty. I sauntered over to the booth where Sid was hemmed in by the three women and turned off my transmitter as soon as I could hear them without it. Sid pushed the one I think was Leslie out of the booth to get up and greet me.

"Hey, love," he said, giving me a quick kiss. "I've got some old friends here. This is Jenna, Leslie, and Cora. And this is my fiancée, Lisa Wycherly."

"Fiancée?" Cora screeched. She was an overly made-up brunette.

I smiled. "Nice to meet you ladies."

Sid helped me into the booth.

Jenna looked at Sid, aghast. "Are you serious? You're getting married?"

Sid grinned. "On the first of March."

"I'll believe it when I see it." Leslie rolled her eyes.

"Give us your address and we'll invite you to do just that," Sid said.

He took charge of collecting the addresses, then helped me out of the booth. We said good night and left the bar.

Back at the house, I emptied my purse on my desk.

"He must have missed it," I grumbled, going through the several bits of paper that had been in my purse.

Sid shook his head and picked up one bit. "Lisa, this receipt is over a year old. For a pair of shoes."

I looked at it and shook my head. "Drat. Those fell apart months ago."

"Then why do you still have the receipt?"

"I don't know."

Sid sighed, dropped the receipt into the wastebasket, and began sorting all the bits of paper into piles. "Alright. Here's a list to pick up shirts, razor blades, soap, nail polish..." He groaned. "This is from last September!"

"I suppose that can go." I dropped the piece of paper into the wastebasket. "What's this?"

The small sheet of blue paper was almost as beat up as the rest of the bits. However, the handwriting on it looked European and was not terribly legible. It looked like a note of some sort, in some odd shorthand. It had a letterhead at the top, too, in a language that I didn't recognize, although it looked like it said, "Yugoslavia."

Sid took the paper from me. "It must be the drop. Still, like this?" He frowned. "It doesn't make sense."

"He didn't have a code or priority rating and said he'd just gotten here from overseas."

Sid shook his head. "Another unprocessed drop?"

"Looks like. We call Henry?"

"Yeah. I'll do it first thing tomorrow."

Sid got the photo of the paper, then I put the paper back into my purse, along with all the other bits of paper.

Still breathing heavily from my run, I stopped and saw a small diner. I checked my watch again. It was probably time to get back to Mae's. I called a cab from the pay phone at the back near the restrooms. While I waited for it to show, I went to the front and ordered some hash browns and an orange juice, paying for them with the last few dollars I had in my pocket. The cab arrived just as I finished the orange juice. The hash browns were long gone.

The cab pulled up in front of Mae's house at almost eight. Maybe a little later.

"Why don't you park it and come on in?" I told the driver. "My money's inside."

He sighed, but agreed. We walked into sheer chaos.

Neil was yelling at Mae. "She can't have gone that far!"

"She's here!" Darby yelled.

"Lisa!" Mae flew at me. "Where have you been? We've been worried sick about you."

Mama flew down the stairs. "Landsakes, Lisle! I like to have died. What did you think you were doing?"

"I went running," I replied. "I've got to find my purse."

I went toward the room where I'd been sleeping.

"Why didn't you tell anyone where you were?" Mae followed me.

"We all got up, and you had plumb disappeared." Mama followed on Mae's heels.

"I went running," I said again. I turned to the cab driver. "I've gotta get my purse. I'll be right back."

Mama and Mae followed me into the guest room, yammering at me every step of the way. I found my purse and pulled out my wallet. It was empty of cash.

"Where's all my money?" I asked.

"Lisle, honey," Mama said. "I know you're tense about this, but you could have told us where you went."

I groaned. "That's right. I gave my last ten to the waiter on Thursday and forgot to get some more cash yesterday. Mae, you got a twenty I can borrow?"

"What?" Mae screeched.

"Twenty dollars so I can pay the cab driver. Come on. You know I'm good for it."

Mae shoved my robe at me. "Lisa, you've got to get into the shower."

"Fine. Will you take care of the cab driver?"

"Yeah, sure. Now hurry up. We've all got to take showers, too." Mae shoved me toward the stairs. "Your stuff is in my bathroom."

"Excuse me," I called to the cab driver as I went up the stairs. "My sister will pay you. Don't leave until she does."

Mae snorted and went to take care of the cab fare while Mama replaced her, pushing me up the stairs.

"Now, Lisle, you can't dawdle too long, but go ahead and relax."

"Yes, Mama."

Alone, at last, I stripped and turned on the water. The shower felt good, but my nerves were still raw. I felt like I was in line for a roller coaster that I both didn't really want to ride and really did want to.

After drying off, I put on my robe, then slipped out of the bathroom into Mae and Neil's bedroom. Sitting on the bed, I picked up the phone on the bedside table and dialed quickly. He answered on the first ring.

"Hi," I said quietly. "I've got to keep it low, so they don't catch me."

He chuckled. "How are you doing?"

"Nervous. You?"

"Surprisingly, me, too."

"Oh, no." I sighed. If he was admitting it, he was in bad shape.

"I wasn't until last night, after you got hauled off." He chuckled again. "That's when it hit me. It's like the adoption. The wedding changes nothing, and yet changes everything."

"Yeah." I swallowed. "You're right." I gulped again. "I went running this morning."

"No kidding."

"Did you run?"

"Of course. I had Nick and Motley with me. We took the usual route. It loses something when you're not here."

"I'm so sorry."

"It's not your fault." He paused. "I had a nice long talk with Stella, too."

"Good."

"She said she thinks I'm doing the right thing."

Stella was, for all intents and purposes, Sid's mother. Even though she was his aunt, she'd raised him even before his mother had died when he was two years old. Stella did not approve of marriage, nor of the Catholic Church, and had been dismayed to find that Sid was marrying me in a religious setting.

"That's terrific," I said.

"She's on the phone," I heard Mama shout to somebody outside the room.

"Uh-oh," I said. "Mama knows I'm on the phone."

"Don't hang up yet."

"I won't until they make me." I took a deep breath. "Just a few more hours."

"I know. Can you believe we're actually doing this?"

"Not really." I had to laugh. "Kinda freaky, isn't it?"

"It most certainly is."

I shut my eyes. "You know, just hearing your voice is calming me down."

"Good. I'm glad you called. I needed it."

"I love you."

"Lisa!" Mama burst through the door. "Are you talking to Sid?"

"Shavings. She caught me."

"You get off that phone this instant! You're not supposed to be talking to him."

"I can hear." Sid chuckled. "I never thought I'd ever say this, but see you in church. I love you."

"Love you, too."

I slowly replaced the receiver onto the hook.

"Honey, you'd better hurry," Mama scolded. "It's almost nine o'clock and Jesse's going to be here by ten. You gotta be ready."

I shook my head. "Mama, it's not going to take that long."

"And talking on the phone with Sid. Did you call him?"

"Yes, Mama." I smiled at her calmly. "We planned it last night. He needed to hear me, and I needed to hear him."

"Oh, Lisle." Mama began sniffing.

I was named for my Grandma Wycherly, who's German, and my parents tend to use the German version of my name as often as not.

"Look at you," Mama continued. "You're all grown up and getting married."

"Mama, I've been grown up for a while now." I got up off the bed.

"I know, sweetheart." She blinked, then put her arms around me. "But you're getting married. That's a whole new step." She sighed, then smiled at me. "You have no idea how proud your daddy and I are of you."

"Thank you, Mama. I love you so much."

We held each other for a couple minutes, then I went downstairs and got my makeup on. I swallowed as I looked at the dress. It had a high collar, slightly puffed long sleeves, rows of silk lace trim running up the front of the bodice. I'd nearly blinded myself trying to get that trim on straight. The lace fabric of the overdress was silk, with tiny rosebuds interspersed throughout. The feel of it was deliciously soft and smooth, as was the light silk underdress. I slid it on over my head. Grandma, who had just gotten dressed herself, sniffled as she buttoned up the back, and tied the sash. The tiny lace ruffle at the hem swished just above my ankles.

Then I sat down on the bed and looked at the two pairs of shoes I'd brought. For months I'd been trying to decide whether to wear a pair of white spike-heeled sandals with a wide band across my toes and an ankle strap, or a pair of white ballet flats. The sandals looked spectacular with the dress but were not the most comfortable shoes I'd ever worn, and I was going to be on my feet a lot that day. The ballet flats were comfortable but kind of blah.

The dress decided it for me, though. I put on one of the sandals, but as I tightened the ankle strap, sure enough, the spike caught on the bottom ruffle. My heart stopped. Thank God, it didn't tear anything. Holding my breath, I disentangled the sandal and slid into the ballet flats. Who was going to be looking at my feet, anyway?

The doorbell rang.

One of those things that a lot of people never get about Sid and me is that I am not freaked out by all his former girlfriends. There's no reason to be. Sid takes his word very seriously, and he had made his promise to be faithful. The other part was that I'd become friends with some of them, such as Angelique Carter, and didn't want to drop the friendships simply because Sid had slept with them at some point or another. Another excellent example was Shawna Daye. I first met her as Sid's hair stylist, who then became my hair stylist. And when she showed up that morning at my sister's house, she came to fix my hair for my wedding to her former lover. The point that almost everybody seemed to miss was the former part.

Shawna, a blond with nice curves, got me settled in the dining room of Mae's place and smiled.

"How are you doing?" she asked as she brushed out my hair.

"Okay," I said. "Kind of getting used to the idea."

Shawna laughed. "You and me both. Would never have figured Sid would get married."

"I wouldn't have figured I would either," I said.

"Then you two deserve each other."

The wreath of daisies and pink rose buds had arrived. The florist had the rest of the flowers at the church.

"That wreath looks perfect." Shawna said. "It will go great with your dress. Why don't you just sit and relax and let me take care of everything?"

"Sure."

I wasn't entirely sure about relaxing, but didn't really care. I let my brain go only to hear wild, cackling laughter from two nights before.

(Friday, February 28)

More accurately, it was 2:48 Friday morning at that point. Neil and my dear friend Frank Lonnergan stood laughing like hyenas in the front door of the house I shared with Sid. They were drunk, or more accurately, they were bombed out of their skulls.

"We're home!" Neil announced merrily. He's tall with red hair.

"Brought Sid back safe and whatever." Frank leaned precariously against the doorjamb. He's roughly the same size as Neil, but with dark hair.

"Where is he?" I asked.

"He's right…" Neil looked around and tried to push his glasses up on his nose. Only he couldn't find his nose. "He's not here."

Neil and Frank looked at each other and burst into laughter. I stepped around the two of them and walked through the tiny front yard to where I could see the driveway and the street below. The limousine was still parked in the street, with the chauffeur walking up the drive. I met him halfway.

"Ma'am, I've got another guy in the back seat still. Dark-haired fellow. I'm not sure if he belongs here or not."

"He does more than those two at the door." I shook my head. "What happened to the fourth guy?"

"Sicker than a dog. We took him home to Encino a couple hours ago. That's why I'm not sure about this guy. Everyone met here."

"I know. Why is he still in the limo?"

"He's out, Ma'am. He passed out around two, or maybe some later. I'm amazed those other two are still on their feet."

I rolled my eyes. "Really? Can you help me get the guy in the limo inside?"

"Sure. He a friend of yours?"

"My fiancé. This was his bachelor party."

The limo driver just shook his head. I had to admit, I'd seen Sid drink my uncles under the table, which was no easy thing. That he was out, and Frank and Neil were still going was totally frightening. Frank and Neil had somehow staggered up to the loft next to Sid's and my bedroom and were singing pseudo-Irish songs written by American Jews. Conchetta, the housekeeper, had made a huge pot of menudo earlier that day. Those boys were going to need it. Once the driver and I had dumped Sid on the living room couch, I picked up a phone and called Mae.

"It's me," I told her. "You wanted me to call when they got home."

"It's almost three in the morning," Mae said with a yawn.

"I know. They got here a few minutes ago. I think Neil and Frank have finally passed out. Your husband was singing Irish tenor."

"Oh, dear God. I didn't think they were going to get that blitzed."

"I didn't, either."

"Get some sleep. Tomorrow's a big day, and then Saturday."

"I don't want to think about it. I'll see you tomorrow. I mean, tonight."

I hung up, sighing. I had teased Sid about Dan Williams' bachelor party, at which they'd indulged in ice cream sundaes. Sid had been appalled. But at that moment, I thought that maybe Dan's idea of a bachelor party hadn't been all that bad.

I got a little sleep, but then the alarm went off at six-thirty, and I stumbled downstairs to get Nick up and ready for school. That turned out to be a waste of time. Nick begged me to let him skip that day, claiming that he couldn't concentrate and would only make his teacher mad at him. Nick was so excited about the wedding, which is why I agreed to let him stay home and called the school office. Mrs. Fleming really didn't like it when Nick skipped, but I later found out from Maria that the teacher had been relieved when Nick hadn't shown. He'd been pretty antsy all week.

Stella, Sid's aunt who raised him, and Sy, her lover, were already up and reading the newspaper in the breakfast room. They were staying with us for the festivities. I told them that we had guests in the house upstairs and asked that they get dressed after breakfast. Stella is a nudist, one of the reasons Sid is perfectly comfortable in his birthday suit no matter who happens to be around. I was almost used to seeing Sy in his altogether. It was part of the compromise Sid and Stella had come to. If she was going to have to respect closed doors, then Sid didn't mind her wandering around buck naked all the time as long as it was just Sid, Nick, and me in the house.

Nick and I made French toast for all of us for breakfast and had a lovely time doing it. Nick looks just like his father and Stella, with dark, wavy hair, bright blue eyes, and a dimple in his chin. Well, Stella's hair is dark gray and Nick wears glasses. His dad wears contact lenses. Nick had turned thirteen exactly two weeks before, and the top of his head was already almost to my nose. I have a strong feeling he's going to be taller than his father, who is only three inches taller than me, and I'm average. Sy is taller, with a rounded belly and full dark gray beard. His hair is also dark gray, and he's bald on top.

I explained about the bachelor party. Stella's eyebrows rose and Nick laughed.

"I'm surprised Sid passed out so fast," Stella said. "He used to hold his booze much better than that."

I laughed. "So, I've heard. I think it's more of a comment on Frank and Neil. Sid drank my uncles under the table last Thanksgiving, and that is not easy to do."

"Hm." Stella looked over at Sy. "We should probably make ourselves scarce for the time being."

Sy smiled and turned to Nick. "Well, my boy, where should we amuse ourselves today?"

"Anyplace but a mall," I blurted.

"Mom!"

Nick wasn't greedy. On the other hand, you could hardly blame him for liking his chances with Stella and Sy and stores with cool stuff in them. Stella and Sy loved playing the indulgent grandparents.

"I know," said Sy. "Whale watching."

"It may be a little late in the day for that," I said. "But a trip to a pier might be fun. Which ones haven't you seen yet?"

With Sy, that was a pretty short list. The man loved being a tourist. I'd thought he'd caught every sight there was in the area over the Christmas holidays, but then he and Stella had visited again at the end of January, and he'd still found stuff to look at. I let them worry about it and pulled together the aspirin bottle, and scooped menudo into mugs to be ready to microwave at the first moan. And, as it turned out, Sy did somehow find a whale watching cruise that left late enough for the three of them to get on it. They left around eight.

Sid stirred around nine a.m. I hit the button on the microwave, got the aspirin bottle, a glass of water, and a spoon. Sid lay on his back with his hand over his eyes. He muttered a curse.

"Sid, are you okay?"

"I feel like somebody has been dancing on my head in steel boots. Was I attacked?"

"No. Just drunk."

"I was afraid of that." He groaned again. "I haven't felt this bad since I woke up from that three-day binge when I got out of the Army." He opened one eye. "You're a hell of a lot better looking than that S.O.B. Landry."

Colonel Landry had been the officer that had roped Sid into intelligence work when Sid was in boot camp, then later sent to Vietnam. We'd since learned that his real name was Dale O'Connor, and he was a congressman with intelligence connections. He'd also pulled some strings in allowing me to officially adopt Nick as a stepparent, even though Sid and I weren't quite married yet.

Sid shut his eye again. "He's not coming to the wedding, is he?"

"Both he and Marge Benson sent regrets."

"Good." He blinked, then cursed. "I still have my contacts in."

It could have been worse. Some months before, Sid had gotten soft lenses, which were easier to sleep in than the hard lenses he'd had.

I put my hand out. "Give them to me. I'll get them into your case. In the meantime, I've got some menudo here for you."

Sid winced. "I suppose I must."

"Here, get a few spoonfuls down and I'll let you have some aspirin."

I helped Sid into a reclining position and fed him some soup.

"Do I want to know what happened?" he asked, pulling the lenses from his eyes, and placing first the right one under the pinkie on my left hand, then the left under my forefinger.

"Well, Henry got sick." I gave him three aspirin tablets and some water while holding onto the lenses.

"Yeah. We took him home around one." Sid knocked back the pills, then some water, and winced from the headache.

"You apparently passed out around two, and then everyone arrived here at ten 'til three. Neil and Frank were still going and polished off a bottle of Chablis."

Sid moaned. "I was saving that."

"They finally passed out. They're still up in the loft. When I last saw them, Neil was wrapped around Frank and telling Mae she needs a shave."

Sid couldn't help chuckling but winced as he did. I took the contact lenses upstairs and got them into the correct partitions of Sid's case and poured wetting solution over them. Neil and Frank both woke up sometime between ten-thirty and eleven. They were in slightly better shape than Sid, but still pretty bad. I distributed mugs and spoons and left them alone while I called Esther and Mae to let them know that neither man was in any shape to drive yet.

I suppose I should have been more annoyed. But none of those guys drink that much normally. I'd seen Neil get plastered at least twice, but no more than that, and I'd known him since I was eight years old.

Sy, Stella, and Nick returned around three, having enjoyed the boat ride, even if they'd only seen one whale. Or maybe they didn't see any. I was too busy getting Frank and Neil upright so that they could get ready for the wedding rehearsal and the dinner afterward.

Sid staggered to his feet around the same time so that we could take my truck and his Beemer to the garage where his Mercedes 450SL was. It was a necessary precaution. Frank had something up his sleeve, probably multiple things. I'd caught Neil and Mae winking at each other several times that week, and it was entirely probable there may have been some revenge inspiring them. [Given what Neil had told me, it was all about the revenge. Seriously, Lisa? The honeymoon suite? The only thing exonerating you was that you were only fourteen at the time. I know we thought for the longest time that it was Frank who'd rigged the shoe stunt. But it was Mae and Neil who pulled that one off. How, I still do not know. – SEH] Sid debated taking another nap, but realized he needed to shave and get dressed for the rehearsal at six.

As we got to the church for the rehearsal, it hit me that I was doing this. I was getting married. For real. Mama and Father John conferred on the procession, then Mama lined us up in the vestibule, putting Daddy at my side.

"Mama, I was going to walk in alone." I glared at her.

"Why would you do that?" she asked.

"Because giving the bride away is archaic and sexist and everything I hate about marriage."

"Oh," sighed my father. He looked so hurt. "I was really looking forward to it."

I shut my eyes. "Oh, crap!"

"Lisa Jane Wycherly!" Mama trembled in fury. "How dare you use language like that, especially in a house of God!"

"I am a grownup!" I hollered in spite of myself. "I will use whatever language I like."

I saw Stella lift an eyebrow.

"Are you going to tell me you're going to hurt your daddy's feelings?"

I looked over at him. "But I hate what it says."

"That's alright, Lisle." Daddy smiled weakly. "I think I understand."

I shrieked. "This isn't fair!"

In the end, I agreed to let Daddy walk me in. But the rehearsal didn't get much better. Nick was really, really nervous and pale as a ghost. Sid didn't look much better, but that was probably the hangover. He seemed okay otherwise. Mae's five kids were unusually hyper, even for them. Darby, who was almost thirteen, was having kittens about the music – he was going to play his violin along with Sy and Stella for the wedding. Janey, one of my bridesmaids and nine and a half, was everywhere but where we needed her. Ellen hid. Well, she is the shy one in the group, and was not quite eight yet. Marty and Mitch, the five-year-old twins, got into the choir loft and started playing with the organ, which did not do much for Darby's kitten fit. John walked us through our paces so fast, I barely knew what was going on.

I was shaking so badly that when we got to the restaurant for the rehearsal dinner, I ran for the ladies' room and refused to leave. Mae and Kathy both tried to get me out, but I just locked myself in one of the stalls. They left and a minute later, I heard the door open.

"Hey, Lisa, it's Esther."

"You gonna try and get me out of here?"

"Why? I just came in to keep you company."

I opened the stall door. "Thanks."

Esther sat on the sink counter and handed me a tissue. "Here you go."

I blew my nose. "I've been acting like such an idiot."

"No, you haven't. I've seen lots worse. I worked at that bridal salon, you know. You should have seen some of those girls. Spoiled brats. They panicked over the least thing. Oh, and the fights! If they weren't fighting with their mothers, they were fighting with their grooms and a lot of times, both. You are sailing through this."

"It doesn't feel like it."

"You got more to deal with, too. Your fiancé has a past and a half, plus he and three of your groomsmen are hung over. Your sort of mother-in-law hates the Church and hates marriage. And then, there's your kid. He's running around out there now, telling everybody his parents are finally getting married."

I had to laugh. "Nick's so excited."

"He showed up those little angels of your sister's. Were they brats tonight."

"Nick was good. Poor thing. He was so nervous. He's so proud of being Sid's best man."

There was a knock on the door and Sid poked his head in.

"May I come in?" he asked.

"No one but us in here." Esther hopped off the counter as Sid came in. "I'll go stand guard."

Sid smiled gently. "You're pretty upset."

"Maybe we should have just shacked up."

He shrugged. "We still can. It's not like all of this is changing anything, really. We've made our promises."

"I know." I took a deep breath. "I just wanted the Sacrament is all."

"Then let's focus on that. All the other hoop-de-do is for everyone else." He came up and pulled me into his arms.

I leaned my forehead against his. "Thanks, Sid."

He lifted my chin and looked into my eyes. "It's going to be alright. We get to define our relationship. No one else does. Not even your parents, and not even if you let your father walk you up the aisle tomorrow."

"He is looking forward to it." I smiled softly. "I love you."

"I love you, too, Lisapet." He kissed me so sweetly. "Think you can face the crowd now?"

I took a deep breath. "Yeah."

I blushed when everyone cheered as we entered. It wasn't just the bridal party and parents. Neil's parents, Malcolm and Ellen O'Malley, were at the dinner since Neil's father and Daddy have been best friends since college. The senior O'Malleys had hosted the parents' lunch the day before. Father John was at the dinner, which I'd thought was an amazing concession on Stella's part, given how she feels about the Church. Stella has good reason to hate Catholicism and priests and she and Sy were hosting the dinner as the parents of the groom. But for some reason, she really likes John. [No surprise there. That's just who John is. – SEH]

Jesse was there because Kathy was one of my bridesmaids. Jesse, a professional photographer, had decided he wanted to take the pictures, so he'd declined to be one of the groomsmen. Frank and Esther were both part of the wedding party, so they were there. Henry and Lydia James were there because Henry was also a groomsman, and they'd brought Angelique Carter. Ange is Henry's secretary as well as a good friend. Stella had also invited Sid's old friend from high school, Tom Freeman, who had come down from San Francisco to attend the wedding.

On my side of the family, my two uncles and their wives were there, as was Grandma Caulfield. My cousin Maggie and her husband, Jed, were not.

That was kind of a weird story. Mama had gotten them an invite to our wedding because Sid and I had gone to their wedding the previous fall. But right near the end of January, Mama called to tell me that Maggie and Jed were breaking up and Maggie wanted to know if I'd mind if she kept the coffeemaker Sid and I had gotten them for their wedding because she used it every day and really liked it. Well, that freaked me out, what with my own ambivalence about getting married. Only Mama said that it was a good thing because Maggie had gotten a really great job in Tallahassee and moved up there from the town in Southern Florida where my folks are from. Jed was supposed to move, but decided he didn't want to. Maggie realized that she was having more fun in Tallahassee than she was with Jed, and told him that if he wanted to stay married, he'd have to move, which made Mama happy because it meant that Maggie had finally grown a backbone.

I told Mama it was fine if Maggie kept the coffeemaker. Then Maggie sent Sid and me a set of six lovely hand-thrown coffee mugs for our wedding with an uncharacteristically sweet note thanking us for being so nice about the coffeemaker, but she wouldn't be able to make the wedding because she couldn't get off work.

The rehearsal dinner was lovely, with good food, some nice bubbly, and lots of laughter. The kids ran around everywhere. We had just been served dessert when Mama and Stella got up. Mama had a big, flat, white box in her hands.

"I promise this will not be at the reception tomorrow," Mama said, handing Sid the box. "But Stella and I thought you both might like to have it, anyway."

I opened the lid to the box and pulled out a huge binder that had been padded and covered with pink, white, and blue striped cotton. Nick hung over our shoulders as I opened the album. The first picture was a recent shot Mae had gotten of Sid and me together with Nick, but the next one featured a black-and-white photo of Stella as a younger woman holding a small infant. Sid's first picture. Mama and Stella had set the photos up in chronological order, so the first few pages were of Sid only, since he's older than me. Sid smiled at my first picture, though, and touched it. It's a shot of Daddy sitting in an easy chair, with Mae, then almost six-years-old, leaning on the chair's arm, looking at a tiny infant in Daddy's arms. I was already a month old at that point and still smaller than most newborns.

"Mom? Is that you?" Nick asked. "Why are you so small?"

"I was born prematurely," I said.

Mama's voice shook. "We almost lost her a few times. She was getting sick all the time when she was little, then roughhousing and getting into trouble as she grew up."

Sid smiled at me. I was still getting into trouble and risking my neck. We kept turning pages. Given how many shots there were of Sid in his birthday suit, even well into his teens, I was glad that the album would not be at the reception.

"Well, you gonna pass that around?" Uncle Leonard hollered. He and my Uncle Stephen are identical twins and Mama's older brothers.

Mama looked up from a picture of Sid and several of his friends without any clothes on sitting around a small living room.

"I don't think so, Leonard. This is just for Sid and Lisa."

Sid and I looked at each other, and I couldn't help giggling. We'd both been worried that Mama would put out an album of our baby pictures at the reception, even though both of us had protested vociferously and repeatedly. Given Mama's response to her brother, I got the feeling that Sid's photos might have deterred her.

There were not a lot of shots of either Sid or me after we'd left high school. But Mama and Stella had included several photos from Nick's baby album, then several shots of the three of us together.

"That's really nice," Sid said, closing the album.

Stella smiled, then tapped on her glass with a clean knife. "I believe it is time to drink a few toasts to our bride and groom. Bill, would you be so good as to make the first toast?"

Daddy grinned as he stood. "Thank you, Stella."

The bottles were passed around and glasses filled. Daddy tapped his glass and paused as the room quieted. His grin was just a touch evil as he looked at Sid.

"Sid, how did you put it once? Yes. That you were the last man on earth that I wanted to see my daughter with."

Sid laughed.

Daddy chuckled. "You were right." He winced. "There's a bit of a problem here, though. My daughter does not seem to care about that. One thing I have learned over the years is that if my Lisle makes up her mind about something, she's usually right. And she has made her mind up about you. Sid, you are a good man. More to the point, you love my girl. Now, I know she is going to tell me that she does not need you to take care of her, and she doesn't. But you damned well better, son. And welcome to the family. To the bride and groom."

We laughed as the others drank from their glasses. But then Stella got up.

"There are a lot of people in this room, and probably even more at the wedding tomorrow, who are surprised to see Sid settling down," she said, then smiled at Sid. "I, however, am not. For one thing, as a boy, Sid was always deeply kind and very loyal and protective of his friends. And while he definitely enjoyed sleeping around, and it was certainly part of the culture at the time, I could see that he was happiest with the two or three young women he called friends. Even back then, I knew that what he really wanted was a relationship." She paused and took a deep breath. "Then there is Lisa. Now, some of you know that Sid and I were estranged for over sixteen years. But last November, Lisa walked into my music school. She somehow managed to convince me that the time was ripe for a reconciliation. I'm still not sure how she knew. I did know the look on Sid's face that afternoon when he saw her walk up. He was happy, and that meant the world to me. Lisa, you gave me my son back. I cannot thank you enough."

I couldn't help but weep, and I was not the only one in the room wiping their eyes. I got up and hugged Stella.

All too soon, the dinner was over, and Mama and Mae tried to pull me to their car. I debated making a fuss and going home with Sid, but my dress and my overnight bag were already over at Mae's place. I put my foot down long enough to spend a couple moments with Sid, kissing him goodnight. We quietly arranged for me to call him the next morning. Then Mama and Mae swooped down and carried me off. I looked back. Sid looked so forlorn.

Shawna finished pinning my hair into a Gibson Girl style, then settled the wreath of fresh daisies and small pink rosebuds around the bun, making sure the ribbons flowed down my back. Mama watched, her eyes filling up again.

She sniffed. "Now, Lisle, have you got your something old, something new?"

"Yes, Mama." I reached across the table for my necklace with the aquamarine and diamond pendant and the matching earrings. "The new is the dress. The old is Sid's class ring."

I had it on under my dress, hanging from a battered nickel chain. You could sort of see it through the lace above where the underlining was. I unhooked my necklace and started to put it on. Shawna took the ends and fastened them under the ribbons.

"I've got my aquamarines for the blue." I put my earrings on. The matching dinner ring that I wore every day sparkled from my right hand. I looked at Mama. "And you said I could borrow your linen hankie."

"Yes." Mama handed it to me. "But where are you going to put it?"

"I have pockets." I smiled as I slid the hankie into my left side one. I had added the pockets to the pattern because I never make anything without pockets.

"You look gorgeous, Lisa," Shawna said, and smiled wistfully.

"You okay?" I asked.

She laughed. "As in, am I in love with Sid?"

"Well, maybe." I shrugged. "Given some of the responses we've been getting, I suspect there is a contract out on me."

"I'm not contributing to it. Sid was fun, but not much more than that." Shawna walked around the chair I was sitting in. "No. I think I just want to be in love."

"It's nice," I said softly.

I closed my eyes. The reality was, I deeply loved Sid, and it did make all the difference in the world. That previous Monday night, Sid's happy sigh as he slid his pants off.

(Monday, February 24)

It was almost midnight at that point, and when you consider that Sid and I generally get up at five-thirty, that's late. We were in the bathroom. I was brushing my teeth prior to stripping for bed. Sid sat on the bench next to the laundry hampers tucked into the huge walk-in closet that we shared.

"I don't know what's making me happier right now," he said, neatly folding his dress slacks before tossing them in the dry-cleaning bin. "The fact that I'm not going to infect you with anything, or that I don't have to wear my jeans tonight."

Sid doesn't trust condoms, which was why the jeans were necessary to protect me from any of his bodily fluids. Given that he was wearing a condom when Nick was conceived (which happened before he'd gotten his vasectomy), I couldn't entirely blame him. I spat into the sink.

"I'm happy that you're going to live," I said, then rinsed my mouth out. I turned and smiled at him. "But then, I was pretty sure you were going to."

Sid got up and kissed me, his hands gently unbuttoning my Oxford shirt. "I do wish I had the energy to deflower you now. But I am looking forward to full body skin contact."

"So am I," I purred.

I let my hands slide down his back and squeezed his buns.

He sighed happily. I finished undressing and staggered after him into the bedroom and slid into bed. Sid snuggled up to me, and while it wasn't full sex, he did have one suggestion that turned out to be a lot of fun, although not entirely relaxing. Still, in the contented afterglow, we held each other and fell asleep.

Kathy and Jesse showed up at Mae's house right on time. Kathy looked gorgeous in the dusty rose Victorian top with the white and blue roses and the navy-blue skirt. Mae and Janey were wearing similar skirts and tops. The big difference was that Kathy and Janey's tops were belted at the waist. Mae's wasn't to accommodate her pregnancy. Neil had already left with Darby and Mama to meet Sid.

Jesse shot at least two rolls of film. I was a little sad that Esther wasn't there, but Mama said she'd be happy with just the shots we could get at Mae's. By eleven, we were all in cars. Daddy drove the O'Malley's van with Mae in the front passenger seat, me, Grandma, and Janey in the middle seat, and the twins and Ellen in the back. My overnight case was under one of the seats.

Daddy steered the van through the light Saturday morning traffic to the freeway through downtown Los Angeles. I took a deep breath. This was it. I was really getting married. Yes, it would be a relationship that Sid and I defined, but still... I had never wanted to get married. That was probably why I'd found Sid so attractive initially. Marriage, as far as he was concerned, was not going to happen. And yet, there we were. I closed my eyes and tried to think of something else. After all, there were other things going on in Sid's and my lives, such as the weird business with the unprocessed drops. Two weeks into February, right before Nick's birthday.

(Wednesday, February 12)

The freezing wind stabbed through me as only a winter Santa Ana wind can, piercingly cold and dry. The sky was a brilliant blue and completely clear. From where I stood in front of the old mission, I could see the San Gabriel mountains, intricately detailed in the icy air. A cab on the street just barely slowed down. The window slid down, and a tiny missile flew from inside the cab, landing near my feet. It was a cannister of film. I picked it up and stashed it in my purse. A moment later, another car slammed to a stop alongside the curb and a man jumped out. He ran straight at me.

Now, a lot of the time, attracting attention is the last thing I want to do. However, there are times when one wants to create the illusion that one is a civilian and, in those cases, it pays to act like one. Which this time meant screaming like a banshee and running away as fast as I could. It's one of the reasons why when I'm working, I tend to wear low-heeled pumps. I had on a wool A-line skirt, and heather blue jacket over a light blue flower-print blouse.

I was barely around the corner when I felt the hit. Almost three hundred pounds of pure muscle landed on my back and knocked me face down.

"Help!" I screamed. "I'm being robbed! Help!"

The man rolled me over and whacked me in the face. "Where is film?"

"Film? What film? Help!"

"In your purse. I saw you put."

"I don't have any film in my purse." I, nonetheless, slid my hand inside, reaching for my key chain and the mace can there. "Wait. Is this it?"

My hand flew out, the spray blowing in the breeze. I shut my eyes just in case. It caught my attacker full in the face. I got my leg up and kicked him where it hurts, then rolled him off me. Gasping and coughing, I ran through the small suburb, changing directions and looking for that second car. I seemed to have ditched it. Well, I thought I had. But as I pulled my truck out of the parking lot where I'd left it, I saw it coming after me. Almost cursing, I drove fast, weaving through the traffic, until I found Interstate 10. I made a last second turn onto the freeway and saw the car behind me skid and slam into another. I kept my foot on the accelerator, weaving through the traffic with one eye on my rear-view mirror. But I had well and truly lost the tail.

By the time I staggered into the office, I was a little winded.

"You okay?" Sid asked, looking worried.

"Yeah. I just got tackled." I looked down at my skirt. There was a gaping hole in the wool. "Drat! I liked this skirt."

"So, what do we have?"

I dropped my purse on the desk and started digging through it. "Another unprocessed drop." I found the film cannister and showed it to Sid.

He shook his head. I went upstairs and changed clothes while he called Jesse. We got Nick from school and took him with us to Jesse and Kathy's condo on Wilshire Boulevard. Nick knows about our side business, even if he doesn't know all the details.

Jesse had the film developed and printed in a relatively short time. He laid the pictures on their dining room table.

"It looks like different angles of some sort of fortress," he said. "Look. See that hole behind those rocks."

"Here's one with some writing on it." I picked up the print.

"That's a Company code." Sid frowned. "Jesse, why don't you go ahead and make a couple extra prints of this one? And get everything on a microdot, please."

"Sure. Do you want me to package it? Once you get me the route, it won't be a problem. It's Kathy's turn to run."

"We'll call you when we know something," I said. "And let me keep the prints. We may want to look at them again."

I stashed the prints in my purse, then we collected Nick and headed home, very puzzled, indeed.

"The question is, do we break the code or not?" Sid asked.

I shrugged. "We could send it up to Blue Shield."

"Let's see what Henry has to say first."

Henry agreed that we wanted to send the microdot to New York and suggested a route. He didn't say anything about the code. We called Jesse and Kathy.

The funny thing was, after that, there was no more business, period, for the next couple weeks. We had gotten cleared to take a honeymoon after the wedding. We couldn't help but wonder if someone upline had gotten the dates wrong. If they had, there wasn't much we could do about it.

I swallowed and looked out the window. Daddy was getting onto Interstate 10 from the 110 Freeway. The dash clock said 11:12.

"Not much longer now," Mae said, reaching back behind her and giving me a playful nudge.

"Yeah," I sighed and blinked.

I looked out the window again and wondered what Sid was doing.

Sid's Voice –

Nick still insists that at that point, I was coming unglued. As to whether or not that was an exaggeration, I can't say. I was ready to go, although the jacket to my tux was still sitting on the end of our bed. Neil had just pulled up after dropping Darby and Mama off at the church. Stella and Sy were already over there. I couldn't believe the troop maneuvers that this production required. Nick and I were in his room. He was in his suit, and I was double-checking his tie, at least visually. I still thought it was a little loose, but we'd agreed. Once he could tie it himself, as long as the knot hit the collar, he could keep it as loose as he liked.

"Alright. Have you got everything?" I asked him.

Nick patted his pockets. "Handkerchief, my wallet..."

"In your breast pocket?"

"Yes, Dad. I have the house keys in my pants, though."

"Those won't show. What about your mother's ring?" I checked my hair in Nick's mirror.

"What about it?"

My heart stopped. "I gave it to you. Remember? You're supposed to put it on the plate thingie when John asks for it."

"Dad, you never gave it to me."

"Nick, this is no time for playing games."

"I'm not playing!" Nick's face had gone pale. "You never gave it to me."

Neil called from the front.

"I did, too!" I yelled.

"When?" Nick cried.

"Fuck! Where the hell is it?"

Neil poked his head in the door. "You guys okay? I heard you all the way at the front door."

"Son of a bitch!" I ran for the garage, as if that would have helped. The garage was empty. I slammed my hand into the doorjamb. "Fucking hell!"

"What's the matter?" Neil asked.

I took a deep breath. "Lisa's wedding ring set. It's at the jewelry store. I took the set there on Monday to get it soldered together. I was going to pick it up yesterday, but I was hung and forgot. And there is no car in the garage that I can take to go pick it up."

"Is that all?" Neil grinned, unflappable, as usual. "Let's go now. We'll swing by the jewelry store and pick it up on the way to church. We've got plenty of time. Where's your tux coat?"

"Upstairs on the bed."

"I'll go get it. You go apologize to Nick."

I rolled my eyes, but did as he said. Neil handed me my jacket and the three of us left. In an attempt to avoid putting seat creases in the back hem of the jacket, I held it on my lap. I should have put it on.

Neil somehow found a parking space on the street near the store on Cañon and thanked Saint Anthony. Lisa did the same thing when she found a good parking spot. I had no idea why. I put it out of my mind. All three of us got out of the car and went into the store.

I was not happy when I saw the clerk. Neil chuckled softly.

"Another one?" he asked me softly.

I sighed. "One of the unhappy ones. I don't get it. I only slept with her three or four times at the most. And I bought several things for Lisa at the same time. I dropped out last year, never heard a peep. Now I'm getting married, and she's pissed."

Martine was blond, with a sharp face and stick thin body. She glared at me as she saw me.

"May I help you?" Her smile was icy cold.

"Yeah, Martine," I said, trying to sound casual. "I left a ring set here on Monday to be soldered together. I need to pick it up."

Martine glared at me again, then ever so slowly went into the back and came out with a plastic bag and some paperwork.

"I'll need to see some ID."

I still had my tux jacket in my hands and reached for the breast pocket. It was empty.

"Where's my billfold?" I asked.

"It wasn't in your jacket?" Neil asked, taking it from me.

"No." I closed my eyes. "I hadn't put it in there because I hadn't put the jacket on yet."

"I'm so sorry, sir," Martine said. "Mr. Anderson is very strict about ID."

"Are you shitting me?" Both my hands landed on the glass case between us. "You know who I am, and I know where the mole is next to your boob. Now, goddammit. Give me the fucking ring! I've already paid for the work."

Martine stepped back a little. "But Mr. Anderson..."

"Mr. Anderson knows me, too." I glared at her. "And I have his home phone number and his car phone number. Do you want me to call him?"

She huffed. I pulled my pocket watch from my vest pocket. The soft tinkling of Minuet in G did little to ease the tension.

"Martine, I am getting married in less than thirty-five minutes. If that ring is not on my bride's finger by the end of it, I will see to it that your ass is fired. Are we clear?"

She put the plastic bag with the wedding set on the case and I grabbed it. Once we got out of the store, Neil took the bag from my hands.

"Don't worry, Sid." He tucked the ring into his pants. "I may as well. I've already got your ring. Mae almost lost it three times this morning."

"Thanks, Neil. See that Nick gets it at the right time. Come on, son." I shook my head. "I can't believe I'm acting this way."

We got in the car as Neil laughed.

"You should have seen me on my wedding day." Neil started the car, then checked to see that Nick was in the back seat and buckled in. "You're lucky you're still on your feet. I almost fainted twice."

The good news was, we got to the church in plenty of time, which really didn't help my nerves any.

Lisa's Voice –

Daddy parked the van on the street in front of the church. Mae scurried in ahead of us, then appeared in one of the side doors and beckoned us in. On the other side of the vestibule, there was a small commotion.

"Cut it out, dammit!" Sid yelped as I was pushed up the stairs to the choir loft.

"Can't I just see him?" I begged as Mae shoved me in the back. Daddy stood behind her.

"Lisa?" Sid called.

"Sid!" I tried to get back down the stairs, but Mae and Daddy would not be moved.

Mae shoved a couple more times, and I was in the choir loft. Sid's curses floated up from the other stairway, with Mama giving him what for at the same time for swearing in church.

"Where's Nick?" I asked.

"You're not seeing him either," Mae said with an evil giggle.

Stella laughed. She sat at the piano with Sy next to her, tuning his cello and chuckling. Darby, holding his violin and bow, rolled his eyes.

"Daddy, you keep her here," Mae said, shoving a small bouquet of daisies and pink roses into my hand.

"I will." Daddy laughed.

"I don't know why I can't see him," I grumbled. "This is ridiculous."

Jesse shook his head. He stood next to the two tripods he'd set up in the center of the loft, each with a different camera. One of the cameras held a huge telephoto lens, the other a more normal-sized one. His cousin, Shaneequa, was acting as his assistant and shooting in the church below.

I did finally get to see Nick. I looked down at the church as my son walked Grandma Caulfield up the aisle. A minute later, Nick turned, looked up, saw me, and waved. Daddy pulled me back into the choir loft, where I could not be seen. Jesse picked up a smaller camera and squeezed off a couple pictures of me.

Nick returned to the aisle, this time with Mama on his arm.

I smiled, my eyes getting misty. "He looks so handsome today."

Daddy pulled me back again before Nick could wave at me. Mae came up the other stairs, behind Stella, Sy, and Darby.

"Any time," she hissed at Stella, who nodded.

Stella looked at Darby and Sy. The three rearranged the sheet music on the stands in front of them, then Stella waved her hand at the other two and counted three.

My heart stopped when I heard the melody. Sid had taken a class in music composition the semester before, and the tune had been his final. It really was a lovely little tune, but Sid was going to be so embarrassed.

[I wasn't embarrassed. Shocked, yes, and a little peeved at Stella, who told me later that if I hadn't wanted anybody else to hear it, I shouldn't have left the music out - and trust me, I hadn't. Frank told me that she'd engineered that little surprise. That was when I began to wonder if any of the music Frank and I had chosen was going to be used. - SEH]

Down in the church, I saw the top of Neil's red hair as he started up the aisle. Henry walked in after Neil, then Frank, then Nick. I barely saw the top of Sid's head when Daddy gently pulled me to the stairs. Near the bottom, I swallowed. Daddy chuckled.

"He's a good man, Lisle. You'll be fine."

"I know, Daddy. I love him so much. It's just..."

"I know. Come on."

We got to the doorway into the church in time to see Mae go up the aisle. Janey, Esther, and Kathy were already at the altar, on the other side from the men. Daddy held me in place just long enough for Mae to get to the altar. In the front row, Mama stood, and the rest of the congregation stood, as well. I shut my eyes. Then Daddy started forward.

It wasn't like I hadn't walked up that aisle before. I did most Sundays as a Eucharistic Minister serving at Mass. Somehow, that day, it stretched forever. Sid stood at the end of it, fidgeting with my class ring, which he wore on his right little finger. I couldn't tell if I wanted to run up the aisle or step as slowly as possible. I focused on Sid. I loved him and the only thing moving me at that moment was thinking about how much he loved me. I heard his voice, my own, as we'd tried to say so over the years.

"There may come a time, Lisa, when we do find ourselves in each other's arms. I wouldn't be averse to it."

"I don't know what's happening to us, but whatever it is, it's happening way too fast."

"Lisa, I have a lot invested in you, too."

"Sid, I'm willing to listen."

"When we come together, it will be with joy, or it will not happen."

"Because I love you, Sid."

"Lisa, I... Lisa, I love you."

[Watching you come up that aisle was possibly the most surreal experience of my life. It wasn't so much that I was getting married. After all, in most ways, we already were. We had made our promises. We knew who and what we were about. What would having a priest involved change? And yet, as I saw you on your daddy's arm, walking toward me, I realized, as I had the night before, that it was going to change everything. - SEH]

Suddenly, I was there. Sid stood across from me. I gave Daddy a quick kiss on the cheek. Jesse got an incredible shot of Daddy giving Sid the stink eye. I looked over at Sid, then saw Nick just beyond him. It didn't matter what we'd rehearsed. I walked over and scooped Nick into a hug. Nick is amazing with hugs. The two of us, my darling son and I, rocked quietly for a second. That picture came out particularly nicely, and the one a second later, with Sid smiling over us. Then Sid took my hand, and we walked up the three steps to where Father John waited for us.

John's amplified voice boomed out over the congregation. "Well, it's about time you two showed up here."

The assembly laughed softly. Sid and I did, too.

"I understand you two are here about this Sacrament thing," John continued, grinning. "So, let's begin. In the name of the Father, the Son, and the Holy Spirit..."

Kathy read the first reading. I had sweat bullets trying to find just the perfect one. Did I hear a word of it? No. Mae sang the responsorial psalm and led us in the response. Stella had moved over to the organ at that point and she and Mae both sounded fabulous. Do I remember which psalm? No. I think the gospel was from the first chapter of St. John, but that's only because I really like that chapter. John read it and it went right past me. John closed the book then looked at where Sid and I were sitting in the front half pew and grinned.

"Well." The priest laughed. "Can you believe today is here? I never thought I'd live to see it. I've been hearing that phrase a lot, both last night at the rehearsal dinner, and today among you, the assembly here. Now, I know that some of you have meant that both Sid and Lisa are about the last people you'd expect to get married, period, let alone to each other. The rest of us have meant that we never thought these two would get around to getting it over with."

Sid and I looked at each other and laughed quietly.

John smiled at us, then looked out over the congregation. "I first met Lisa when she joined the parish, shortly after Sid hired her. It wasn't too long before I met Sid himself. Even back then, I began to see something very special happening. As time passed, I waited as patiently as I could as it grew and flourished. There were troubles. As if Sid's many girlfriends weren't enough, Lisa had to go and get engaged to the wrong man. Neither of them was willing to own up to what was happening between them. But it worked out, as it always does, if we are patient and let the Lord work. I won't say it was easy. It never is. But what did I see happening? A marriage. A marriage in formation. Here were two people who were building a commitment to a life-sustaining relationship. Sid and Lisa have struggled to build this relationship. Both of them..." John looked directly at me, and I flushed. "Both of them had to learn how to love, and it wasn't an easy lesson. So, now we're here today to celebrate that love and to support it. Sid, Lisa, I hate to say this to you now, but your struggles are just beginning. Lisa, in some ways, it will be a little easier on you because you know what a good marriage is. It will be your job, then, to keep that ideal before the two of you. Sid, in some ways, it will be a little easier on you because you know where the pitfalls are. Your job will be to watch out for them and protect both of you from them. As you both already know, marriage is not easy. It's not something that just happens and it's all happily ever after. But it is a good and blessed thing. It is what brings us life. And it is why you two are here today." John grinned again. "Now that I've got you two completely petrified, are you ready to get this over with?"

Sid and I laughed and nodded. We got up and walked to the space in front of the altar as John came over. I recognized the altar server from the teen group and smiled at her as she held the marriage book. I looked over at Sid. His gentle blue eyes shone with warmth. I took a deep breath. This was the Sacrament. It was why we were there. Sid had been right. The rest of the hoop-de-do was for my family. This was the part that counted.

There were the traditional vows. Of course, we committed ourselves to our lifetimes. We already had. When John asked us if we would accept children as gifts from God and raise them in the Faith, I glanced at Mae's swollen belly and said I would, knowing it would take a miracle for that to happen. Nick snickered, then hissed an "ow!" as Sid consented.

John asked for the rings. I turned to Mae and went pale at the panicked look on her face.

"I don't have it!" she whispered.

"Dad, you never gave it to me!" Nick hissed loudly.

"Excuse me." Neil butted in calmly and dropped the rings onto the silver plate. That was another priceless shot Jesse got.

Sid and I both started laughing. But Sid was serious when he took my hand and slid the ring onto my finger. There was something about the way he said the word when he promised me his fidelity that assured me he would never be unfaithful. He had already promised me that before. It was still special when he reaffirmed it. I placed the ring on his finger and tried to say the same thing I had before when we'd originally made our promises.

Mass went on. Sid and I kneeled at the two kneelers that had been placed before the altar. A soft chorus of snickers filtered up from the congregation. I looked at Sid and he shrugged.

It felt a little strange having Sid next to me, but I liked it. I received Communion. Sid didn't. I felt a little sad, but Sid is an atheist. It was how he was raised, and I respect that.

Finally, John returned to the altar and began cleaning vessels. Stella had gone back to the piano in the loft. The only problem is that the music caused another ripple of giggles among the congregation.

"What?" Sid looked at me and frowned. "It's Beethoven, Pathétique Sonata, second movement."

I chuckled. "It's also Billy Joel. 'This night is mine.'"

Sid nodded. "Frank."

"I believe so."

Sid shifted. "I hope I can stand after this. I don't think I've spent this much time on my knees in my life, and that includes an extended stint during the Sex Olympics."

Which was actually nonsense. We hadn't been on our knees very long at all. And Sid got up alright. John pronounced the final blessing over us.

"You are coming to the reception, aren't you?" I hissed at the priest.

"Wouldn't miss it," John whispered, putting his hand over his body mike. He removed his hand. "And now, my brothers and sisters, I present to you our newest married couple, Lisa and Sid."

There was plenty of cheering, but I didn't entirely hear it. Sid and I were too wrapped up in a warm, wonderful, passionate kiss.

"Put some tongue in it!" someone yelled.

Sid and I shook with suppressed laughter because I already had.

Stella got on the organ and immediately demonstrated the meaning of pulling all the stops out, almost blasting us with Mendelssohn's Wedding March from the ballet A Midsummer Night's Dream. Okay, it is the tune that's the second most associated with weddings after the "Here Comes the Bride" tune from Richard Wagner's Lohengrin. I hate "Here Comes the Bride," but my favorite play in the world is A Midsummer Night's Dream, by William Shakespeare. So, I was happy with Mendelssohn.

It was a lot faster going out than it was going in. Giddy and out of breath, Sid and I stopped in the vestibule, and I grinned at him.

"We did it!" I gasped.

"We did." Sid laughed. "We're officially married!" He pulled me into his arms and kissed me. "I'm so glad we are."

Laughing, Mae and Nick walked in.

"Should I?" Sid looked at me.

"Definitely," I said.

Sid took Mae's face in his hands and kissed her with his passionate best.

"Neil!" Mae yelped.

Then she recovered herself. She had work to do. As the rest of the wedding party landed near the door, she pushed everybody into place for the receiving line until Mama and Daddy walked out. Then Mama took over. Stella, still upstairs, had finished with Mendelssohn, and launched into a Bach fugue.

"Why isn't Stella down here?" Mama asked as the rest of the congregation ambled into the vestibule and lined up to greet us.

"She's having fun, Mama," I said. "You're not going to deprive her of that, are you?"

Mama got into her place after me and rolled her eyes.

I was amazed at how many of Sid's old friends had shown. Admittedly, that group was at least two-thirds female, and several of those women had worn black. One of them had even put on widow's weeds.

"I don't believe it!" crowed two of the younger examples.

"We don't either," I said to them.

"Lisa, my beloved, this is Sandi and Denise," Sid said.

"We've met," I said.

The girls rolled their eyes.

Sandi, a petite brunette, smiled. "Sid, we really thought you were joking when we got the invitation. I know. You told us, but we couldn't believe you'd actually do it."

"Well, we did." Sid grinned and squeezed me.

I introduced the women to my mother and father, and Sandi and Denise moved on quickly.

Now, there are not many people in our side business who know our real names, nor do we know theirs. It's generally safer that way. There are Kathy and Jesse, but we'd been friends long before they were recruited into the business. However, when the head of Quickline had heard that Sid and I were getting married, she asked us to give her a list of people we'd like to have at the wedding. Sid and I had agonized over the decision, but finally agreed that there were four people we'd like to see, all from a case we'd worked together eighteen months before, plus a couple of others. Two names were not approved, but Marissa Maldonado and Karen Bischorn were. To be honest, Marissa, who had dark hair and a timid mien, already knew Sid's and my names and address because she usually worked in Systems and had to know our real identities to run paychecks and other things. Karen, also known as Blue Shield, was a code specialist with neatly cut brown hair who worked in San Francisco.

Marissa hugged Sid.

"It's so nice to see you alive," she hissed at him. Sid had narrowly escaped an explosion. "I mean, I knew you were, but it's nice to see it."

Nick, who was standing next to Sid on the other side from me, looked at her strangely and shrugged. Marissa attacked me next.

"I knew you two had a thing for each other!"

I laughed. "I never said we didn't."

"And his kid!" Marissa giggled. "Oh, my god! He's adorable."

I smiled. "That's my boy."

I introduced Karen and Marissa to my mother, then greeted several of the teens from the youth group I helped lead. A tall, matronly woman stepped up and introduced herself as Lillian Ward. Sid and I had met her a few times, but mostly knew her as the Dragon, the head of Operation Quickline. We also knew the couple behind her, Marian and Andrew. Marian was petite, although still taller than my mother, with a pert nose and fluffy hair cut short. Andrew was significantly taller with a horsey face. Both were a pair of rather frightening British CID agents who had taken a liking to us for some reason. I wasn't entirely surprised to see Marian and Andrew. When the Dragon - I mean Lillian - had sent back her RSVP, it had been for three people attending.

"Congratulations, you two," Lillian said, bussing Sid on the cheek.

"Thank you, Lillian," I said, and introduced her to Mama.

"Good to meet you, Mrs. Wycherly," Lillian shook Mama's hand. "I've known Sid and Lisa for a good long time. It's such a delight to see them getting married."

Andrew stepped up to me and kissed my hand. "Congratulations and best wishes, love."

"Thanks, Andrew," Sid said, his eyes narrowing.

I turned to my parents. "Mama, Daddy, this is Andrew and Marian." I stopped. I had no idea what their last names were. "We know them through the writing business."

"Well, nice to meet you," said Mama.

I really didn't like the leer Andrew gave my mother, nor did Daddy, but there were more people to greet.

Another elegant older woman walked up shortly after Lillian, but I felt considerably more warmth toward Hattie Mitchell. She had been one of our editors and had been involved in a couple of other situations but had a high enough security clearance that it wasn't a problem. She was also yet another woman Sid had slept with.

The big surprise was when Tom Freeman and Angelique Carter wandered out of the church and through the receiving line. Well, we knew they were there. We'd seen them the night before. That they were arm in arm was what shocked us.

"We had a great time last night," Tom told us.

"We really did." Angelique grinned happily. "We haven't stopped talking since we had dinner."

I laughed. "That's terrific! I'm so glad for you guys."

"I am, too," said Sid.

Tom punched him in the shoulder and Sid winced. Okay, Tom is a big guy, with receding blond hair and glasses.

"We'll catch up with you two later," Tom said, and moved on.

As the church emptied and the crowd around the front thinned, Sid and I told Jesse that we didn't need the traditional group shots around the altar. Jesse agreed, although Mama pushed for and got several family group shots outside the church.

Then Neil and Mae dragged Sid and me to their van, still parked out front of the church, but now decked out with streamers and paper roses, for the ride to the reception. I snuggled against Sid and tried breathing deeply, as the horns from the cars behind us sounded gleefully.

"You okay?" Sid asked me softly.

"Oh, yeah. Just trying to get used to it." I looked at him. "At least we're together and they don't have any more excuses to separate us."

"They'd better not." Sid squeezed me, and the two of us simply relaxed into each other.

My thoughts went wandering again to the first week of February and the phone in our office ringing...

(Tuesday, February 4)

It was my day to pick up the calls, so I grabbed it. It was Sid's personal line, as opposed to the business line we used for our writing business. We were shutting that personal line down since he hadn't really gotten very many calls on it for the past eleven months. He'd dropped out of the singles scene in late March the year before and it was as though no one had noticed. Well, until that week, no one had seemed to notice.

"Is Sid there?" asked an uneasy female voice.

"May I ask who's calling?"

"Um. Shelley Friedman."

"Let me see if he's available." I put her on hold and looked at Sid, who was sitting at the desk facing mine. "Shelley Friedman?"

"Huh. Haven't heard from her in forever. Wait." Sid suddenly chuckled.

I grinned. "She's on the guest list, isn't she?"

We'd sent the invitations to the wedding out a few days before and were waiting for the shockwaves.

"Yep." Sid put his hand on the phone set. "We were on the board together for Hedonists, Incorporated. Wanna listen in?"

"Are you kidding? Of course, I do."

Sid punched the buttons for the speaker phone. "Hello, Shelley. It's been a while."

"Yeah. I'd heard a rumor that you'd dropped out of things."

"I have."

"Oh. Well, Sid, I had to call. Somebody is playing an awful joke on you."

"Really? What's going on?" Sid winked at me.

"I just received an invitation to your wedding. Can you believe that?"

"You did? Who am I marrying?"

"A Lisa Jane Wycherly. Isn't she that little ice cube of a secretary of yours?"

"Well, she's actually my partner now."

Shelley sounded surprised. "Oh. The invite says something about a Catholic church."

"That sounds right."

"You mean other people got them?"

"I would imagine so. We sent out about a hundred and fifty of them." I could see Sid trying not to laugh.

"Oh, my god! Your phone must be ringing off the hook!"

"Not yet. You're the first one."

"Sid, this is awful. Do you have any idea who did this?"

"Shelley, Lisa and I sent them out. Well, we paid a couple teenagers to address them."

She gasped. "Sid, are you trying to tell me you're getting married?"

"I'm telling you. Lisa and I are getting married."

"Have you completely lost your marbles?" [That was not the way she phrased it. – SEH]

"No. Just my heart."

"But... But... She's been telling you no for how long?"

"That's not the issue, Shelley." Sid smiled, but I could hear his voice getting a little tight. "It's not about the sex in this case. I love her, and I mean the real thing."

"Sid, darling. I'm sure it's just a phase. Be patient. It will pass."

Sid laughed loudly. "A- I don't want it to, and B- It's not going to pass. Lisa and I have worked too long and hard at this relationship. It's time to publicly acknowledge that."

"I have no idea what you're talking about."

"Come to the wedding. Maybe you'll see."

"I'll think about it."

"Okay. Talk to you later then."

The horns of the cars in procession behind us were going full tilt.

"What are you thinking about?" he asked quietly.

"Shelley Friedman."

Sid nodded. "I was glad she showed."

"Think she figured it out?"

He sighed a little. "I doubt it. Her kind wouldn't."

"You were her kind once."

"Not quite." He shook his head. "I was never a true hedonist. Too many values, like being nice to people. And the pursuit of pleasure was never the focus of my life." He looked at me. "How are you doing?"

"Better. Not so nervous. You?"

"Me, too." He smiled and blew out his breath. "We got the important part done with. Now, all we have to do is get through the party." He shifted. "And then the wedding night."

I looked at him. "You're not nervous about that, are you?"

"Not per se. Just a lot to live up to."

I sighed. "You don't have to live up to anything."

I swallowed. Between the oral sex and the fact that I loved him, that was going to be easy. Me making it worth all he'd given up. That was more worrisome, although he hadn't been complaining at all. He smiled at me and pressed his lips to my temple.

"You're right, honey." He squeezed me again. "It's just a party. And the rest of it, we work out between ourselves."

"Exactly."

It wasn't just a party, and we both knew it. There was also my general terror of large gatherings. However, I knew pretty much everyone there, so it was the easier part of the day to get through.

When we got to the hotel, Jesse pulled us aside to get a few more photos with the parents and wedding party as the rest of the guests arrived. There was more cheering when Sid and I finally entered the room. A small jazz/rock band was setting up at one end, while canned music played from unseen speakers. The guests mostly stood around on the eventual dance floor as waiters served hors d'oeuvres and sparkling cider in tall, straight glasses. There was Champagne (the real stuff, not just sparkling wine) available in flutes, but it was only served at two bars set up on either side of the room. We did have quite a few teenagers there from the youth group, and the bartenders were very good at carding folks. I got a few bites of hors d'oeuvres, and a glass of Champagne before Frank picked up a mike near the band and asked everybody to take their seats so that lunch could be served.

"Oh, and please make sure you have a full glass of something," Frank said. "We will have the traditional toast to the bride and groom in just a minute."

I'm not sure how it happened, but while Nick held a tall, straight glass as he stood next to Frank, the color of the liquid inside looked a lot more like the bubbly than cider. Nick did like wine, especially Champagne. As soon as everyone was seated, Frank handed the mike to Nick. My boy grinned.

"You suckers," he said, looking at us and laughing. I gave him a rather severe look, but the little stinker was undeterred. "Dad, you copped out. Still, I can't help being really glad you did. It's like I told the judge at the adoption hearing the other day. We're a real family now. We weren't always. I was only sometimes around. Mom did her thing. Dad did his. Okay. Dad did a lot of his." There was general laughter and one loud sob. "Then Mom got Dad to behave and is probably the only woman in the world who could have. And now, I've got a family again. And two middle names. To Dad and Mom, who finally got their crap together and got married. It's about time."

Everyone drank, although it sure looked like Mama wanted to take Nick to task over his language. Marlou Parks, who had been the best friend of Nick's first mom, Rachel, went over to Nick and gave him a big hug. I was so happy to see her.

Frank took the mike and broke in again. "Before we are served our lunch, Father John, would you please come up and say grace?"

Shaking his head, John lumbered up to the mike. "Grace."

There was mostly laughter, but a few kids booed.

"What?" John asked. "I thought I was off duty. Alright. In the name of the Father, the Son, and the Holy Spirit. Father, we thank you for the gift of Sid and Lisa and their love. Please continue to bless it and the food we are about to eat. We pray in gratitude in your Son's name. Amen." About half the guests muttered amen in response, then John cleared his throat. "I have one other thought to share, and I will keep it brief. I'm hungry, too. I think it is particularly telling that Jesus' first miracle was at the Wedding at Cana. First off, he may have given his mother some attitude, but he did do what she asked him to do. Secondly, he opted to keep the party rolling. Sid, Lisa, we've got plenty of water. It's going to be a good day."

Then a crew of waiters appeared, and everyone was served their salad.

"Wedding at Cana?" Sy asked. He was sitting next to me at a table near the far end of the room.

We'd opted not to have a head table. Sid was on my other side, with Mama on his other side.

"When Jesus turned the water into wine," I said.

Sy suddenly nodded and chuckled.

I picked at my salad.

"Are you okay?" Sid asked.

"Okay enough."

"You're not eating."

"I know. I'm just not hungry." My appetite is usually voracious, so I could understand Sid being concerned.

"It's not your period." Sid looked at me. He knew that because I always put a piece of tape on the bathroom mirror when I start so that I don't forget to do my breast exam when I finish. "You took the tape down Thursday morning."

I shrugged. "It must be all the excitement, but I'm not that hungry for some reason."

I got some food down me, but only about half the plate. Jesse and Shaneequa alternated between eating and shooting pictures. I'm not sure who got it, but one of them got a terrific shot of one of Sid's former girlfriends, who was either a model or an actress, wearing gold lame pants and holding Irene Sanchez's baby Miriam with Irene sitting primly and modestly nearby. [Delanna Monte, and she was a model. – SEH]

After Sid and I had finished eating, we wandered hand in hand between the tables, saying hello and chatting with our friends. Shelley Friedman completely scandalized Dan and Sarah Williams by grabbing Sid between the legs.

"Just so you know what you're missing," she told him.

Sid laughed and removed her hand. "I'm not missing a thing, Shelley."

He looked at me with a lascivious grin and I flushed. Okay, I may have gotten a feel or two while we were eating.

There were several kids running around. Carl and Erin MacArthur had their two little ones, the oldest was, I think, four. Nick had invited Josh Sandoval and his family, so Josh's two younger brothers were playing with Janey and Ellen. Marty and Mitch never stop running, only this time they were playing hide and seek under the tables with Erin's oldest. Nick's other two friends and their families were there, as well, and the younger siblings ran about. Several other of my Single Adult friends, who were now married, had their babies and toddlers with them. The Guitar Choir had their spouses with them, along with their kids, who ranged in age from infant to late teens.

Jesse talked to Frank, who got up and made the next announcement.

"It is time to cut the cake! Sid, Lisa, come on up to the cake table." Frank grinned.

I rolled my eyes. Sid nodded that we should go with it. I watched as he set the knife into the bottom layer.

"Now, the two of you have to cut it together," Mama said.

"Why?" I asked. "Sid's the cook. I'm not."

Sid laughed and cut a small slice, put it on a plate, and tried to hand it to Mama. Jesse's camera whirred almost as if he were shooting video.

"No!" Mama protested. "You feed it to each other."

"I'm not having any cake," Sid said.

"What?" I asked. "Why not?"

"I don't want any cake." Sid's voice got a little tight.

"Do you have to be so picky?" I snapped.

"Lisa, that cake is loaded with processed flour, sugar, fats."

"That's real butter in that frosting."

"Cholesterol!"

Even as we glared at each other, the people around us shifted uncomfortably. We looked at each other.

Sid sighed. "It's not the cake. I just don't want to play games with feeding it to each other."

"Then why didn't you say so?"

"You got on me about the health thing."

"Oh. Sorry." I smiled sheepishly at him.

"I'm sorry, too."

Mae laughed. "Actually, they're doing pretty good," she said to someone. "That's their first fight today."

"But what about the picture?" Mama asked.

I looked at Sid. "I've got an idea."

He suddenly grinned. "Really?"

"You wanna go with me?"

He nodded. [Are you kidding? You had that look on your face, so I knew it was going to be fun. – SEH] I used my forefinger and scooped up some frosting from the cake plate that Sid still held. He looked a little befuddled when I drew a line of frosting down his cheek, but laughed when I reached over and licked it off. Yeah, that picture came out really nicely. So did the ones after that, as Sid put my finger in his mouth and sucked the rest of the frosting off it.

The chorus of cat calls rose over the sounds of scandalized disgust. Then Frank interrupted over the mike.

"You know, you two, you've got all night for that kind of thing," he teased. "Alright. We're going to keep things moving with the next wedding tradition, the bride and groom's first dance as a married couple. So, I'd like to introduce the Guitar Choir right now. Come on up, gang."

The group of singers walked up to just below the little stage where the band was waiting.

"Sid," Frank continued. "You've become quite a special part of our little group. Some of you may not know, but last winter, I finally convinced Sid to accompany the choir."

"It was extortion!" Sid called.

"Okay, there may have been a bet involved. You see, the youth group has a touch football game on Thanksgiving Weekend, and a certain amount of pomp and silliness has become part of it, including a Turkey Queen. Some years, the queen has been elected for her looks. Other years, he hasn't. Last October, Sid foolishly bet me that I wouldn't get elected Turkey Queen."

Sid laughed and shook his head. "You rigged it."

Frank grinned. "Hell, yes. I was desperate for a good accompanist. And I have to say, Sid, you've been terrific about making good on it. In gratitude, the Choir has decided to provide the music for your first dance."

Frank blew the notes on the pitch pipe as Sid led me to the dance floor. Frank had done a phenomenal job on the vocal arrangement of "You and Me Against the World." It's an odd tune for a love song, but for Sid and me, it spoke volumes about the isolation we often felt because of our side business. No one knew that, of course, except Kathy and Jesse, because they're part of it.

Then Frank turned things over to the band, and, of course, the first tune they played was Rod Stewart's "Tonight's the Night."

Sid and I danced that together, then did all the other usual dances, me with Daddy, Sid with Mama, then Sy and Stella. I danced with Nick and Sid danced with Janey. The other guests began filling the dance floor. Tom and Angelique spent more time dancing with each other than anyone else at the wedding.

We got one kerfuffle. Uncle Leonard happened to be dancing with Lillian when he got fresh. A second later, and so fast no one knew how she'd done it, she had him in a headlock. Uncle Leonard is not that tall but is otherwise large and used to throwing his weight around. Lillian is tall, but not that filled out. She gave him a little shake, then dumped him on the dance floor.

"You certainly know some interesting people, Lisle," Mama said, her voice a little shaky.

Daddy thought it was hysterical, but Aunt Amanda, Leonard's wife, was furious.

When the band declared a break, Frank decided it was time to throw the bouquet. We had a bit of a problem finding enough of my single friends to make a group, and most of Sid's single female friends were already gone or still in mourning. It was okay. I had a surprise for them. Instead of being fixed into a plastic holder, I'd convinced the florist to just bundle the flowers together. She also showed me how to break the string that held them together, which I did just before tossing the bouquet into the air over my shoulder. The flowers went everywhere to gales of laughter.

Sid and I were not going to get out of the garter toss, however. They seated me on a chair while the returning band played the usual strip tune.

"The higher it is, the better the luck," one of my uncles hollered.

Esther Nguyen came up as Sid lifted my skirt just enough to get his hand inside.

"Sid, maybe you better go look for it," Esther said.

"Maybe I should." Sid started to put his head under my skirt.

"Sid, will you please behave yourself?" Mama groaned.

Sid sighed loudly. "Isn't this what I married her for?"

However, he kept his head outside my dress. I had placed the garter just above my knee, but that didn't stop Sid from reaching all the way up and grabbing a feel. I flushed again, mostly because it felt so very nice. Sid retrieved the garter. One of the youth group teens leaped a full foot or two off the floor to snag it out of the air. Jesse's photo caught him right at the top of the leap.

The band began playing again, and the afternoon wore on pleasantly. Uncle Stephen got a little loud and the hotel staff had to confiscate the bottle of Grandma Caulfield's corn liquor on the table. I'd seen Sid get a snort – he'd had it before and really liked it. Nick tried a sip, too, and shook his head violently. Andrew tried propositioning Lety Sandoval, but Ramon, her husband, shut that down quickly. I would have thought Andrew stood a better chance with some of Sid's ex-girlfriends, but he didn't seem to take much interest in them.

The room slowly emptied out. Andrew and Marian found Sid and me together and made their farewells.

"It was a lovely wedding, darling," Marian said to me, then smiled at both of us. "We'll see the two of you shortly."

Sid and I smiled but couldn't figure out what she'd meant. It's not as though we had time to think about it. Someone else wanted to say goodbye and wish us well.

We were saying goodbye to Sister Maria Campos when Ellen and Janey came running up.

"Uncle Sid, Aunt Lisa, you guys gotta come outside!" Janey said as she and her sister pulled on our hands.

"Okay, we're coming!" I said.

Outside, my jaw dropped. Mae and Neil's van had been festooned and then some. Shaving cream, streamers, toilet paper, cans, pompoms, balloons, not to mention a veritable rainbow of tempera paint. "Tonight's the night!" had been painted just under "Just Married" on the back. "Cherries Jubilee!" ran across the right side, and that was the cleanest stuff. The rest, oh, my god... One of Sid's friends (and I think I know who) had put all of Sid's old Sex Olympics records on the left side, along with "Class of '68, Most Likely To..."

Sid's grin got a little tight, but he laughed anyway.

"Most positions?" I looked at him and grinned.

"That poor girl!" Aunt Marie told Aunt Amanda.

Mae came up and nudged me. "You lucky dog. Best all-around four years in a row."

My face burned. "Well, I knew that." I saw something else. "Sid, they goofed. They put sixty-nine all over the van and you graduated from high school in '68."

He came up and pulled me close to him. "That's not what that's about."

"It's not?"

"Monday night," he whispered, nuzzling my ear.

My eyebrows lifted. "Oh. That was fun."

"Now, you two gotta get back inside," Mama said, tugging on my elbow.

"Why?" I asked.

"So, we can throw the rice."

"Forget it!" I started for the van.

I wasn't near fast enough. Yelling broke loose and rice was everywhere. Sid and I turned our backs to the onslaught and tried to open the side door, but it was locked.

"Too bad I don't have my lock picks," Sid whispered.

Mae and Neil waited until the deluge had stopped before opening the doors. Sid and I scrambled in. Sid shut the side door as Neil started the engine. Banging and rattling rocked the van.

"What the hell is that?" Sid yelped.

Mae and Neil looked at each other.

"Gravel in the hubcaps," they said together.

I laughed, but Sid had other things on his mind. Satisfied that there wasn't any threat, he began kissing me and the next thing I knew, I was flat on my back with him on top of me. Mae reached around behind her and swatted him.

"Oh, for Heaven's sakes? Can't you two wait until you're alone?"

"Why?" Sid asked.

I sighed happily as his kisses moved along my jaw and started down my neck.

"Uh-oh," he said quietly. "I am going to put in a formal request that this be the last high collar you wear. Seriously. No turtlenecks, either. I want access at all times."

"I see. Does this mean no more closed shirts and ties?"

He sighed. "You drive a hard bargain, woman. We'll see."

"Then we'll see about the turtlenecks."

He laughed, then nuzzled my ear. I cooed.

"I'm told I was pretty good in a back seat at one time," he whispered.

"You still are."

"Watch the hanky panky back there!" Neil called.

"I'm watching! I'm watching," I called back.

"Come on!" Mae swatted Sid again. "Behave!"

"I am," Sid said righteously. "I'm behaving like I married her."

A minute later, Sid did lift his head. "Are we getting on the freeway?"

"We're taking the long way back to your house," Neil said. "Give the rest of the family a chance to get over there."

"Okay." Sid shrugged and pushed me down onto the back seat again.

I enjoyed the necking in kind of a dreamy stupor. At the same time, my thoughts wandered. Again, to early January.

(Monday, January 6)

I was entering a new query letter into the computer when Sid wandered into our office. He'd been to lunch with Henry James. That was not unusual. The two went to lunch regularly, and usually just for the fun of it. Sid did not usually come back from those outings looking bewildered, though.

"Are you okay?" I asked.

Sid slid onto his desk chair. "I think so. We need to talk about our honeymoon."

I looked at him. "Weren't we talking about Hawaii?"

"Yeah. But you said you'd rather go to England."

"I said I didn't think we could."

I have my Master of Arts in English Literature. I wanted to go to England and then some. The problem was, because of our side business, Sid and I had to get any trips outside the U.S. cleared upline. Hawaii may not have been the preferred option, but it was an acceptable alternative.

"Henry actually suggested going to England." Sid shrugged. "Which makes sense. He knows what a Shakespeare freak you are."

"But what about you? Don't you want to bask indolently in the sun?"

"I don't care." Sid shrugged.

"Really?" I looked at him. "That used to be your favorite way to go on vacation."

He winced. "It was a favorite way to get laid." He sighed and mused. "I had a lot of fun with Sy this past holiday.

It's entirely possible that tourism could be a new passion." He looked at me. "Do you still want to go to England?"

"Are you kidding? I'd love it! Do you want to?"

"Yeah. It sounds like fun." He sat up a little. "I'll have to research some flights, but I'm guessing with the time change and everything, we'll have to spend the wedding night in L.A. Is that okay?"

"Sure." I thought. "Any reason we can't spend it here at the house?"

Sid grinned. "Besides our families?"

"That's why the bedroom was soundproofed and we have locks on the doors."

"True." He looked at me. "You know, given how the timing on my last AIDS test works out, we might have to wait until the wedding night for me to deflower you. I suppose if we find a way for that to happen before the wedding night, then spending it here is less of an issue."

"And if we have to wait until the wedding night, then it's even better if we do it here." I smiled as he looked at me in wonder. "When we finally get to have full sexual intercourse for the first time, I'd rather do it in our own bed than anywhere else."

Sid leaned back in his chair and sighed. He was feeling the urge. I shifted. I couldn't help but feel it, too.

I have no idea where we were when Neil finally pulled off the freeway and didn't get back on again. We stopped for a red light and Neil rolled down his window and laughed.

"Thanks, but we're not the ones," he called to someone outside. "They're in the back. They couldn't wait."

"You should see all the looks we're getting," Mae said, turning toward us again.

"Why do you think we're down here?" Sid replied.

"Yeah. Right," Neil sniggered.

The sun was about an hour away from setting when we finally pulled up into the driveway of our house in Beverly Hills. Neil had done his work well. The people back at the house included Nick, who had let everybody in, Mama, Daddy, Sy and Stella, Frank and Esther, Kathy and Jesse, the O'Malley kids, and that was it. Jesse got a great shot of Sid, Nick, and me, still in our wedding clothes on the stairs to the second floor. We eventually framed it and hung it in our bedroom.

Sid and I went on into our bedroom to change into more comfortable clothes. We weren't the only ones. By the time the two of us came downstairs, even Kathy and Jesse and Frank and Esther had found sweatpants or jeans and t-shirts and sweatshirts to put on. Stella seemed a tad perturbed that she had to put on a running suit just to be decent. On the other hand, she was willing to concede that not everyone was more comfortable in their natural state, even if she thought it was ridiculous. I had on my oldest pair of jeans and a sweatshirt that I'd cut the neckband out of. [Nor did you put a bra on, and the way that neckless sweatshirt fell over your bare shoulder... - SEH] Sid was wearing his tight jeans, his sleeveless undershirt, and a dress shirt over that, which he'd left unbuttoned. Nick had on the pajamas he seldom wore.

Conchetta Ramirez, our housekeeper, had left a complete buffet worth of food in the refrigerator. She'd been at the wedding and reception, and we'd invited her to the house, but she'd decided not to join us. There were several trays of enchiladas, beans and rice, and a smaller tray of her wonderful chiles rellenos. Sid and I loved them for the way the dish seared our nasal passages to the back of our sinuses. Daddy and Esther were also big fans. For some reason, everyone else seemed to prefer the enchiladas.

Kathy and Mama had gotten the food heated up and on the dining area table. Everyone over thirteen settled into the living room. The kids ate and landed in the rumpus room at the back of the house and started arguing over which video to watch. A pile of wedding presents sat on the ebony baby grand piano. There was also a significant stack of cards. The kids eventually settled on looking at Back to the Future.

I picked at a chile as Mama handed Sid the stack of cards. One of our three cats, Long John Silver, came out of hiding and jumped into Sid's lap. Sid finished his chile quickly, then began going through the cards, most of them from former girlfriends who were not happy about Sid getting married. Those messages were not of the sort one wanted to read aloud.

"Best in the city?" I grumbled as he showed me one. "What's wrong with her? At least three said best on the West Coast."

"Best what?" Mama asked.

I pointed at the rumpus room. "Probably best not to say."

Stella snorted. "It's simply normal, natural human be-havior. Nothing to be ashamed of."

The sound of ticking clocks spilled out from the rum-pus room. Mae got up and turned the sound on the TV down to a chorus of groans.

With the cards opened, we moved on to the presents that people had brought. Several minutes into Back to the Future, Mama put a large box on my lap. The card was from Uncle Stephen and Aunt Marie and addressed to Mr. and Mrs. Sid Hackbirn, which annoyed me a lot. The present though... Once the paper came off, it revealed a brown corrugated box that had been taped at the top. There was plenty of tissue paper and I had to pull the object out to get the paper from around it. When the last piece fell from the gift, the wooden mounting board faced me. The rest of the room gasped. I turned it around. It was a stuffed and mounted possum.

"You made a time machine out of a DeLorean?" Michael J. Fox yelped from the other room.

Loud laughter drowned out the next line.

Sid got up out of the chair next to me. "I think I'll just take this straight out to the trash."

Mama sighed. "I think so, honey."

We got two more blenders. Mama said we could always use an extra. I rolled my eyes as Sid pointed out that we'd already gotten twelve at the teen Bible Study and another two from the shower Janet and Sylvia had thrown. Most of the other gifts were mundane, except for the small box that Sy presented.

Sid opened it, pulled the tissue paper away, and smiled. It was a guidebook to London. Yellow sticky notes poked out between the pages. As we looked at it, notes on lined paper were stuck between pages, and several items were highlighted.

"It's from our trip last summer," Sy said. "I hope you find it useful."

I laughed. "We will. Thank you so much!"

Fortunately, we got through the presents in record time – there weren't that many, thank Heaven. It had gotten around that we didn't really need or want any. Several people had sent theirs to the house in the week or two before. The movie in the other room was still going when a jaw-cracking yawn shook me.

Sid laughed and got up. "Oh, honey. I'm guessing it's time we went upstairs."

"I should think so," said Stella.

"But wait," said Sy. Somehow, he pulled a lute, yes, a real lute, from behind his chair. "Fortunately, I was able to borrow this from a colleague of mine at UCLA. I think we should take advantage of a very old wedding custom and sing the bride and groom to their connubial couch. Oh, and, Stella, the sweet wine to make the groom gentle."

"I'm not worried about that," I said as Sid helped me up.

"Still a little riesling is a nice touch." Stella handed Sid and me each a glass of light gold liquid.

Sid held me as I leaned next to him, and we sipped our wine. The tune was bawdy, but kid-safe in that the kids wouldn't get the Elizabethan language. Sy sang in a cheery baritone, and eventually followed Sid and me, singing away, as we made our way up the stairs to our bedroom. We waved at everybody, then went into our room. Sid locked the door, then checked that the door to our workroom was also locked, and then the bathroom door into the workroom, as well.

I looked at him and smiled. "So, this is it."

"Yeah." He looked at me tenderly. "I guess it is." He paused. "Do you mind? I need to use the bathroom."

"Sure."

I debated getting undressed, but we usually like that part. So, I wandered over to the bed, instead, and sat down on the side, setting my wineglass on the nightstand. I'm not sure what happened after that because I fell asleep.

[You were out cold. At least, that's how I found you. I admit, I was taking my time in the bathroom. When I saw you there and heard that cute little whistling snore of yours, I couldn't help smiling. I rolled you over so that I could get the covers pulled back. That's when I discovered the bed had been short-sheeted. Mae and Neil again. Still don't know when that happened. It made getting you shifted around enough to re-make the bed interesting. Then I finally got your flip-flops off, along with the rest of your clothes, and slid you back onto your pillow. I got undressed, got into bed, then reached over and kissed the side of your head.

"Thank you," I whispered, and turned out the lights. – SEH]

March 2 – 3, 1986

I awoke to darkness and silence. The darkness was familiar. It was how our room always looks in the middle of the night. The silence was a touch off. You see, Sid talks in his sleep. If he's quiet, he's usually awake. I rolled onto my back and saw his profile next to me. He was also laying on his back, another tip-off that he wasn't sleeping. I lifted my head to look at the clock radio on his bedside table. Sid is very nearsighted, and the clock is on his side of the bed so that he can see it without his contact lenses.

It was just after two a.m.

"You're awake." I muttered, letting my head fall back onto the pillow.

"Yeah."

"Is that why I'm awake?"

"Don't think so."

I sighed. "I fell asleep on you, didn't I?"

"It's alright. You were obviously tired." He rolled onto his side and pulled me next to him.

"It's still our wedding night, right?"

"Of course."

"Good. Close your eyes."

"Huh?"

"Close your eyes. I want to turn the lights on."

He chuckled. I gave him half a minute, then shut my eyes and turned on the lights next to the bed. I rolled over and faced him.

"So, what's going on?" I asked.

"What do you mean?"

"You're not feeling me up. You're not grinning lasciviously."

"It's the middle of the night, Lisa."

"And when has that ever stopped you?"

He sighed. "Point taken." He sighed again. "I may be having a little trouble getting started."

"Really?" I snuggled closer to him. "What's the problem?"

"Sex Olympics records." He winced. "I gotta say, the reception was a lot of fun. And the cards we got. But it all did ramp up the expectations."

"I thought we agreed those didn't matter."

He looked at me. "Come off it, Lisa. You can't tell me that there isn't something in the back of your brain wondering how good it will be?"

"Of course, there is." I giggled. "But that has a heck of a lot more to do with what we've been doing than anything I read on the side of Mae's van today."

"Really?"

"Really." I reached over and touched his cheek. "Why do you think I got so peeved when your former friend said best in the city? I know how good you are that way."

"But there's so much that could go wrong. You could even be one of those women who like oral sex better than regular sex."

I smiled. "I do like oral sex."

"You most certainly do." He sighed and looked away. "And it's been almost a year since I last had full intercourse, sharply increasing the odds that I'll go off too fast."

"So what? Sid, my dearest. When you and I got into the oral thing last summer, it was mind-blowing at first. But I knew that wasn't going to last, and it didn't. And that was fine. Things settled down, and, yes, we've had a few times when I couldn't wait to get you under my skirt. A few times when we were just being silly. That really weird thing that happened at that motel near Dulles last fall. And some other times that blew my mind, and even a few times when things were a little perfunctory. But it was all good and delicious and yummy. Why would full intercourse be any different? If you don't blow my mind tonight, you will at some point. Even if you don't, it will still be good. I love you, Sid. That's the important thing. Not whether or not you beat me to the punch."

He laughed a little. "How do you do it? You're so naive and yet so knowing."

"I don't know. I just know that I love you."

"And I love you." He sighed and kissed me. "I love you so much."

"Kiss me again like that."

He did. It was so good, and it led exactly where it should have, which was even more amazing than I would have thought. We were still breathing a little heavily when he looked down at me.

"That wasn't just sex," he gasped.

"Oh? What the heck was it?"

"We just made love."

"Duh."

He kissed me so hard it almost bruised my lips. "No. Real love."

"Okay."

He rolled over, and I snuggled next to him.

"By the way, you blew my mind," I whispered.

He chuckled. "I don't think we need a postmortem, but that's good to know."

"Mmmm."

"You blew mine, too."

"That's nice. Thank you, Sid."

"Thank you, my sweet Lisa."

My eyes popped open. "You know. I'm hungry."

He laughed loudly and nuzzled my ear. "Then maybe we should do something about that."

I found a robe and tossed a pair of running shorts at him. We had the kids in the house, and I didn't want to assume they were asleep. The leftover chiles rellenos were in the fridge. I microwaved a plate full. Sid hoisted himself onto the kitchen counter and watched while I ate standing next to him.

"You know," I said around a big mouthful of chile and cheese. "I'm really glad we decided to stay here tonight."

He smiled. "I am, too."

"You sure you don't want some?" I asked.

"I'll have a bite."

I fed it to him, then burped. He laughed loudly. As I finished eating, he pulled the plate and fork from my hands and washed them. I slid up behind him and played with his chest.

"Oh, my god," he sighed, putting my plate in the second sink. "I'm young again."

[Now, I know why you found that line from L.A. Story so funny. – SEH]

"What do you mean?"

"Let's just say I haven't recharged this fast since I was a teen." He turned and pressed against me.

"Oh."

"Would you mind if we took advantage of this?"

I giggled. "Mind? Not in the least. But the kids. We'd better get upstairs."

Which we did, and it was more than lovely, and we finally fell asleep together.

[Yes, it was mind-blowing sex. But it was so much more than that. If I had known just how amazing making love with you would be, even as far back as the summer of '83, I probably would have been faithful. But you would never have known that, so perhaps it was best that things fell out the way they did. – SEH]

Oddly enough, it was Sid cursing that woke me.

"What?" I mumbled.

"It's after eight-thirty."

"I guess we were pretty sleepy."

"I guess we were." Sid slipped over next to me and nuzzled my ear.

"Does your nuzzling mean we're going to do this again?" I asked, hopefully.

"What? Two times in one night isn't enough for you?" He was laughing, so it was okay.

I smiled at him. "If it's this good, is there really enough?"

"You know. We should probably test that theory." And he kissed me so warmly.

The only problem was the phone rang while we were engaged. I couldn't believe it, although I'd sort of seen it before. Sid didn't miss a beat while he got the phone off the hook.

"Are you two awake yet?" I heard Mama ask through the receiver. "We're supposed to go to brunch before seeing you two off at the airport."

Sid let out a happy sigh. "We're a little busy right now."

"Oh, my god!" Mama screeched and the phone on her end clattered onto some surface.

Stella's voice was a touch distant, but grew louder. "What are you so embarrassed about? They're just having sex." She'd picked up the receiver on her end. "Sid, when are the two of you going to be ready? The children are getting hungry."

"Give us forty-five minutes, maybe an hour." Sid sighed again. He did hang up.

"That was weird." I whispered.

"You okay?" He shifted position a little and I couldn't help it. I yelped happily.

"Oh, yeah."

It was a bit more than an hour, but we took a shower together, which was supposed to save time and didn't, then we dressed casually in sweaters and jeans. When we got downstairs, the kids clamored how hungry they were, so Sid and I made sure we had all our luggage for our trip. We rode with Mama and Daddy. Mae and company rode in their van, which was still decorated, and Sy and Stella had Darby and Nick in their rental car. At the hotel where the brunch was, Mama held me back.

"Are you alright?" she asked. "I mean, after the phone call this morning."

I laughed. "I'm fine. Yeah, it was a little weird, but I should have known it was going to happen. There isn't much that will put Sid off his paces."

"But still…"

"Mama, you have no idea how many times I've been on your end of the phone call."

"Oh, dear Lord." Mama snorted. "Well, I do not care how normal and natural that behavior is, there are some things that are not meant to be shared."

"I'll try to let Sid know."

The brunch was a buffet, which thrilled me, especially since my normal appetite was back. I don't know if Sid was relieved or appalled. [Both. – SEH] We made it to the airport well before our flight, and we had a lovely time chatting as we waited for our plane. It felt weird, though. Sid and I don't like to call attention to our traveling, so we usually wait at the airport by ourselves, or with Nick, if he's coming. However, when Sy and Stella had come for their visit at the end of the previous January, Sid and I had taken them to lunch with Henry and Lydia. Strangely, Henry had spilled the beans about our honeymoon plans. Stella told Mama, and then everyone knew.

When they called our flight, there were hugs all around. Poor Nick got double reminders to do his homework and otherwise behave. He held the two of us tightly right before we left. It was hard for him to let us go. He was always afraid that something would happen, and he'd never see us again. Given that it had barely been eight months since his first mother had died, it was understandable. At least we weren't working that trip. Us working really freaked him out because he knew how dangerous things could get. Stella had asked to stay with Nick at our house while we were gone, so I knew he'd have someone around who loved him deeply, and that was the most important part.

"We'll see you, son," Sid said, giving him a kiss on the cheek and one last squeeze.

"We'll miss you," I told him as we held each other one more time.

"I'll miss you, too," sighed Nick, then he grinned. "Have a good time."

I kissed his cheek, and Sid got my hand. We waved, then got on the plane.

We were traveling first class, which is Sid's usual preference (and Lord knows, we can afford it), so we had plenty of time to get settled in our seats as the rest of the passengers boarded. Sid pulled down the tray table and took out his contact lenses.

"You know," he said as he put the lenses and solutions back into his carryon. "It has been a really fun week."

"It's been a long one, that's for sure." I thumbed through the inflight magazine. Sid and I had written for them before, and I couldn't remember if we had an article in that issue or not.

"As much fun as it's been, I cannot tell you how glad I am to finally be left alone with you." He smiled and stroked my hand.

"I'm glad, too." I rolled my shoulders. "And no work, too. Just vacation."

We both sighed happily, then Sid yawned. Several minutes later, the plane began to taxi, and Sid was asleep, coming awake right after takeoff just long enough to recline his seat and go back to sleep. The plane flew into the coming night on the East Coast. The roar of the plane almost lulled me to sleep, but I couldn't keep my eyes closed. Instead, in my head, I heard a phone ringing.

(Thursday, January 16)

Sid was making a pickup, so I got the call. It was the Dragon, which was strange. We seldom spoke directly to her unless something was going on with a case.

"Henry told me you and Sid are going to England for your honeymoon," she said.

"That was fast." I blinked. "So, we're cleared?"

Sid and I had only finalized the decision a couple days before, even though we'd talked about it for over a week or so. I knew Sid had called Henry. Still, it usually took several days, more likely a week, to get clearance to leave the country.

"Of course. It helps when you know the boss." The Dragon chuckled. "Anyway, I need to get your passports through, and while I'm at it, will you need a new driver's license and Social Security card?"

We got all our IDs and car registrations, both for our real selves and for our various aliases, through Quickline. I suspect it was a way for them to keep tabs on us, but it also meant no waiting in line at the DMV, so I didn't mind so much.

"Are we changing aliases?" I asked.

"Oh, no. The Devereauxs are still in effect. But you are getting married. It suddenly dawned on me that I shouldn't assume that you're taking Sid's name."

I sighed. "Why wouldn't you? Everyone else is. But, no, I'm not taking Sid's name. I'm keeping my own."

"Excellent. I'm glad I checked."

"And thanks for asking."

Sid returned home with another unprocessed drop. We got the film developed, called Henry, and sent it on its way. It was a CIA code. Sid got out a notepad and began playing around with it.

"Should you be doing that?" I asked.

He shrugged. "Why not?"

"We don't have Need to Know."

"And when has that stopped us?"

I sighed. "Good point."

He glared at the letters, then scribbled something down. "The thing is, between those first two unprocessed drops and this, there's something awfully strange going on. I want to be sure we're on top of whatever we get through here, just in case."

Which made sense, so I let it go.

The other interesting thing was, when I picked up the passports the next week, in addition to passports for Sid, Nick, and myself, there was a set for Charles, Linda, and Ryan Devereaux. Ryan was Nick's alias for when we traveled under that name. Given that Quickline is strictly domestic, I wondered why we'd need passports for our aliases. Sid was just as surprised. So, we called Henry. We'd been doing a lot of that, it seemed.

"It will just make it easier for you to travel," Henry said. "That's all. Don't worry about it."

"We're not worried," Sid said. "We just want to know what's going on."

"You'll find out soon enough. Don't borrow trouble."

It was a ten-hour flight. I'd been reading, but I was getting bored. About halfway in, somewhere over the Atlantic Ocean, Sid woke up and blinked.

Now, I'm sure it comes as no surprise that when it comes to sex, Sid is pretty much up for anything. What we had discovered in those months before the wedding, while we were waiting for his AIDS tests to come up negative, was that I was adventurous, too. So, I can't entirely blame Sid for thinking what he did when I asked if he'd ever had sex on a commercial flight. Of course he had. Which led to me asking how one did that because I was curious. The meal had been served - I'd eaten Sid's as well as mine since I knew he wasn't going to, being asleep. There was a movie running, but it wasn't anything I wanted to see. So, I asked questions and found out that, among other ways, that the restroom was the easiest.

But then, about fifteen minutes later, I went to the restroom to use it for the intended purpose. I don't know why I was surprised when Sid knocked on the door, and when I opened it, slid into the tiny space with me.

Afterward, when I slid back into my seat, his seat was still reclined, but he was awake.

"Did you have fun?" he asked, smiling softly at me.

"Yeah." I shrugged. "I guess we can check that one off the list."

He closed his eyes and sighed. "So, those questions were not you asking to have sex."

"Um. No." I winced. "I was just bored. Sorry."

"Honey, you've gotta get more direct about what you do and don't want. It's really hard to tell sometimes."

"I'm sorry."

"It's just part of the learning process." He blinked.

"I guess. It's just that I do want to a lot of the time."

"Want what?"

"To make love?" I blushed. "I guess sometimes I don't even know what I want. I just like it a lot."

He shook his head and grinned. "Like what a lot?"

"Like sex."

He pulled a blanket from the seat pouch in front. "Now, I am putting this on as a blanket and nothing else. I am not asking for anything. I just want to go back to sleep. See? That's how the direct thing works."

I giggled. "Okay."

His hand slid out from underneath the blanket, but it was only to hold mine. A minute later, he was mumbling away.

I did get a little sleep after that but was feeling pretty dopey when the plane flew over Ireland, then began its descent into Heathrow Airport. Sid woke up and got his contacts back in his eyes before they told us to put the tray table up. Once the plane got to the gate and we made our way off, the first thing Sid did was find a pay phone. There was only one problem.

"Do we have any British change yet?" Sid asked as he read the placard on the phone.

"Not yet. I've got about forty pounds in cash, and we've got traveler's checks."

Sid shook his head. "It doesn't look like it takes calling cards, either. We'd better get some change. Dragon…

I mean, Lillian said to check in before we pick up our luggage."

We found a duty-free shop. I bought some mints and got the coins we needed. Fortunately, it was a British number we were to call.

"You're here in London?" Sid asked after giving a caller code and presumably getting the receiver.

He was not happy with the answer, but said yes a couple more times, then hung up.

"Lillian's here," he told me.

"Why?" I asked.

We headed toward the baggage claim.

"She said we didn't have Need to Know yet." Sid sighed and shook his head. "Something's up. She also said that there will be a car for us that will take us to our hotel."

"This couldn't be some weird wedding present, could it?"

Sid shrugged; his face pained. "We can but hope."

We got our luggage and waited in line at customs. We hadn't brought any weapons with us, so we weren't terribly worried on that front. We hadn't even brought our personal transmitters or our armored running shoes. After all, we were on our honeymoon, on vacation.

It was almost eleven in the morning local time when we got through customs. As promised, there was a man in a black suit and tie and white shirt holding up a card that said, "Hackbirn," on it. Sid waved at him, and he nodded.

"Good morning, sir, ma'am," he said as we approached him. "I am Mr. Quimby, and I am at your service. To which hotel am I driving you?"

Sid told him. The man took charge of our luggage and the next thing we knew, we were in the back seat of a Rolls Royce limousine.

"We weren't sure if there would be a breakfast on the plane," Mr. Quimby said, handing us a basket. "So, there is one in this hamper here. Alas, cold. I'm afraid we could not be certain the plane would arrive on time. I hope that will be satisfactory."

"More than," I said. "They served a little something on the plane, but it wasn't much."

Sid tried not to smirk. However, even he'd had to agree that the stale croissants and jam were not overly generous.

"Then you'll have elevenses. There's tea in the flask and milk in the refrigerator in front of you. Sugar, if you like, is also in the hamper."

It was a rather nice spread, with scones, and clotted cream, and two different jams. The teacups, saucers, and little plates were all Spode bone china. There were also finger sandwiches of different kinds. What there wasn't was fresh fruit of any kind or anything whole grain.

"Are you going to be okay?" I asked Sid softly as the car pulled away from the curb.

"I'll find a way."

"You brought your Metamucil, right?"

"I'd sooner leave home without my American Express card." Sid shifted.

I sighed. As much as I give Sid grief about his finicky eating habits, I have to concede that his system can get tetchy, especially when we're traveling.

He smiled at me. "I knew what I was up against when we decided to come here. I'll be fine."

I picked up a scone and bit into it. "Oh my god, this is heavenly!"

Sid tried one with some cream on it and agreed that it was incredibly tasty. We both had some tea, as well, and were feeling well fed when we got to the hotel near Grosvenor Square. It was a four-star bed-and-breakfast inn, and perfectly luxurious while still charming. The woman at the desk was quite efficient and happy to let us know that even though it was barely noon at that point, our room was ready.

"Oh, and Mr. Hackbirn, Ms. Wycherly, we were asked to give you this." She handed Sid an envelope of heavy rag stationery, the super fancy kind.

"Thank you," said Sid.

We followed the bellhop to the lift, then to our room. It was lovely, filled with antiques, and had a full bathroom.

"Giggerty geggerty!" I exclaimed.

"What?" Sid looked at me.

I laughed. "Just a British book I read as a kid."

I think he'd been bracing himself for such moments. [Nah. I was enjoying them. - SEH] I took a deep breath and looked out the window that overlooked the back garden.

"Oh, Sid, look! They've got a sculpture garden out there."

Sid looked. "Very nice."

"This is perfect." I sighed. "Now, we need to get some lunch before the pubs close." I dug through my purse. "Sy's guidebook should be in here. Here it is. Let's see... Grosvenor Square. There's got to be something in the neighborhood or reasonably close by. Or maybe we should ask the desk clerk. They usually know the places that the locals like."

Sid held up the envelope the clerk had given us. "We should probably check this out first."

I sighed. "Sure."

Sid opened the envelope, which contained a nice note card with a hand-written invitation on it from the Earl and Countess of Graymere to dinner that night, cocktail dress suggested.

"Who are they?" I asked.

"I don't know," said Sid. "But Lillian said we should accept any invitations we receive."

I looked at the card. The handwriting was atrocious, but oddly familiar. I dug into my purse.

"Remember that pick up on the blue piece of paper?" I said.

Sid's eyes rolled. "Don't tell me. It's still in that mess you call a purse."

I stuck my tongue out at him. "And here it is."

The handwriting on the blue bit of paper was the same as on the invitation.

Sid sighed. "In other words, we don't have a choice about accepting."

"Probably not." I frowned. "Do we have cocktail dress?"

"Of course." Sid sighed, glaring at the invitation card. "Now, what do we do?"

I jammed the guidebook, the invitation card, and the blue bit of paper back into my purse and slung it over my shoulder.

"We see as much of London as we can before somebody decides we have something else to do," I said.

Sid smiled. We left the room and found the nearest pub and ordered lunch. I thumbed through the guidebook as we ate.

"You don't know that we're going to be able to do any of that," Sid said.

"I don't care." I glared at him defiantly. "I'm going to do the best I can." I checked my watch. "Given the proximity and how much time we have left, I think our best opportunity this afternoon would be running through the British Museum. Are you going to be okay if we can't read every tag and count brush strokes?"

Sid laughed. "I'll manage."

"I want to be sure we catch the Rosetta Stone and the Parthenon friezes."

"Sounds good."

I had to concede it wasn't the best way to visit the British Museum, but there wasn't much else we could do. We called Nick, back in the States, around three (which was around seven in the morning there) to let him know that we'd gotten in okay, then had a proper British tea at the museum's restaurant. After all, dinner wasn't going to be until eight, with cocktails at seven. It was not at all the way Sid and I usually ate, but there wasn't much we could do. We got to do a quick run through Covent Garden, but most of the shops there were closing, and then we had to get back to the hotel to change for dinner. Sid put on a three-piece suit. My straight dress had a yellow silk lining under a flower-print chiffon overlay with ruffles at the neck and bottom and long sleeves, and I wore a pair of nice spike heels, plus a pretty gold necklace with a modern pendant of wavy lines studded with diamonds. We both put on trench coats over our finery, just in case.

We were ready shortly before seven to find out that Mr. Quimby was back.

"With the Countess' compliments, I am here to drive you to dinner," he said, passively.

So, we got in the back of the Rolls and soon arrived at a bright white Georgian townhouse among a row of others. Mr. Quimby opened the limo door for us and, since it had started raining, held an umbrella over our heads as he brought us up to the doorstep. A butler had the door open immediately and ushered us inside.

I tried to keep my jaw from dropping and did not entirely succeed. The hallway was dark paneled and lit by a crystal chandelier hung over a sweeping staircase with burnished wood banister and steps and Persian carpet on those same steps. Landscapes and a couple portraits darkened by age hung on the wall in ornate frames. The butler took our trench coats.

"The Earl and Countess regret that they have been unavoidably delayed," said the butler, a youngish man with dark hair. "However, they asked that you join their other guests in the drawing room for cocktails."

"Thank you," said Sid.

You need to understand that Sid and I live in Beverly Hills, one of the most affluent places in the country, if not the world. That we live there has more to do with Sid's frame of mind when he first landed in the Los Angeles area, namely that the house was the first place that looked livable. He'd just graduated from college after having inherited a small fortune from a then nameless relative. He bought the house, then went to work, turning his small fortune into a decent pile. At least, that was the visible part of his life. He was also a member of Quickline, which was why he'd moved to Los Angeles from the Bay Area.

Given our neighbors and the area, in general, we know what serious money looks like. The London townhouse eclipsed anything we'd ever seen before. This wasn't just wealth; this was generations of inherited privilege. Antiques that some ancestor had bought new. The house looked like a museum. The drawing room was also paneled in dark wood. Deep green velvet drapes covered the windows. More darkened portraits and a few hunt scenes were scattered around the walls. The two sofas and several chairs had to be Eighteenth Century. The mantle around the huge fireplace was marble and intricately carved. A full ebony grand piano sat in front of the windows, and I saw Sid's fingers twitch as his eyes fell on the instrument.

But the opulence was the least of the surprises.

"Here they are!" crowed Lydia James in her delightful, soothing voice.

She was a tall woman with dark gray hair, cut short and feathered. Henry, also tall, balding, and whose face had a permanent flush, smiled from her side. Both held cut crystal old-fashioned glasses with something amber inside. Lillian Ward, in full matronly grace, sat on one of the sofas with a martini glass in her hand. Near her, standing ramrod erect, was a tallish man with thinning reddish gray hair, probably in his mid-sixties. He had his arm around a woman in her early forties who looked like she'd been a model in her younger years and was still keeping herself up.

Lydia came over and gave me a warm hug, as did Henry. I went over to Lillian, who also stood and bussed me on the cheek.

Lillian smiled and nodded at the tall man. "I'm told you've met Congressman Dale O'Connor."

"Yes," I said simply.

Sid finished giving Lillian a quick kiss on the cheek and glared at O'Connor. "I've known Dale for a good many years."

"We have, indeed," O'Connor said. "Sid, Lisa, this is my wife, Adrienne."

I shook her hand. "Nice to meet you."

"Likewise." She smiled very warmly at Sid, who ignored it.

"I'm mixing the cocktails this evening until their Lord and Ladyship get here," O'Connor announced. "What'll it be? I can recommend the scotch."

"Sounds good," said Sid, coolly. "With a little water. Lisa?"

"Um. I prefer single malt if there's any." I swallowed, hoping like crazy I'd done that right. I really hated the smoky Islay scotches and knew a lot of the hard-core scotch fans loved them.

"Of course." O'Connor went over to a breakfront and poured the liquor from cut crystal decanters.

The scotch was fantastic, though I sipped it gingerly. There were hors d'oeuvres, too, and I nibbled, but couldn't remember what was there.

"I wonder how much longer they're going to be on that call," Adrienne said, looking at a canape with a sigh.

"Oh, I doubt they're on a call," Lillian said with a grin as Adrienne smirked. Lillian smiled at me. "They're not normally very pretentious, but she does occasionally like to make an entrance."

"Why shouldn't I?" Marian stood in the doorway to the room wearing a lovely chiffon gown in blue, then swept inside, Andrew behind her. "What's the point of a centuries-old name and all sorts of fusty ancestry if one can't make hay with it occasionally?" She smiled as she saw Sid and me. "Hello, darlings. I'm so glad you're here! Did you have a pleasant flight?"

She gave Sid a loud kiss on the lips, then came over and kissed my cheeks. I stepped back as Andrew approached and gave him my hand, which he kissed rather warmly, then he turned and shook Sid's hand.

"It was good," said Sid. "Uh…"

"Oh, darling, we're friends," Marian said, patting his arm. "Just call us Marian and Andrew. We only use our titles when we're trying to make a point."

"So, you're the Countess…" I gulped.

"Surprised?" Marian laughed. "No matter. Dale, would you be so kind as to mix up a couple of gin and tonics for Andrew and me? And don't be your usual stingy self and make them good and stiff. Oh, lovely. We've got the hors d'oeuvres. Lisa, dear, did you try the duck confit? It's marvelous."

It was marvelous. Still, I clung to Sid for dear life. I think the only reason I didn't run and hide was that I already knew everyone there, except for Adrienne. Sid, with his more polished urban survival skills, was managing quite nicely, even if he was also a little overwhelmed. [That only lasted for an instant. I was more worried about you. And wondering what the hell was up. - SEH] I couldn't help but feel as if the dinner were more than a welcome to England party. I had no idea if either Adrienne or Lydia knew anything about our side business. Lydia, I knew, had some inkling that her husband did classified work and had probably figured out that Sid and I were involved in it somehow. But she had the good sense and grace to act as if she didn't. Adrienne was an unknown quantity.

"Sid, darling, I understand you play the piano quite beautifully," Marian said, sliding up to his other side. "Would you be so good as to play something for us?"

"Sure." Sid set his glass down on an end table next to one of the sofas, then opened the keyboard and ran his fingers across the keys. "Would a little Chopin do?"

"Sounds wonderful," Marian said.

Sid glanced at me as he settled himself on the bench and smiled. His fingers gently touched the keys in a couple chords first. Then he slid into Prelude Number Fifteen, which is my favorite of the Chopin Preludes, Opus 28.

There was soft applause as he finished. Sid's eyes found mine and I couldn't help smiling.

Adrienne sighed. There was no mistaking her hungry look at my husband. I'm not sure what shocked me more, that I was so jealous or that I'd just mentally referred to Sid as my husband. Well, he was. But still... I fidgeted with the ring set on my left finger, feeling the band as part of it. I'd worn the set many times before, but that had been part of a role I'd played. This time, it was real. I was really married.

A bell softly rang, and Marian announced it was dinner. Andrew took my arm, then led us into the dining room and seated me next to him at the head of the table. Sid had Marian on his arm and seated her at the end across from Andrew, then seated Lillian on the other side from where he was to sit. O'Connor sat across from me, and Henry on my other side, with Adrienne on his other side next to Lillian. Lydia sat between O'Connor and Sid. I saw the preponderance of silverware on the table and realized that we were having at least five courses. I looked over at Sid, who smiled pleasantly at Lillian. He's even better at place settings than I am, so I was fairly sure he knew what he was up against.

Footmen poured a white wine into our glasses and Andrew stood.

"I think, before we begin, we should drink a toast to our newest travel club members, Sid and Lisa." He raised his glass as the others mumbled their assent, and they drank.

I looked over at Sid, whose bare wisp of a shrug still managed to speak volumes.

The first course came, three oysters on their shells, perfectly chilled.

"I do not like discussing business over dinner," Marian announced, after eating one of her oysters with great relish. "However, I fear we must. Dale, would you be so good?"

"The Yugoslavians?" O'Connor asked, noisily slurping down his second oyster.

"I fear that may enter into it." Marian glared at O'Connor. "But that is not why we are gathered here tonight."

I was puzzled. I had figured that Lydia knew more about our secret business than she'd let on. But Adrienne was still there, and it was clear that we were going to be discussing top secret business. I could only assume that both Adrienne and Lydia had the clearances.

I looked at Lillian and then got a good look at Henry's face. Neither of them betrayed anything. Henry cleared his throat.

"Sid, Lisa." He shifted in his seat, then took a large gulp of wine. "We are making some changes in the operation. As you know, we've had to rebuild two lines over the past couple years. What you may not have realized was that we also needed to make repairs on the Red line, as well."

"Our line," said Sid.

"You two have been the hub team for that line for six years." Henry paused. "About three and a half since Lisa joined you, Sid."

Sid's eyes narrowed as he looked at Henry. "Nineteen-eighty. How much of this has to do with Lydia getting breast cancer that year?"

"Everything," Lydia said, then ate her last oyster. "I was Henry's partner, but had to retire because of the cancer."

"I've been trying to retire since then," Henry continued. "The problem was, you needed a partner, and that partner would need enough training and experience to keep up."

O'Connor sat back in his chair, his oysters long gone. "Sid, the intent was always that you were going to replace Henry at some point. That's why you were sent to L.A. in seventy-six, after you graduated from college."

"What about Eric?" Sid asked. "I thought he was your partner."

"Eric was more of a hub than a floater." Henry sighed. "He was supposed to be your partner, but then Eric was killed in May of eighty-one, which is when I started pushing you to find a partner. We've been limping along for the past four years, trying to get all the pieces into place."

"Not to mention restoring two lines," Lillian grumbled.

Marian waved her fingers, and the three footmen sprang into action and removed our plates. I had to figure that the footmen had security clearances for our conversation. No one seemed to notice that they were there otherwise.

"So, now you and Lisa are ready," Henry said. "I'll be around until July, but in the meantime, you two are now the floaters for Los Angeles and San Francisco."

Sid's eyes widened. "That's... Wow."

"You mean we're being promoted?" I asked, looking between Henry and Lillian.

"Exactly," Lillian said. "That's why we're all here now."

The footmen placed small bowls of perfectly clear yellow bouillon in front of us. More white wine was poured, and I'd barely finished my first glass.

"This is going to be your training trip," Marian said. She took a sip of her bouillon and sighed happily.

"What?" I yelped. "We're on our honeymoon!"

Lydia smirked at her husband.

Henry shrugged. "I know. I'm afraid that can't be helped. We needed a good cover to get you two over here. Not that you'll need it after this."

"I don't understand," Sid said.

"It's a matter of establishing a visible friendship," Marian said. "You are friends with Henry and Lydia, and with Lillian, and now with us. I must say that wedding invitation helped a great deal."

O'Connor snorted. "It's not going to do us a lot of good if those Yugoslavians decide that Sid and Lisa are the targets of their plot."

"Why on earth would they do that?" Marian asked, glaring at O'Connor.

"Oh, please." O'Connor rolled his eyes. "We've known about the plot for over two months. They should have moved on it before now."

Both Marian and Lillian sighed.

"I'm afraid he's right about that," Lillian said, then sipped from her wineglass. "Sid and Lisa are the only new Americans in your circle."

"That's assuming any Americans connected to us are part of the plot," Andrew said. "We do not know that to be the case. We simply know that getting the American government to negotiate is the intended goal."

Marian noticed that we'd all finished our bouillon and signaled the footmen.

"But our government won't negotiate," Sid said.

Marian sighed. "We've had several bits and pieces of intelligence that the thinking on the part of our plotters seems to be that if they get someone with a high enough profile, your government will be forced to."

"Well, that lets us out as a target." Sid smiled as a footman placed a plate in front of him with a bit of white fish on it covered over with julienned vegetables and a creamy sauce. "We make a point of keeping a low profile."

More wine was poured, this one with just a hint of creaminess. [It was a Chablis and an amazing one, at that. - SEH]

Lillian sighed. "Which makes your pronouncements of doom all the more annoying, Dale." She put up a hand to stop O'Connor's protest. "Yes, you have a point on the timing, but that's all. If Sid and Lisa need to know what's going on, it's only part of their training, and because Marian and Andrew are wrapped up in it somehow."

"I agree," said Marian. She looked at me kindly. "We're going to make this as leisurely as possible. I'm not completely insensitive to a honeymoon, for Heaven's sakes. Now, Henry, dear, would you please explain the process?"

Henry nodded and finished a bite of fish. "Alright. As you two know, floaters oversee their respective lines. There are four floater teams, each connected to a specific port of entry. Miami is the Yellow line; New York is Green; Seattle, Blue; and L.A., Red. Each of those four ports of entry has four hub teams, one from each of the lines, so there are sixteen hubs. Quickline mostly services operatives in Europe and South America, although we do occasionally serve operatives in Israel. The CIA has another courier branch servicing incoming intel from the rest of the Middle East, Asia, and the Pacific Rim. All calls for service go through Lillian first. She knows who's where and doing what. Floaters pick up the packages, process them, then assign the route, going through a hub team as the first stop."

"Why?" I asked.

Henry chuckled. "As you two may have noticed these past couple months, packages coming in from overseas have a high likelihood of having tails with them. Floaters and hub teams are generally more experienced and better at losing said tails. Not always, but generally. Also, floaters and hubs are more likely to get called on to handle investigations when those come up. Since floaters also must know everyone on their line, they know their people by their real names. Now, the reason we're here in Europe is that you two need to know our allies' courier system."

"Alas," said Marian, looking over the table. Sid was still nibbling at his fish, as was Lillian. "It does occasionally happen that one of our couriers or one of yours can't quite make it to a port of entry in the States. So, we've developed a series of caches, if you will, where information can be dropped and all you must do is go in and get it. Well, avoiding the usual observation and such."

Sid rolled his eyes and pushed back his plate. "Which is, of course, the trick."

Andrew chuckled and smiled at me. "If we didn't know you two would be good at it, you would not now be here."

Marian looked at Lillian, saw that she was done, and signaled the footmen again. I looked over at Sid. The poor darling had already eaten at this one meal more than he normally ate all day. The only thing mitigating it was that the food was beyond phenomenally good. Me, I was in hog Heaven. Well, not entirely. I couldn't believe it, but I was starting to fill up, not a common occurrence at all.

The next course almost made me cry. Roast saddle of lamb. I love lamb and almost never get it because of Sid's ban on red meat at the house. This one came with a red currant emulsion, of all things, and it was divine.

"While you will need to learn some of our codes," Marian said. "The important part of all of this is that you need to visit each of these drop-off stations and familiarize yourselves with them. The nice part is they're scattered all over the Continent, which will make a rather nice tour of Europe for you." She looked at me. "Lisa, you seem rather nonplussed."

I winced. "Well, no. I mean, a tour of Europe does sound lovely. I don't want to be ungrateful."

Sid rolled his eyes. "What Lisa is trying to say is that she was hoping to spend more time in England. Where all, lover?"

"The Lake District. Stratford Upon Avon. Especially Stratford. Oxford. Westminster Abbey. Maybe the Tower of London." I sank into myself. "I have my Masters in English Literature."

Marian laughed. "How lovely. Oh, I do wish we could do all of that. Well, we shall the next time you come, and there will be a next time. I can promise you that."

"That sounds nice," I said with a smile that I didn't feel.

"In any case, we will do what we can to make things run smoothly." Marian smiled warmly, then rolled her eyes. "Obviously, we can't make any promises. Still, I think we'll manage a nice visit for you, after all."

Henry grinned. "Lisa is a big Shakespeare fan."

"Indeed," said Andrew. He smiled. "I do believe we can manage a day trip to Stratford Upon Avon tomorrow, can't we?"

"Of course we can," said Marian. "Would you like that, dear?"

"I'd love it," I gasped, blinking back tears. "I love Shakespeare."

"And we'll all be standing by," Lillian said, sending O'Connor a quick glare.

"Well, Lydia and I are going to have to leave tomorrow," Henry said, a pall of sadness settling over the both of them.

Sid caught his breath. "The cancer's back, isn't it?"

Lydia nodded. "We have our next appointment on Wednesday. It's not all bad news, though."

I reached over to him. "We'll be here, Henry. And I'll be praying for the two of you."

He smiled. "I appreciate it."

Lydia smiled at me. "We both do."

We turned back to our food. After a pause, Marian went back to covering the drop-off stations, which didn't really mean much. O'Connor wanted to talk more about the plot by the Yugoslavians, but Marian did not, for some reason. I couldn't help but hope it was because Sid and I really didn't need to be on top of that case, although I was a little worried that O'Connor seemed to think we'd be targets.

We moved on to a lovely salad, then cheese, and a dessert that was... Well, frighteningly intense, given what we'd already eaten. It was a wheel of pastry filled with clotted cream and bits of candied fruit. The top had been sprinkled with powdered sugar, and we were offered cream to pour over it. Of course, I tried it. It was delicious, although I couldn't eat that much of it. Sid nibbled, but really didn't have any appetite left and he doesn't really care for sweets, anyway.

After dinner, we made our way out of the townhouse. There were three taxi cabs waiting for us. Sid and I staggered to the last of them, Marian's promise to pick us up at nine in the morning ringing in our ears.

Sid snuggled up next to me and nuzzled my ear happily. I wasn't quite so happy.

"This is amazing," he whispered.

"What?"

"We got promoted, honey. That's enormously big."

"We're working on our honeymoon." I tried not to sulk.

"Okay. That part sucks. But promotions don't happen very often in this biz. It says a lot that they were planning this for us."

"They could have said something." I looked at him. "I know you're happy. That's the important thing."

Sid's eyes narrowed. "As long as you're happy, too."

I took a deep breath and thought about it. "Yeah. I guess I am. Except for working on our honeymoon."

He chuckled. "Except for that."

Back at the hotel, Sid spent quite a few minutes in the bathroom and seemed okay. I washed up, then stripped for bed. He smiled as I slid under the covers.

"How are you feeling tonight?" he asked.

"Tired. You?"

"Pretty tired, too. But I'm open to making love if you are." He slid over and pulled me next to him.

"Oh. Am I allowed mixed feelings?"

He laughed. "Of course. What's going on?"

I yawned. "I'm really tired, but I really want to make love, too. It feels so good."

"Ah." He chuckled. "I may just have a way around that."

It was a nice way to make love and be tired at the same time. We fell asleep quickly afterward.

I was chatting with someone, I couldn't tell who, but then I was in a closet, my Smith and Wesson Model Thirteen in my hand. Sid was on the other side of the door and another man. I shot. Bright red blood splattered against the wall. I couldn't escape it. It was my fault... My fault.

I came awake gasping and sitting up. Sid rubbed my back.

"It was just a dream, honey." His voice was soothing, and I clung to him. "You're alright. I'm here and it was just a dream."

I got a hold of myself. "Okay."

He smiled softly. "Are you sure?"

"I think so."

"Was it the usual?"

I nodded. "Yeah. I don't know why. I didn't have one leading up to the wedding. Why now?"

"Could be all sorts of things." He squeezed me gently. "Let's face it, we're not on vacation anymore. It's probably that."

"Yeah." I sighed, then looked at him. "Can we... Um..."

"Um, what?" Sid obviously knew but wasn't going to let me get away without saying it.

"Um. Make love?"

He chuckled warmly and kissed the back of my neck. "Of course, my darling."

I got to breakfast in the hotel dining room at just after eight, and a bit ahead of Sid that morning. I'd put on my beloved blue Shetland wool sweater over an Oxford shirt and some nice jeans. I also had on my beloved and dirty gray deck shoes. When the waiter came by, I made a special request, and she was happy to fetch it. Sid showed up a moment later, wearing nice jeans and his blue argyle sweater over one of his white dress shirts. He didn't look entirely happy.

"Are you feeling okay?" I asked.

He made a bit of a face. "My old caffeine habit. It's not really a headache yet."

"Maybe you'd better stay off it, then."

He chuckled. "In Merry Olde England? I guarantee you, we'll be drinking tea all day. I'll be fine."

The waiter returned with a glass of prune juice and a stack of whole wheat toast. She placed a bowl of fruit in front of Sid. Unfortunately, it had come from a can. Sid looked at me.

"Did you?"

"Of course," I said. "I'll be getting the traditional breakfast, though. They've got kippers. I've never tried them before."

My plate arrived with several huge rashers of bacon, two fried eggs, a fried tomato, a sausage, toast, and the kipper, a smoked, salty fish. I shared the tomato and the fish with Sid. We both agreed that the kipper was a touch too salty for our liking. I cleaned my plate handily and drank two cups of tea. Sid surprised me by ordering a cup of coffee.

"Given all the tea, no point in not," he said. The reality was he loved coffee. He just had a small problem with the caffeine. "It sure smells good."

Right before nine, I ran up to our room to get my purse, pausing only to put our big SLR camera into the bag. I sighed. Usually, Sid carried the camera because I often had my Model Thirteen revolver in the purse, and it's one big gun. Both it and a single lens reflex camera weighed a lot. Unfortunately, the gun was at home.

When I got back down to the lobby, Marian and Andrew had arrived. They bundled us off to their car, a large Mercedes convertible sedan with the top down, and the next thing we knew, we were flying up the motorway to Stratford Upon Avon. I was, at first, a touch nervous about the top being down, but it was one of those rare sunny days in England, with a bright blue sky and white puffy clouds drifting lazily along. Marian loaned me a scarf, so that I didn't get my hair blowing in my face. It was not even ten-thirty when we got to Shakespeare's birthplace.

Given that Stratford is just over a hundred miles away from London, we should not have gotten there that fast. How do I put this? Andrew made Sid and me look like slowpokes, and Sid and I are well known for our lead feet. If I don't know exactly how fast we were going, it's because the speedometer in the car was set for kilometers, not miles. I'm not sure I wanted to. The British countryside flew by in a blur.

Stratford was charming. We did a tour of the Anne Hathaway cottage and Shakespeare's birthplace and school room. Sid and I found several watercolors and an oil painting that we bought. We ate lunch at a pub. We looked at the Bard's grave at Trinity Church. We walked along the river's edge. I would have loved to see a show at the theater there, but it was the off-season, and the Royal Shakespeare Company was in London.

The only problem I had was that it seemed like Marian was trying to get Sid's attention, while Sid was clearly annoyed with Andrew for some reason.

Sometime close to two, Marian suggested that we head back toward London with a stop off in Oxford.

"That sounds wonderful!" I gasped. "One of my favorite books of all time, Gaudy Night, it's set there."

"A Lord Peter fan?" Marian looked bemused.

"Very much," I said, blushing.

"Well, I love Oxford, myself," Marian said, eyeing Sid. "Our two sons are at the university, although Eric is at Trinity and James is at Christ Church. They're far too busy for Mum and Dad to visit. Our daughter is away at school, as well, these days, but she's not in uni yet."

"You have children?" I asked.

"Well, they're mostly grown." Marian smiled. "If you have a title, you must procreate. So, we have the heir, a second son, and our daughter. And, thanks to the boys, we have an easy excuse to come to Oxford on a regular basis. There are some delightful shops there, and not only a lovely tearoom, but one of my favorite restaurants. We'll have tea, do a bit of shopping, then look at some of the colleges, and finish off with dinner. How does that sound, Sid?"

"If Lisa's happy, I am." He smiled at me.

I gazed at him fondly. "I'd like that."

We got into town just in time for Sid and me to collect several pounds' worth of change and find a phone booth. It was close to three in the afternoon, and we wanted to call Nick. He picked up right away. School was boring, as usual, although Stella had helped him with his geography homework. Sy had gone back to New York and would return in another week.

"When are you guys coming back?" Nick asked me.

"We told you we weren't sure," I said, looking a little anxiously at Sid.

"Oh." Nick's voice suddenly got tense. "Something come up?"

"Nothing serious, my sweet guy. It's good news. It just means we're not sure when we'll get home is all." I blinked back tears. "If you don't hear from us, it doesn't mean anything. We're just having a good time."

"Okay."

"You be good. We love you."

The operator chimed in that we needed to add more change, and Sid held up his hands. We were out.

"We'll try to call tomorrow."

"I love you, Mom."

The call cut off.

"What's the matter?" Sid asked.

"He's figured out that we're working."

Sid sighed. "There's nothing we can do about that."

I wasn't entirely surprised that Marian had ulterior motives regarding the shopping portion of our visit to Oxford.

"You had no way of knowing," she said as we finished tea. "But there is a party tomorrow night. You two need to be there to assess the guests. The problem is, it's formal dress and most people do not travel with that in mind."

"I have a dinner jacket with me," Sid said. Well, he wasn't most people. "But why would we be needed to assess the guests?"

Marian rolled her eyes. "It's one of Dale's fancies. Unfortunately, he's right just often enough. I loved the cocktail dress, Lisa, but do you have anything with you that's floor-length?"

I glanced at Sid. "No. I don't think so."

Sid often packed for both of us, so I didn't always know what we had.

"I know the perfect shop," Marian said. "Sid, you and Andrew can explore someplace else."

Sid smiled softly at me. "I'll go with you two. I'm more curious about why this party is so important."

Marian sighed, then smiled right at him. "Suspects, darling. I can't say more than that. We don't want to prejudice you against anyone. Your unfiltered impressions will be the most helpful."

Sid nodded, then got up. "Well then, let's get to this shop of yours."

Marian was a little surprised that Sid was so interested in dress shopping, but she really didn't know Sid that well. At the shop, Marian pulled gown after gown from the racks, but Sid found the perfect one almost immediately. It was a lovely navy-blue strapless dress with princess lines and the center section gathered into the sides, and a full gathered skirt that started around the lower part of my hips. I smiled as I saw myself in the mirror.

"This is it," I said.

"Quite nice." Andrew nodded, and I noticed Sid shooting him a quick glare.

"I have to agree," Marian said with a touch of shock. She looked at Sid. "Who would have thought?"

I laughed and went back to the changing room. I already knew that I had heels to go with it and, of course, my aquamarines.

The only problem was, after we left the shop, it was obvious that we had a tail on us. Andrew and Marian ignored it, so Sid and I did as well. Sometimes that is the most effective thing you can do, especially if you don't want to give yourself away as an operative.

We wandered through Balliol and Somerville colleges, but then had to find a pub, as it was getting dark, and the restaurant wouldn't open for another hour and a half or so. I was not entirely surprised to see Dale O'Connor enter the pub and spot us.

"You guys have a tail," he announced as he came up to our table.

"Yes, we know." Marian's eyes glittered. "Is he still out front?"

"Yeah. Smallish guy with a gray raincoat and hat."

"Sounds about right. Would you like a pint?"

"Yeah. Sure." O'Connor slid into a chair at our table as Marian signaled the waiter.

The four of us were sharing a bottle of red wine.

"So, why haven't you taken him out?" O'Connor grumbled once the waiter brought the pint of dark brown beer.

"To what end?" Marian asked. "Honestly, Dale, you have no sense of finesse."

I tried not to gag as I remembered Andrew calmly killing a man that first time Sid and I had met him.

"Okay." O'Connor wiped some foam from his upper lip. "I get you don't want to expose yourselves as operatives, but we gotta get on top of these Yugoslavians."

Andrew rolled his eyes. "Getting on top won't do us any good if we give away the game in the process. We have no confirmation on who the target is, and barely any on the point of the plot."

O'Connor wasn't swayed. "I got your note from the Yugoslavian Embassy in mid-January. It specifically said high-level Americans."

Marian grimaced. "I do not believe so."

"It most certainly did." O'Connor solidly put his half-empty glass on the table.

"That's easy for you to say," Marian countered. "Do you have the note with you?"

O'Connor shifted. "Of course not."

Sid glanced at me. "We do."

O'Connor, Marian, and Andrew all riveted their attention on Sid and me. I briefly debated playing dumb, but knew that wouldn't work.

"We have the original note with us," I said softly, pulling my purse from where it hung on the back of my chair.

There are, in fact, multiple incarnations of my purse, as the darned things do tend to wear out. The one constant is that they all are exceptionally large. [Your purse is that black hole to another dimension whence go all the missing socks from the dryer, ballpoint pens that are never there when you need them, and other such ephemera. - SEH]

The current one was made of tan leather and had multiple pockets that I'd thought I'd organized. But I did remember into which pocket I'd stuffed the blue bit of paper that we'd received in January. I pulled it out.

"Is this it?" I asked, laying it on the table and smoothing it out.

Marian's eyes widened. "It is. How did you get it?"

"We got four unprocessed drops," Sid said. "All between the second week of January and the middle of February. This was one of them."

"Henry was showing us how to route them," I added. I looked at O'Connor. "Where were you in mid-January? At home in Tahoe or in Washington?"

O'Connor frowned. "In D.C. Why?"

"I thought so." I looked at Sid. "That's where we sent the processed version of this."

"We didn't look too closely at it either," Sid said, smiling. "We assumed we didn't have Need to Know."

I rolled my eyes. "That and it was really hard to read."

Andrew laughed and looked fondly at Marian.

She shook her head. "I'm afraid my handwriting can be rather difficult. And I was using my usual shorthand. It will be well worth it for you two to learn to read it. Fortunately, Henry recognized it and got it sent to Dale right away." She leaned over the paper. "Alright. It says, 'Croats developing plan for kidnapping to force Americans to negotiate.' Nothing there about who the target is."

O'Connor glared. "We have additional intelligence that the target is high profile."

"Into which category you fall," Marian replied. "And we're only supposing that the target is an American because that's who the Croatians want to negotiate with."

"That doesn't let Sid and Lisa out," O'Connor grumbled. "If the Yugoslavians want to force a negotiation, then kidnapping the daughter of one of my constituents could be a way to do it."

Marian, Andrew, and Sid looked puzzled, but it dawned on me what O'Connor meant.

"That's right," I said. "Mama and Daddy live in your district."

"Oh, for Heaven's sakes," Marian groaned. "This isn't about you getting re-elected, Dale. How could anyone have planned such a thing?"

"I'm not saying they planned it that way," O'Connor said, shifting. "But, yeah, it's another election year. Any reasonably astute person might conclude that putting me in a tough situation that way might make it more likely that I'd negotiate." He shifted again. "When did you pick up your tail?"

"Right after the dress shop," said Sid. He looked at Marian. "Did anyone else besides O'Connor know we'd be here?"

"Oh, dear." Marian frowned. "Practically everyone, I'm afraid. Sid, darling, while you were calling your son, I called Gwen, our hostess for tomorrow night, to confirm that you would be joining us and happened to mention we were here doing a bit of shopping. It wouldn't have been hard to find us after that, given that I prefer the same shops."

Andrew snorted. "Gwen loves to chat. I'm sure that entire circle knew within minutes."

"That doesn't help us much," O'Connor grumbled.

Marian checked her watch. "We should be going to dinner shortly. Dale, would you like to join us?"

"Nah. I've got to go keep Adrienne from spending all my money." O'Connor drained his glass and stood.

"If you see Lillian, please tell her we'll be at the usual place around seven-thirty." Marian smiled.

"Will do." O'Connor shook his head and left.

Marian sighed in relief. "Gone, at last." She looked at us. "Please do not take this the wrong way, but he can be rather odious."

Sid snorted. "We know."

"He got Nick's adoption pushed through," I said.

"For which he will soon be expecting payment." Marian made a face as she sipped the last of her wine.

"I don't doubt that for a second," Sid said.

I sighed. "He said that he was trying to make up to you."

"We'll see how far that gets us." Sid shook his head.

He offered to pay the tab, but Marian and Andrew said it was already taken care of.

Marian took Sid's arm as we left the pub. "You two are our guests for the remainder of this trip. It's the least we can do after hijacking your honeymoon."

"That's very kind of you," Sid said, subtly putting a little space between himself and Marian.

Andrew took my arm, and I added distance as well. The night air was nippy, and I was glad I had on my Shetland wool.

"I hope we're not too casually dressed for dinner," Sid said. He patted Marian's arm, then turned and gently pulled me away from Andrew and under his arm.

Marian tittered briefly. "No. It shan't be a problem at all. It's a lovely little French place, family owned. And wonderfully good food." She paused. "I hope you weren't expecting some great multi-course extravaganza with white tablecloths and cut crystal."

"I don't know what we were expecting," I said, shifting closer to Sid. "But a little family-owned place sounds great."

Marian looked at both Sid and me with a particularly penetrating look. She smiled. "Yes. I thought as much. Always nice to know when one's instincts are proved correct."

Our biggest problem, however, turned out to be getting to the restaurant in one piece. It was on a narrow side street, in the middle of the block, with several dark doorways between the main street and the front door.

We had just turned onto the side street when the five men jumped out of the doorways. The almost fun part was watching Andrew swing into action like a Kung Fu master. I started screaming, assuming that we were trying to keep our covers as civilians. Andrew punched and kicked, and the next thing I knew, Sid got a few licks in, and I may have tripped one or two guys. Marian tossed one fellow over her back, then stood apart and watched, laughing, of all things.

Three of the men ran as the shrill police whistle echoed through the tiny street. Andrew finished off one of the two remaining men. The other was out cold. It wasn't long before police constables swarmed the street, with some sort of supervisor or other apologizing to their Lord and Ladyship about the fracas.

Andrew and Marian soothingly shook them off, and we finally made our way to the restaurant.

"How...?" Sid asked as soon as the coppers were gone.

Marian laughed. "Everyone knows that Andrew is a fifth-degree black belt in karate. Sadly, this is not the first time someone has decided to attack us. And oddly enough, it has never been attached to anything espionage related."

"It seems mostly related to the fact that we are peers," said Andrew, meticulously dusting off his own sweater. "I have no idea why."

I worked hard and succeeded in not rolling my eyes. I remembered how Lillian had once described the two as being rather medieval. Lillian, in person, walked up just then.

"I saw a bunch of police escorting a couple of men away from here," she said, looking at the four of us. "Did I miss some excitement?"

"Just the usual nonsense," Marian said.

"I'm sorry I missed it." Lillian smiled, then looked at Sid and me. "Well, have you two had a good day?"

"It's been pleasant," Sid said.

"We got to see a lot," I said. I smiled. It wasn't as much I'd wanted, but there was no help for that.

Marian saw to getting our table. It was a tiny place, maybe ten tables total, and definitely catered to the local, rather than the tourist trade, a very good thing to my mind. If the staff treated Marian and Andrew with a certain respect, it was that due to old and favored customers rather than fancy titles.

Marian didn't give us a chance to peruse the menu. She simply told the waiter to let the chef decide, then ordered a bottle of Champagne to go with whatever starter we'd get.

We started with some late season mussels, steamed in broth.

Marian sighed happily after tasting one. "I must confess, I was a little skeptical when I saw these. We really are just past the season for good moules."

"I was wondering about that," Lillian said, then looked at Sid and me. "So, do you have any questions about your new role?"

Sid glanced my way, then shrugged. "More about our cover here. I get that we're all supposed to be friends."

"Actually," Lillian said. "We're all members of a travel club."

"It's a loose group of people who like to travel together," Marian said. "We've set it up that we met the two of you through Henry and Lydia, the summer of the Olympics."

"Which we did," Sid said, eyeing her carefully. "Well, at least, officially."

"That does help, doesn't it?" Marian tittered.

We had met Marian and Andrew on an even earlier case, but hadn't really had any time to get to know them.

The waiter came by and cleared the table of the bowls of mussel shells.

"I know you two through Henry," Lillian said. "And Henry set up an invitation for you to join our group as a wedding present. That's why we waited until after the wedding for your first trip with us."

Andrew cleared his throat. "Do be aware that our group members include several people who are not operatives. We accept them as cover."

"Gwen Flowers, for example," Marian said. "She's hosting the party tomorrow night, and that's why you're invited. She wants to meet our new club members. Also, there are several spouses who are not operatives. It's actually a rather large group, but we rarely travel together at the same time."

"Well, we have a couple social meetings," Lillian said, then paused as the waiter returned with four serving plates.

One held lamb chops cooked to just pink, another had a full side of some white fish covered in a buttery yellow sauce, a third featured a dark red sauce and what turned out to be melt-in-your-mouth tender chunks of beef. The final plate had a whole chicken in pieces with the skin roasted to a perfect golden, crispy brown.

"The club was set up because too many of our domestic couriers weren't able to get the intelligence where it needed to be, simply because they didn't know what was going on here." Lillian continued as we passed around the serving plates. "So, we set up a visible way for our various liaisons to connect with our floaters. That's why everybody knows each other by their real names. And you'll need to know the names of your line members and create a visible reason to know them so that you can work with them, as needed."

I took something from each of the serving plates. The waiter reappeared with another bottle of Champagne, this time a pink one, a bottle of Bordeaux, and a bottle of Chablis. The three bottles were opened, and the Champagne and Chablis were settled into an ice bucket set up at the side of the table.

"We also need to set up our schedule for your little tour," Marian said, pouring a glass of the Bordeaux for herself.

I looked at Sid. "We need to be home by the twenty-seventh."

"Oh?" Marian asked.

"We have a few commitments we've made." Sid smiled but didn't say anything more. He had a bit of chicken breast on his plate and some of the fish and had filled his wineglass with the Chablis.

I wasn't sure if he was uncomfortable explaining those commitments. [Perhaps a little. It was more that I didn't want to give either Marian or Lillian an excuse to talk us into staying longer. - SEH] We needed to be home the day of the twenty-seventh because Sid was playing the organ that night for Holy Thursday mass. In fact, he was playing at all three of the Easter Triduum services (Holy Thursday, Good Friday, and Easter Vigil). The more important part was that Nick would be on Easter vacation from school that following week and I really wanted to spend that time with him rather than running around Europe. I poured some of the pink Champagne into my glass and nearly cried, it was so good.

"Hm." Marian pulled a small pocket calendar out of her purse. "I do believe that will be possible. Gwen has been talking about spending the weekend in Gstaad, so that will get that stop taken care of. Why don't we do Venice after that, then Vienna?" She closed her eyes. "In terms of the map, Wiesbaden would make sense as the next stop. No. No. It doesn't matter. We'll do Brussels after Vienna, then Wiesbaden, then Paris, Copenhagen, then Athens." Marian counted the squares on the calendar. "We'll have at least two days, if not more, in each stop and get you home on the twenty-seventh. That will also give you some time to be tourists, which would not hurt your cover at all."

Sid looked at me, and I shrugged.

"That sounds good," Sid said, then shifted. "O'Connor hinted that we might get tied up in something involving Yugoslavians?"

He looked at Lillian, who rolled her eyes.

"It seems pretty unlikely," Lillian said.

Sid shook his head. "Except that we were attacked this evening before we got here."

"Darling, we explained," said Marian. "Andrew and I get attacked all the time. The IRA, primarily. Our diplomatic work has not favored them, I'm afraid."

"Still, is there any way to get the police reports?" Sid asked. "I'm not sure how that works here."

Andrew nodded. "That might, in fact, be a good idea." He looked at Marian. "Would you like to fetch the report, or shall I?"

"You might as well." Marian shuddered. "I cannot tell you how annoying it is to be patted on the head by a constable who can't understand that a woman would want such a thing. It's such a damnable nuisance being a woman sometimes."

I didn't say so, but I had to admit I heartily agreed with her.

"We also have to coordinate with someone on the staff for that break in on Thursday," Andrew said.

Lillian chuckled. "And yet, you have two of our better break-in artists at our table right now."

Andrew also laughed. "As I recall, we do."

Sid shook his head. "We don't have any of our tools or weapons. Or even the right clothes."

"That shouldn't be a problem." Marian pointed at me. "I know you can pull together what you need quite easily."

She had a point. She'd asked me to do the same the summer of 1984, right before the Olympics.

I bit my lip. "We'll still need lock picks and keys. Plus time to look the target over."

"We'll have Mr. Quimby brief you when the time comes." Marian looked over the platters on the table, then took some of the beef in wine sauce. "He'll be able to provide lock picks at the very least, and probably keys as well."

"But we also need hardware," I said. "And allover ski masks, gloves, cargo pants, black sweatshirts. Where can we get all that?"

"Marks and Spencer, I would think," Lillian said.

"That won't help me," Sid grumbled. "I can't buy off the rack."

"That's right." I pulled a notebook from my purse. "Maybe if we can get to the store tomorrow, I can get the pants hemmed before the party tomorrow night."

"Oh, for Heaven's sakes," Marian said. "Just make up a list of what you need, and we'll see that you have it."

"Fine." I dove back into my purse. "I'll need my calculator, and I think I have a metric conversion chart in my organizer."

I had the list put together with our measurements converted to centimeters in short order, then gave it to Sid to approve. He did, then handed the list to Marian, who looked at it in surprise.

"Crotch depth?" she asked. "What's that?"

"How deep the pants should be from the waist to where the legs meet," I said. "Sid likes his fairly shallow."

"I like a snug fit," Sid said, smiling at me. We'd tussled over that one before.

"Well, I'm sure we can arrange accommodation," Marian said, eying Sid as if he were being served up on one of the plates in front of us.

Sid ignored her hungry smile and grinned at me, shaking his head. "I'm afraid we're working, my darling."

I smiled back. "Could be worse. Now, if we can just avoid people shooting at us, that would be nice."

Our dinners were followed by a lovely and very dense chocolate cake. Even Sid ate most of his. I was also a little surprised when he ordered some coffee to go with his cake. I wasn't surprised when he picked up the cup and breathed in deeply. I guess it was good coffee. I didn't really care for it that much.

Lillian prevailed upon Marian and Andrew to let her drive Sid and me back to London. I was glad. Both Marian and Andrew had been drinking heavily. Come to think of it, I'd had more than a couple glasses of wine myself. Lillian had me sit up front with her while Sid sat in the back of the rented Ford sedan.

"I wanted a few minutes to check in with you two," Lillian said as she pulled onto the motorway to London.

"We had a mostly pleasant day," Sid said.

Lillian glanced at me.

"We did," I said. "I'm glad I got to see Stratford and a little bit of Oxford."

"Well, I would like to apologize for hijacking your honeymoon. Still, it has made things easier."

"Why couldn't you have just told us?" Sid asked.

Lillian chuckled. "And risk you putting your foot down and going someplace else? Sid, you have quite the record for insubordination."

Sid laughed, and I giggled a little.

"You're not much better, Lisa." Lillian still smiled. "The problem is things have been down on the Red line for far too long. And now that Lydia's cancer is back, Henry needs to be able to focus on her. Which is why we need you two functional immediately."

"I suppose so," said Sid.

"Our world is changing." Lillian sighed. "Glasnost. There are rumors the Soviet Union is going to break apart. Yugoslavia is practically a powder keg of ethnic conflicts. We still have our fingers in the Afghanistan war. Not to mention the rest of the Middle East. Oh, and the Irish Republican Army. We're also involved all over the place in South America, and that's not getting any more relaxed. Nor have I touched on Africa."

I shrugged. "Sounds like business as usual to me."

"In some ways." Lillian looked at me again. "And how are you two doing with our friends?"

"Well enough," Sid grumbled.

Lillian sighed. "Many of us are an acquired taste, I'm afraid."

"I like Marian and Andrew," I said. "I don't know why, but I do."

"We try to avoid personality conflicts," Lillian said. "But that can't always be done. Fortunately, most of our group is very professional. One of the reasons no one has taken out Dale O'Connor. He's damn good at what he does, and he is a very good judge of character."

Sid laughed. "He'd have to be to have seen me as a spy."

"Oh, that's right. You two have a history."

Sid choked. "You could say that."

Lillian chuckled. "He does have a rather paternalistic attitude toward you."

"Not that it's done him any good," Sid said.

"I hope it's not going to cause any problems."

"It won't once he gets it into his head that I'm not in the Army anymore. But, as you said, sometimes it's about being professional."

"True." Lillian chuckled.

Sid cleared his throat. "Oh, and what's a yellow card?"

"That. It's a code that got deprecated." Lillian glanced at him in the rearview mirror. "It was a caller/receiver for floaters. You two would have had a red card. How did you find out about it?"

"An enemy caught me about eighteen months back and asked me for my yellow card." Sid sounded mildly annoyed. "He seemed to think it was an actual card."

"That's... interesting."

She chose not to elaborate. But I got the weird feeling that she didn't because she knew we'd be really angry if she did. That is the aggravating part of the spy biz, but there's not much we can do about it. [As much as I hate making the concession, in retrospect, Lillian had a point about that one. The issue with the yellow line had been dealt with effectively, with no little thanks to our own efforts. And I'm not entirely sure that knowing about that little tidbit would have made our lives any easier that summer of 1984, or later in fall '85. – SEH]

Lillian didn't get out of the car when we got back to the hotel. Sid talked to the desk clerk about a tour for the next morning, then took my hand and led me up the stairs to our room. I had to admit, I was feeling a little strange. We'd had a pretty nice day, but all I could think about was Marian lusting after Sid. And Sid drinking coffee and not worrying about what he ate. I didn't know what to make of either. Fortunately, it wasn't that late when we slid inside the room and shut the door.

I smiled at Sid and grabbed his sweater to pull it off him. He caught my hands.

"What are you doing?" he asked.

I looked at him, puzzled. "Um. Making love?"

"Sweetheart, if that was what you're doing, we'd be in bed right now."

"What?" I looked at him. "You like it when I get aggressive."

Which he does, by the way.

"You're not being aggressive. You're being... I'm not sure, but this isn't about the two of us."

I felt myself shrinking. "I don't understand."

Sid pulled me over to the bed and we sat down next to each other. "I don't either, Lisa. What's going on?"

I felt panicked. "I don't know!"

"Does this have anything to do with Marian?"

I tried not to sob. "Maybe."

"Okay. What has got you upset about her?"

"She's lusting after you."

"So?" Sid touched my face.

"Sid, I know you're not going to go for it. I really do trust you." I blinked my eyes. "I just want to be worth it for you."

"What do you mean?" Sid was truly puzzled.

"You gave up sleeping around for me."

"No, I didn't."

"Yes, you did."

Sid looked away, then looked back at me. "I gave up sleeping around because I was getting bored silly with it. Yes, you had a lot to do with why I was so bored. But I stopped because I wanted to. That's why you accepted it. Remember?"

I shut my eyes. "I know. I just feel like I should be making it up to you. You did get a lot out of sex."

"I still do." He smiled so warmly at me. "But it's sex with you that matters. Not with anyone else."

"Even someone as sexy as Marian?"

Sid shook his head. "Marian has nothing on you. Do you remember at our wedding reception when Shelley Friedman grabbed me?"

I laughed. "The look on Dan and Sarah's faces."

"Yeah, but do you remember what I said about it? That I wasn't missing a thing? That's because I'm not, and Shelley's a pretty sexy woman. Marian is, too. But you've got them both beat by a mile."

"I'm glad you think so."

Sid groaned. "Why can't you see just how truly sensuous and sexy you are?"

"What do you mean?" I felt myself sinking even further into myself, if that makes sense.

"Lisapet, how many times do I have to tell you? You are incredibly sexy. I've always known that."

"Well, yeah. You see me that way." I sniffed and snuggled next to him.

"Not just me. In fact, I've been getting a little annoyed that you're leading Andrew on, then complaining about how Marian is going after me."

"I'm not leading Andrew on."

Sid snorted. "You most certainly are."

"I am not!" I glared at him. "I mostly ignore him. And besides, why would he be interested in me?"

Sid almost gaped. "You really don't see it."

"See what?"

"Lisa, you are one of the most sensual women I have ever met in my life."

"I know. You see me that way. But I'm not, really."

Sid sighed and pressed his lips to my temple. "Like hell, you're not. What, for crying out loud, do you think got me excited?"

"Being female?"

"Not even close." He rolled his eyes.

I made a face. "Sid, I know you love me, but that has more to do with our relationship than me being some sexy little tart."

"True." He sighed. "It does. But that doesn't mean you aren't a really sexy little tart." He squeezed me ever closer than we were. "I really wish you could see just how desirable and beautiful you are. Yes. The fact that I love you makes all the difference in the world. But one of the things I fell in love with was your sensuality. The way you touch fabric and utterly enjoy the feel of it. You sipped that pink Champagne tonight and loved it so much that I swear I got excited watching you. And the way you eat. You love the flavors so much."

"But it also appalls you."

He chuckled. "Okay, the sheer amount you consume is pretty scary. But you enjoy it so much. You get teary-eyed looking at a sunset or a beautiful painting. Or listening to some piece of music that touches you. Lisa, that's what makes you such an incredible lover. You feel things and embrace the passion."

"That's easy." I sighed. "You make me feel so good."

"I couldn't if you didn't enjoy the feeling so much." He nuzzled my ear, then lifted the hair on the back of my head and softly kissed the back of my neck.

I sighed loudly with the delicious feel of it.

"You really like that, huh?" he whispered.

"Oh, my god, I do. I don't know why, but it really gets me excited."

He laughed softly. "Well, well, well. Looks like I've just found one of your erogenous zones."

"Wasn't that some cheesy book from the seventies?"

"It was very cheesy, but there may be some truth to it." He nuzzled my ear again.

"So, where are your erogenous zones?"

"It depends."

"On what?"

He looked a little guilty. "Different people, different situations. Not that any of that matters now." He laughed again. "I guess you're just going to have to explore and find out what gets me hot. Besides you just being you."

He kissed me softly. And I did a fair amount of exploring. For some reason, when I kissed the insides of his wrists, that got him. Of course, by that point, we were both in a state, which made things nicely intense.

The weird thing is, I still don't see myself as being all that sexy. But he sees me that way, and that's all that really matters.

March 5, 1986

Sid let me sleep in a little the next morning. As I laid in bed, I could hear him singing something from some opera as he took a bath. This being an older and more European hotel, there wasn't a shower. The only reason we had a private bathroom was because it was a four-star establishment.

I couldn't tell what specifically Sid was singing, partly because I don't know opera that well, and partly because he was trying not to sing too loudly. I smiled. He didn't want me to know he was singing, which meant he was feeling pretty happy about the previous night's lovemaking. It was one of the few things that carried over from when he'd been sleeping around. He'd have a good night and the next morning he'd be singing All Day, All Night, Maryann. Determined not to give me even the least reason to distrust him, he avoided his old habits and anything close to them almost relentlessly. He still couldn't help singing after good lovemaking, though, and I couldn't help but giggle that his former girlfriends got a crude little folk ditty, and I got grand opera.

I closed my eyes and thought about the coming day. After our morning bus tour, we were going to meet Marian and Andrew around two that afternoon to tour the

Tower of London and see the crown jewels. I was glad that our cover required us to do a lot of what I'd wanted to do, anyway. I couldn't help but wonder how I'd ended up where I was. Married. A spy. Sleeping with a man before I'd married him. None of that was anything I'd imagined when I was a kid. In my head, I heard myself oohing over something.

(December 1963)

I was five and looking at the Sears Catalog Wish Book. That December catalog was the highlight of my year for so long. Yes, it was fun poring over the ladies' formal dresses, but the toys. So many wonderful fun things. Mama sat next to me.

"That's what I want from Santa!" I pointed to a bright red fire engine pedal car.

"But, honey, that's for little boys," Mama said.

"Mama, they don't have those little cars for girls. Girls just get a bunch of dumb dolls and ovens and play schools. The boys get all the good toys. I want a Vacuform and a fire truck."

"But you're a little girl."

I suddenly threw the catalog across the room. "I hate being a girl!"

"Lisa Jane!" Mama gaped, then realized I had burst into sobs. "Sweetheart, what's the matter?"

"Mrs. Sorenson says I can't be a fireman when I grow up because I'm a girl. Only boys are firemen."

Mama pulled me into her lap, sighing. "Well, that's true, Lisle. But there are a lot of good careers for women. You can be a teacher. You can be a nurse. You can work in a store. You can be a secretary."

"What's that?"

"Well, you write down what your boss says and type up his letters and keep his papers in the right place. It's a really fun job."

"I want to be a fireman. I want to jump out of a plane and shovel dirt on fire and save people."

Mama sighed. "We'll see, sweetheart."

I didn't get the fire truck, but I did get a pedal car. I also got an Easy-Bake Oven, which sat in a corner in my room until Mae decided she wanted to play with it, even though she was eleven at the time.

"Hey." Sid came in from the bathroom, his chin freshly shaved and still wet. "You want to get your bath?"

"Sure." I lay on my back and blinked at the ceiling above me.

"You okay?"

I smiled. "I'm fine. I was just thinking about how when I was a little kid, I had only four career options and that I've pretty much blown through all of them."

"Only four?"

"Nurse, shop clerk, teacher, and secretary. That's not counting being a mom. That was a given. And come to think of it, I'm that, too. The only thing I haven't been is a nurse. Undercover counter-espionage agent wasn't even an option. At least, not for me. Little girls didn't get to do things like that."

Sid chuckled as he opened the room's closet. "Fortunately for me, big girls do, and you're damn good at it. Now, we do want to enjoy breakfast before catching our bus."

Sighing, I got out of bed and into the bathroom.

The bus tour was a lot of fun. We were rushed through Westminster Abbey, but I got to spend some time enjoying the Poet's Corner.

We had fish and chips for lunch. Again, Sid surprised me by having some, although we had to get some antacids from a chemist's shop. We also collected as many pound coins as we could, then met Marian and Andrew at the Tower of London a little before two. We were at the part of the tour where you get in line for the crown jewels when three o'clock rolled around. It being early March, the line was relatively short. Sid also saw a pay phone in the immediate area, so we held off getting in line while Sid and I called Nick.

After the crown jewels, we still had a little time to wander around the main courtyard. Sid nodded at me and somehow managed to get Andrew walking along with him. I held Marian back.

Marian looked over at the two men and sighed. "I dare say Andrew is getting a talking to."

"I'm afraid so." I winced. "But I also have to talk to you."

"I'm not surprised." Marian laughed softly. "Well, you have nothing to worry about. He's been perfectly circumspect, more's the pity."

"Oh, I know. I trust him completely. It's just kind of hard watching you keep making a play for him. I'll admit

I have been feeling like I had to compete with you, but Sid straightened me out on that last night. Still, I like you and Andrew, which is why it's so annoying when you go after Sid. I want to keep liking you."

Marian's eyes widened. "And yet…"

I flushed. "Marian, I'm terribly sorry. I truly did not realize that I was leading Andrew on. I was just trying to be nice, and I thought I was mostly ignoring him."

"In some ways, you were." Marian shook her head and looked over at Sid and Andrew. "Lisa, I do believe that it is I who owes you an apology. I have been rather beastly about Sid. Not that he isn't quite attractive."

"Yes, he is." My voice took on a slight edge.

Marian let out the ladylike version of a snort. "That only made it easier. You see, darling, the problem isn't him. Or you, really. It's my husband. He quite fancies you."

"That's what Sid said." I shrugged. "I don't know why."

Marian looked at me. "You truly don't, do you? Well, that makes no difference. However, if I've been bad about your husband, it is only a rather juvenile attempt to wrest my husband's attention back to me."

"You mean you're jealous of me?" I swallowed.

"A little." Marian sighed. "Neither Andrew nor I have really worried about any sexual wanderings on the part of the other. We sometimes must in order get secrets, and other times, it's never really meant anything. I suspect any liaison between you and Andrew wouldn't, either. The problem is, he can't have you, and that sort of thing does make him a little obsessive. It's quite irritating." She looked toward Andrew and her face grew soft. "I used to think I was in love with him. Perhaps I still am."

[The funny thing was, Andrew was crazy in love with Marian. You did get him stirred up. He was shocked, that first summer we met them in Paris, to find that we were not lovers. In fact, he wondered if I had known what I really had in you, and I assured him I had. As for our honeymoon, things between him and Marian had gotten a little flat, and he was hoping a little jealousy might add a spark. Now, I realize I still am possibly the last person on earth to consult for relationship advice, but this was only too easy.

"Forget making her jealous," I told him. "Just focus on how much you love her and let her know that you do."

In fact, I suggested that he play the same game at that evening's party that I asked you to play. - SEH]

By that time, it was getting late in the afternoon, and I could see the Yeoman Warders (what people call Beefeaters, but they really don't like being called Beefeaters) looking askance at us. We retreated to a tea-room and had a full late tea while I quoted Shakespeare and Sid laughed. It would have been dinner, but Marian said that there would be a very well-stocked buffet at the party that night. My stomach twisted. I really did not want to go to that party, but it seemed like we had little choice.

One of the really great (and, okay, really annoying) parts of Sid knowing me so well is that it is incredibly hard for me to hide what I'm feeling or thinking. [Except when you're playing poker. - SEH] So, when we finally got back to our hotel room to get dressed for the party, Sid was totally on to me.

"Honey, it's just a party," he said as he got out his dinner jacket and slacks with the satin stripe on the sides.

Dinner jacket, my left foot. Yes, I realize that's the proper name for the suit in question, but only Sid would pack a bleeding tuxedo for a vacation.

"It's a room filled with people we don't know," I grumbled.

He laughed and gently grabbed my arm. "My darling Lisapet. You never fail to amaze me. You are easily the bravest person I have ever met. I have seen you jump off a building with someone shooting at you. You have faced so many people with guns trained on you. You put yourself between kidnappers and their target. This is merely a social occasion."

I made a face and Sid laughed.

"You'll be more than fine," he whispered, touching my face. "If anything, you will be the belle of the ball."

"I don't want to be the belle of the ball. That means I'll have to talk to people."

Sid laughed even harder. "That's okay, my sweet. In fact, I've got a great idea, if you don't mind me alluding to my dark and infamous past."

"Why would I?"

He pulled me next to him and just held me for a moment. "Okay. Every so often, there would be a woman that I really wanted to make love to. Sometimes it was the whole saw her across the crowded room thing. Sometimes I knew she was going to be there. Sometimes we'd known each other, and I just wanted to spice things up. So, what I'd do was totally focus my attention on her, and the more coy she was, the better it got. I swear, I could have somebody else undressing me and I wouldn't notice. Why don't we try this? Let me attempt to seduce you."

I giggled. "You've already done that."

"Doesn't mean I can't do it again." His hand ever so gently cupped my face. "At least, I hope I can."

Oh, lord, it was so hard not to kiss him.

"Okay," I said weakly.

"Alright. I'll get shaved while you get your makeup on. In fact, I think we have just enough room in that bathroom for that to happen. Then we'll get you into your dress and then we'll get me into that tux. And no matter what, no love making until we come back here after the party. I don't care how much we want to. We're going to save it for when we come back. Okay?"

"Um. I wouldn't mind a fast one right now."

He shook his head. "Absolutely not. I'm saving it for later."

"Oh, shavings."

That rat. He really knew what he was doing. He zipped me into my dress, but it was no accident that his hand gently ran down the back of my neck. He only let me rub the insides of his wrists as I got his cufflinks inserted into his sleeves. In short, both of us were in a state by the time Mr. Quimby rang from downstairs that the limo was ready for us. Oddly enough, Marian and Andrew were in the limo and in pretty much the same state as we were.

"I almost wish we hadn't agreed to go," Marian said with a sideways smile at Andrew. "Oh, but we have news for you."

"Yes," said Andrew. "My contact at the Oxford police finally spoke to me. You were right about that attack yesterday. The two men apprehended were Croatians."

"Croatia is part of the Yugoslavian republic," Marian added, and sighed. "Yugoslavia, of course, is made up of several diverse ethnic groups, slapped together after World

War One, and is now getting ready to explode. The Serbians are the larger population group, but the Croatians are anxious for diplomatic recognition."

"Which is why they want to negotiate with the U.S." I sat back and frowned. "Still, why not try normal channels?"

Marian shrugged. "I believe that might have something to do with your CIA. Someone there seems to believe that keeping Yugoslavia in a state of conflict will serve your best interests."

"Can't see how it would," said Sid.

"Neither can we." Andrew shook his head. "But that is the CIA for you."

Sid and I glanced at each other and tried not to roll our eyes. We were not fond of the CIA. A few minutes later, we had arrived at the party and Mr. Quimby held open the car door.

As Sid and I walked into the Flowers townhouse, Sid held me back in the hall.

"You know, I am counting on you to be coy," he whispered.

"And you do not make it easy on a girl," I whispered back. "But I'll manage."

I walked ahead of him for a moment as he laughed.

It made the party almost bearable. We were directed to a large room that I suppose would have been a ballroom, except that it wasn't huge. Only two crystal chandeliers were needed to light it up. Chairs were scattered throughout. There was no band or live music, although there was some quiet music coming through unseen speakers. As Marian had said, there was a nice buffet set up at one end of the room, with two full bars on either side. I am no good at estimating the size of a crowd, although Sid said there were less than fifty people there. Dale and Adrienne O'Connor were there and immediately took possession of us as we walked in.

"We'll introduce you to Gwen and her son," Dale said, gently pushing us toward a matron with a full figure and a beige lace dress.

The man with her was about my age, maybe a little younger, with full, dark hair, brown eyes, and the manner of someone who knew he was irresistible. In truth, he was pretty easy to resist, but somehow, he hadn't figured that out.

"Gwen. Mark," Dale said, somewhat loudly. "I'd like you to meet our new club members, Sid and Lisa Hack-birn."

"Good to meet you," I said, retreating into polite ritual, shaking hands with Gwen first, then Mark.

Gwen looked confused. "I thought one of you was a Ms. Wycherly. Like the playwright."

Sid bent over Gwen's ear. "I'm sorry if it's confusing. Apparently, Dale didn't get the memo. Lisa's keeping her maiden name."

"How modern." Gwen smiled at me. "I was told you two have just been married."

"We have," I said, softly.

"Good to have you two on board," Mark said.

"Oh, you're a member of the club, too?" Sid asked.

"Not really." Mark laughed, flashing teeth that were too white to be real. "Call me and Beatrice hangers-on. Mum needs the support every so often."

"Lady Beatrice is Mark's wife," Gwen said, her chest swelling. "She's right over there. The lovely little brunette in the lavender dress."

Sid looked over at the woman in question and his smile suddenly got very tight.

"Well, lovely to meet you." And he pulled me away.

I looked at him, then at the woman in the lavender dress. "Are you kidding?"

He sighed. "I'm afraid not. There's a story behind it, but, yeah, it was the usual two weeks."

I closed my eyes. "Is she going to hate me?"

"I doubt it. I didn't know you yet. And she's married now."

I sighed. "That should help."

I really didn't mind Sid's former girlfriends, except for the ones who had it in for me for taking him away from the singles scene. I mean, I didn't blame them for being upset. I just wished they didn't want to take it out on me that Sid had given up sleeping around, even if I was the reason he had.

He chuckled. "This doesn't change my objective for the evening."

"I should be so lucky."

His eyebrow lifted, but I pushed ahead toward the buffet.

I thanked God for Sid's little cat-and-mouse game. I do not do small talk well at all. [You do it quite well. You just don't like it. - SEH] Having to avoid Sid's advances while at the same time teasing him took a fair amount of my concentration, which meant that mindless banter with total strangers was not as utterly terrifying as I normally found it. Instead, it was only mildly terrifying. In fact, things went well enough that Gwen Flowers was quite taken with me and wanted to be sure that Sid and I would join her and some of the others (I had to assume that meant Lillian, Dale and Adrienne, and Marian and Andrew) and go to Gstaad for the weekend.

"Marian did say something about that," I said with a smile. "It sounds like fun."

"Oh, good." Gwen beamed. "Mark and Beatrice are also going. It's going to be delightful."

I looked across the room and almost gasped aloud as Sid caught my eyes and rubbed the back of his neck. I lifted my wrist and rubbed it and was gratified to see him catching his breath as well. Some minutes later, I slid up to Sid. He put his hand on my shoulder.

"You seem to be having a little fun, at least," he said softly.

"So-so." I winced.

"I am this close to finding a restroom or a broom closet and dragging you in with me."

I chuckled. "You said no way until we get back to the hotel."

"A guy can change his mind, can't he?"

"Are you going to be able to recharge by the time we get back to the hotel?"

Sid caught his breath. "That's it. Unless you really, really want to stay, I think it's time to leave."

I agreed, but was debating how to say that when the slender brunette in the lavender dress approached us.

"Well, hello, Sid," she said rather breathlessly. "What a coincidence to find you here."

"Isn't it?" He looked at me. "Beatrice, please let me introduce my fi— I mean, my wife, Lisa Wycherly." It was the first time he'd called me that. I felt like I should have liked it more than I did. "Lisa, Lady Beatrice…"

"Flowers," she said, then looked at me with a weak smile. "I suppose I shouldn't say anything."

Sid chuckled. "Lisa is well aware of my raucous past."

"Yes, well, my husband, Mark, is not aware of mine." She smiled, then looked back at where Mark Flowers was chatting with some other men.

"I am nothing if not discreet," Sid said. "It's good seeing you again. How long have you and Mark been married?"

"About a year and a half. You?"

Sid grinned. "Today's the fifth? Then about five days."

"Oh!"

"Well, one has to come up for air every now and then." Sid laughed. He looked around the room and found what he was looking for. "Anyway, Lisa and I were just talking about getting back to the hotel. If you'll excuse us."

"Nice meeting you, Lady Beatrice," I said.

"Lovely meeting you." She smiled. If she still seemed nervous, I didn't think I had anything to do with it.

Sid led me to where Marian and Andrew were chatting with another couple whose names I'd already forgotten.

"Oh, hello, darlings," Marian said, her hand holding one of Andrew's.

Sid nodded at the other couple, then turned to Marian and Andrew. "I think Lisa and I are going to call it a night. We'll get a cab back to the hotel."

"Oh, don't bother," Marian said. "We were about to leave ourselves. Genevieve, Darren, lovely seeing you again."

The other couple nodded. Then the four of us made our farewells to Gwen.

"Oh, and Marian, I am so looking forward to having you at the school opening tomorrow," Gwen said. "Mark and Beatrice will be there as well."

"So, I've heard. We'll see you then, dear." Marian kissed both her cheeks, as did Andrew.

Sid and I each shook her hand, and we left the house.

Once we were in the Rolls Royce limo, Marian sighed and slipped her shoes off.

"I am so glad you two decided to leave early," she said. "The only good part about that ghastly school opening is that you two will have a chance to search Mark Flowers' flat."

"The break-in," Sid said.

"Yes." Marian rolled her shoulders as Andrew watched her appreciatively. "And I'd be interested to know your impression of him."

"Pretty unimpressive," I grumbled.

"I'd have to say the same," said Sid, giving my shoulders a squeeze. "Why are you looking at him?"

"Mark Flowers has been seen talking to the men we believe to be the ringleaders of the plot," Marian said. "The only problem is that we don't know why. Mark doesn't have any visible reason to be talking to them, beyond being involved in whatever they're plotting. We're hoping you'll be able to find something telling in his flat. Quimby will pick you up in the morning. You'll have to visit the shops, anyway, for your ski gear. May as well take the day to go shopping. Once we're certain that Mark and Beatrice are at that blasted opening, we'll call Quimby on the car's radio phone, and you two can break into the flat. Quimby has the building plans and security information."

"And keys, ma'am," Mr. Quimby said from the driver's seat.

"What about the clothes?" I asked. "We'll either need to be wearing them in the morning or have some way of changing into them."

"I'll have them in the car, ma'am," Mr. Quimby said. "We have curtains. You'll be able to change in complete privacy."

"Thanks," I said. I looked at Sid. "Then we're for it, I guess."

"Sounds like a plan." He smiled, and I could tell he was not thinking about break-ins.

Andrew's eyebrows lifted, then he looked over at Marian.

I slid my hand over to Sid and stroked the inside of his wrist, and his thumb brushed the back of my neck.

March 6 – 9, 1986

S id nudged me out of bed at six the next morning to go running. I complained loudly, especially since we'd gotten to sleep relatively late the night before, never mind that we'd gotten back to the hotel early.

"Honey, I know," he said, smiling. "But we are working, and we've been eating an awful lot and not getting a lot of exercise."

"We walked all over the place yesterday."

"I know. But if we run now, we'll be able to relax over breakfast."

I went along with it, never mind that I really didn't want to. Sid was right. We were working and even if we hadn't been, we needed to stay in shape.

The thing that surprised me, though, was that he was wearing his glasses. He truly hates how he looks in them, even though I find them very stylish with dark rims.

"Why?" I asked as we took off.

"I want to see where I'm going." Sid shrugged, gasping a little with the exercise.

"You don't wear your glasses when we're running at home."

He chuckled. "No. I run blind."

"You mean you don't put your contacts in before we run?"

"Not really, especially if we're just running the usual route. I mean, sometimes I want to see stuff, and I put the lenses in, then take them out again before getting in the shower."

"Can't you wear them in the shower?" I gasped a little myself as Sid stepped up our pace as we hit a small park near the hotel.

"No. It hurts like hell if I get soap in my eyes and, to be honest, I have flushed one or two down the drain."

"But you're wearing your glasses now."

"You keep saying you like how I look in them."

"I do." I tried not to choke as I said the words.

We were married. We'd really done it. That had to be why he didn't worry as much about he looked. Sid had always been incredibly vain. I couldn't help but wonder if being married meant that he'd let himself go.

[Not quite, although, at that moment, I thought it was just about being in London and wanting to see. But as I think about it, I was finally realizing that I didn't have to protect my reputation as the super-lover anymore. I still wanted to look good, and always will. And I still don't like how I look in glasses, never mind that I wear them full time now. But I didn't *need* to look good, and, yeah, that I was a married man was why I no longer needed to, and it was a relief. – SEH]

Mr. Quimby showed up on the dot at nine and took us to the ski shop. We got in before the place had opened and found that everything we needed had been ordered and was ready for us to try on, including a pair of black all-over ski masks. I loved the buttery yellow ski overalls and the matching boots. Plus, there was another Shetland wool sweater, dyed to match the ski overalls. There were jackets and hats. Sid got an outfit in purple, black, and blue, which really played up his eyes.

We got out of there in plenty of time to get to Harrod's. We went a little nuts in the stationery department - the fountain pens were amazing. Sid had gotten me hooked on writing with them, and our collection grew by several pens. The menswear department was big enough that there were suits for shorter men (Sid is barely three inches taller than me, and I'm average), and while he would have needed too many alterations to buy a suit or two, the fit was close enough for us to determine that he looks incredibly good in an Italian cut. He bought a couple unstructured blazers, though.

I didn't really see anything I liked in the women's wear department, except for the Dress Stuart plaid kilt that I got, and the only reason I avoided the store's fabric department was that I knew I was headed someplace else. I found several lovely sweaters and other goodies for Mae's kids, and even more goodies for Nick.

The other interesting thing was that we were having everything shipped home. We were traveling as ourselves. It didn't make sense not to.

We could probably have spent all day at Harrod's, but there were two other stops that we wanted to make, and we were painfully aware that we had to have our shopping done before tea-time. That was when Gwen Flowers and her son and daughter-in-law were going to be doing that whatever opening someplace outside of London. Actually, we needed to be done with shopping before then so that we could have a conference with Mr. Quimby regarding our target.

Our next stop was Liberty of London, and I will confess that I went a little crazy in the fabric and yarn departments. [A *little*? - SEH] I bought yards of gorgeous cotton lawns and amazing woolens, not to mention skein after skein of wool yarn, including a heather green Scottish wool so beautiful I knew I wanted to make the sweater right then and there. So, I bought needles, stitch holders, markers, yarn snips, and a retractable tape measure. I got some of my own back when Sid landed in the housewares department at Fortnum and Mason. [Fair enough. - SEH] Sid went after some lovely Wedgwood plates featuring various classical composers, a full set of Spode china, not to mention two different sizes of Waterford crystal wine glasses.

We had an early tea at Fortnum and Mason, which was phenomenal. The clotted cream, alone, almost made me cry, not to mention the jams and marmalades. We also bought a whole bunch of loose-leaf tea.

"What about your caffeine headaches?" I asked Sid as he poured what had to have been his fourth cup that day, although it was only the second cup at our tea-time meal.

He shrugged. "I have no idea. It may be the tea or the fact that I'm not drinking as much as I used to. I could go through about eight cups of coffee in one day, once upon a time."

"Conchetta told me that you'd drink two pots of coffee a day."

His shrug was a little guilty. "Okay. Maybe I did. But even here, I'm not doing that much. Truth be told, I'm going with the gift horse on this one."

Our next step was to get as many pound coins as we could and call Nick. The boy's problems with his teacher, Mrs. Fleming, were ongoing. Apparently, she didn't understand seventh grade math as well as Nick did and had asked him to explain it to his classmates. Stella seemed sure that the teacher was lacking. Sid and I wanted to believe that she was helping Nick to be more confident in his own abilities. Either way, there wasn't much we could do about it right then. We consoled Nick, reminded him that we'd be home as soon as we could and that we'd be home before Easter, then hung up as the operator demanded still more coins.

Mr. Quimby was as good as his word about the curtains on the Rolls limo. Before he could pull them, though, we went over the plans on the Flowers' building and their apartment, excuse me, flat. Sid and I changed into our break-in clothes and made sure we had our various tools, gloves, sweatshirts, and masks as Mr. Quimby drove us over to the building.

We went up to the apartment on the service elevator, then put on our masks and gloves. I was surprised that there was almost no video surveillance, and what there was focused on the front of the building. As Sid had said earlier, I was going with that gift horse. The elevator left us in a tiny lobby with two doors. We knew which one we wanted, and the key worked.

Sid slid into the flat before I did. Usually, I go first because I'm the better shot. But we didn't have guns this time. We landed in a kitchen decorated in white and gray. It was utterly empty. I mean no dishes, no pots, or pans. Nothing. Not even any food, and you would have thought there would have been some leftovers in the refrigerator.

We still went through every cupboard, looking for false panels. Nothing.

The fridge and freezer were completely empty, too.

"How do they eat?" I whispered to Sid.

He shrugged. We went through the trash bin under the sink, but there were only a few takeout containers in there, and no false panels or backs under the sink.

The rest of the flat was the same. It was nicely decorated in a very Fifties Modern style. But nothing, and I do mean nothing, showed up as suspicious. We pulled up carpet. We checked every closet and cupboard for hidden panels. We went through every bit of paper there, searched under cushions, felt under every piece of furniture. Nothing.

That was weird. Truth be told, most people hide something. Maybe it's a porn addiction, usually it's something pretty mild. But someplace this clean was suspicious. The only problem was that it didn't tell us what to be suspicious of.

We had been there almost an hour, which is a long time when you're searching a place, when we looked at each other and shrugged. Using the one transmitter we had, we signaled our ride, then took the service elevator to the street, and while riding down, took off our masks, gloves, and sweatshirts. If Mr. Quimby had been driving anything but a Rolls Royce limo, it wouldn't have looked odd at all. We had our regular clothes in the back seat with us.

Sid looked at me and grinned. "Are you up for another adventure?"

"Besides the break-in?"

Sid's chuckle left no doubt about that part.

"Um. Why not?" I said, still wondering what I had let myself in for.

Sid slid the curtain open between Mr. Quimby and the back of the Rolls. "Mr. Quimby, would you mind finding us a nice, quiet place to park, then taking a good twenty-minute walk?"

"Very good, sir."

Sid shut the glass partition between the driver and the back closed, then made sure the curtains all around the back of the limo were fully drawn.

"What are you thinking?" I asked, both hopeful and worried.

Sid grinned. "We've got to change clothes. Why not have some fun in the meantime?"

That was kind of the problem. I couldn't resist. Okay, we ended up meeting Marian and Andrew considerably later than we should have. But once we got to the pub, it was obvious what had kept us. Gwen, Mark, and Beatrice Flowers were sitting at the table, too, and I saw Mark sniffing as I ran to the restroom to clean up a little.

One other good thing was that I had kept a bag from Liberty with me, the one that had the yarn and tools for the sweater I really wanted to make. As Marian and Andrew ordered another bottle of Bordeaux, I got out my notebook and started doing a little math.

"What are you doing?" Marian finally asked as I measured the front half of the Shetland sweater I was wearing.

"Setting up a cable pattern." I looked up at her and flushed. "It's just this wool I got at Liberty. It's so gorgeous. I want the sweater."

I held up a ball from the sack in my purse and let Marian, Gwen, and Beatrice squeeze it. Beatrice was less than enthused. Marian almost got it.

"That is rather nice," she said, although I strongly suspected she was just trying to be kind to me.

I shrugged. "It's something I love."

I looked at the label on the skein, then cast on twenty stitches on one side of the circular needle and slid a row counter onto the other side.

Sid sat back and watched while I knitted, and the others went on about how boring their afternoon had been. I had my gauge swatch knitted in no time, which meant I could finish my math. I do knit and sew my own clothes. But that is as domesticated as I get. The knitting and sewing happened because I kept getting pneumonia every year until I was seven or so, and Mama needed something to keep me quiet and occupied while I was recuperating.

The conversation had wandered off someplace else by the time I had cast on enough stitches for both the front and the back of the sweater. I was using a circular needle, even though I was knitting the sweater in rows. It's a way of making sure everything lines up and possibly a more complicated way of doing things, but it's the sort of thing I don't even think about anymore. Sid kept up with the banter because he's good at that sort of thing.

Eventually, the Flowers family left, and we went on to an Indian restaurant that Marian and Andrew said was very popular. It certainly was busy, and Sid and I noticed with satisfaction that the customers were just as likely to be from Asia as Europe.

"Do be careful," Marian said as we perused the menu. "The food can get rather spicy here."

"Sounds great." Sid grinned at me.

The waitress, apparently, had dealt with far too many people of European extraction swearing they could handle spicy only to find they couldn't. She brought us a little sample and seemed shocked (and pleased) when both Sid and I thought it was somewhat mild. The platters that came out after that were amazing. Not surprisingly, the waitress knew Marian and Andrew, and there were platters seasoned more to their tastes.

"So, what did you find today?" Marian asked once we'd all filled our respective plates.

"Nothing," said Sid.

"Odd." Andrew's eyebrows rose. "Quimby said you spent almost a full hour there."

"We were really looking," I said. "But it was almost as if no one lived there. We found the usual personal items and clothes, but that's it. No false panels, no papers of any kind, not even anything hiding in plain sight."

"It was almost too clean, which kind of bothers me." Sid scooped up some sauce onto a piece of naan.

"That is oddly telling," said Marian. "We had the same problem with Lady Beatrice a few years back. We even had someone on your side investigate her when she went over your way."

Sid choked. "When?"

Andrew looked over at Marian. "It was spring, nineteen eighty-two, wasn't it?"

"It was," said Sid. "If you sent the request through Henry, then I did the investigation."

"Oh, my god!" I suddenly laughed. "The long story from last night, right?"

"I don't understand," said Marian.

Sid sighed. "My profligate past. Lady Beatrice remembered me last night. She'd spent just under two weeks staying at my place in the spring of eighty-two. Henry had asked me to check her out, so I did."

"And did you find anything?" Andrew asked.

Sid shook his head. "I went through everything she had. I found nothing. If she was communicating with anyone, she did it when she was in the bathroom, and I have no idea how because I was watching for radio signals and there was no phone in the bathroom."

"What about when you were asleep?" I asked. "You do sleep pretty deeply."

Sid shook his head. "I had a silent alarm to register when someone used the phone or sent a wireless transmission. Nothing registered. And the house security didn't register anyone coming or leaving. Not to mention she was a complete airhead. I couldn't wait until she took off." He grimaced. "She wasn't even that good in bed."

Marian's eyes widened, and she looked at me.

I shrugged. "It's his past. I don't worry about it."

"Yeah," said Sid, shifting. "The only problem we've been having recently is with some ladies who resent Lisa for taking me away from the singles scene, which is ridiculous. I left that scene almost a year ago and now they're getting mad?"

I winced. "Honey, I'm guessing they were thinking you'd come back. Getting married means you're not going to be back for a long while, maybe not ever."

"Definitely not ever." He reached over and took my hand. "Anyway, none of this has anything to do with Lady Beatrice and Mark Flowers. And, by the way, Beatrice seemed more worried that her husband would find out about me than anything else."

"Hm," said Marian. "I dare say it will take a bit of finesse to find out whether that is the case or if they suspect you, Sid."

"I don't see why they would." Sid shrugged. "She didn't see me searching anything of hers, not that there was anything to find. The fact that she was staying at my house made it a lot easier."

"Alas," said Andrew. "We can't know for sure. The best we can conclude is that we are alerted to a potential problem." He looked at Sid and me. "As we said earlier, your job will be to focus on the drop-off stations. And we do have an early morning tomorrow."

"We do, indeed." Sid smiled at me as I rolled my eyes.

I made sure that Sid and I had a couple of the antacids from the previous day. They didn't entirely help. We offered to take a cab back to the hotel. Marian and Andrew insisted we ride with them in the Rolls. Sid made a point of lowering the window just a touch in spite of the late winter/early spring chill. Well, we were getting gassy at that point - the big downside of a meal like we'd just eaten.

That didn't stop Sid from getting amorous when we got back to the hotel room. If anything, he was more amorous than usual, which might seem a little odd given the state of our digestive tracts. We made love making all kinds of different noises, and if the air was more than a little fragrant, that didn't seem to matter.

We cuddled afterward, and I burped.

"Excuse me," I whispered.

He laughed and burped himself. "Excuse me, too."

"Oh, dear. We are a pair, aren't we?"

"So what?" He nuzzled my ear and squeezed me. "We're the best kind of lovers. Isn't that what your great aunt said?"

"You mean because we can pass gas around each other?"

"Exactly. I didn't really get that until tonight. It was so great to have a wonderful meal like that, then come back and make love without having to worry about what my gut was doing or that you were going to run away, screaming in terror."

I looked at him, indignant. "Who did that to you?"

"Nobody. At least, not that I heard, and truth be told, I didn't really give anybody a chance to. I didn't want to take the risk. Had to keep my reputation going." He squeezed me again. "That's the best part about being with you. I do sometimes worry about disappointing you, but that's because I don't want you to be disappointed. Before, it was that I didn't want some woman running around complaining that I wasn't as good in bed as everyone said I was. It was all about my reputation. But now, I don't have to be Superman anymore. I can't tell you what a relief that is."

"I'm glad because I don't need Superman. Not that you aren't pretty super. I just need you."

"As I need you, my love."

We snuggled for a little bit longer, then fell asleep.

We were out of the hotel far too early that next morning, but we had an early flight out of Heathrow to Switzerland. Now, skiing in Switzerland has never been at the top of my must-do list. On the other hand, you can't have spent as much time on skis as I have and not want to ski in the Swiss Alps. So, by the time we landed, I was getting excited. I still had to wait.

Marian decided she wanted a late breakfast at a small cafe in the town, and then we'd have to get to the drop-off station. Our luggage was, presumably, on its way to where we'd be staying. Andrew had explained that their staff was made up of CID agents in training. Many of them took undercover assignments as domestic staff in various places in Eastern Europe and in the Soviet Union. The training they got as chauffeurs, butlers, maids, and footmen made them quite desirable. And it also made traveling with Marian and Andrew insanely easy. Their staff did everything, including pack and unpack.

From the cafe, we went to a charming little chalet on the edge of the equally charming little city of Gstaad.

"This is where you'll be staying," Marian said as we stood before the door. "Not only do the drop-off stations provide a relatively safe place to hide information, they also serve as safe houses. Assuming, of course, that one can get to one without being followed."

Andrew smiled. "They're part of a chain of vacation homes for hire owned by a corporation that, eh, may just be owned by us. It would not be easy to find that out, however. The vast majority of the homes owned by the chain are, in fact, exactly that. There are just some that are, shall we say, harder to reserve than others."

"Unfortunately, we can't always let them stand empty." Marian made a face. "It would be too suspicious. We usually hire them to the other travel club members, particularly the ones who are with us as cover. Agents dropping off information generally know to only come during the wee hours of the morning."

Sid glanced at them suspiciously. "The O'Connors aren't staying here, are they?"

Andrew laughed. "Not at all. After Quimby's report yesterday afternoon, we convinced Dale that he and Adrienne might find our preferred hotel significantly quieter."

Sid laughed, but I flushed vermilion as I realized the chauffeur had not gone on a walk after all. Marian and Andrew looked at me quizzically.

Sid slung his arm across my shoulders. "Lisa's not quite used to being such a woman of the world."

There really wasn't much I could say.

"Very well." Andrew flashed a brief smile, then pointed to the small read-out screen on the lock. "The cipher locks, themselves, are a bit of genius. If a civilian enters an entry code, the door simply unlocks, as one would expect. However, if an agent uses one of the special entry codes, the lock sends an alert to one of the monitor teams. The lock also flashes an alert if the place has been hired to notify the agent that there might be people inside."

"It also flashes an alert if there are other agents on the premises," Marian added. "Either way, any entering agent knows to either come back later or get in and out."

"That is why it's important that you make sure you set the lock every time you leave." Andrew handed us a small notebook. "You will also need to memorize the code book, since the code changes weekly."

Sid flipped through the book as I thought of something.

"What if we're staying here, then leave, then another agent comes and wants to stay?" I asked.

"There's a code for that, too," Andrew said, then nodded at Sid. "We don't get a lot of overlap, however."

Sid entered several numbers into the lock's keypad. The yellow backed read-out flashed a code. Sid handed me the book. The flashing code meant that all was clear for entry, and I could hear a bolt click back.

"The important part of a drop-off station," Marian continued as we walked into the front room. "Is that in each one, you will find a series of items in a specific order. Well, usually they are in a certain order. The signal is Forget-Me-Nots. Whatever the decor, there will be some image of that particular flower. The image never hides anything. After that, in a counterclockwise circle, you will find a clock, a table lamp, a chair, a picture frame, and a wastebasket. The idea is that things are supposed to be hidden according to the phases of the moon, except that most of those idiots can't remember what phase the moon is in, so you need to check everything. That's why it's so important that you familiarize yourself with each station. Chairs, lamps, and wastebaskets do get moved every so often. The monitoring team comes to clean up and put things back after every entry, but that doesn't always help."

"As for the accommodations, they should be quite adequate," Andrew said. "And in this case, you'll be quite alone."

I blushed again, but Sid grinned.

"Always nice to know," he said, shamelessly.

"Very well, then," Marian said. "Find our hiding spaces." She smiled disingenuously at me. "The sooner you do, the sooner you'll get to the slopes."

The front room had a high peaked ceiling and was open to the floor above. Dark wood stairs lined one wall, and I could see two doors over the balcony above. The furniture was comfortable and overstuffed with a dark blue abstract pattern. A Persian carpet covered the gleaming dark wood floor in front of a huge fireplace. I saw Sid mulling something over, but then he turned his attention to the primary purpose of our visit.

The small purple flowers decorated a vase on the fireplace mantle. To the left of that was a real Swiss cuckoo clock, and we found that the door in the front opened. The table lamp was round, fat, and ceramic, but the hiding place was in the brass bottom. A wing-back chair was next, and the back detached. The picture frame surrounding a landscape had room for several canisters of film. There was a false bottom in the wastebasket.

The luggage arrived as we finished. Marian and Andrew assured us there would be a car available for our use, then went off to get checked in at their preferred hotel.

We were on the slopes outside that hotel by noon. Even Sid wanted to get skiing as fast as we could. It was probably a little catty of me, but when we got to the slopes, I was surprised to see Adrienne skiing. She followed Dale down the run as Sid and I got in line for the lift. Sid saw something else, too.

He nodded at Dale. "You think you could take him in a race?"

I snorted. "With one pole behind my back. Why?"

Sid just laughed. "I'm thinking we can squirt some cider in his ear."

I rolled my eyes. Sid's favorite musical, bar none, is Guys and Dolls. I think he relates to the whole Sky Masterson falling for the mission lady story line. But one of Masterson's better lines is that you don't take sucker bets because as soon as you bet that someone can't make a card jump out of a deck and squirt cider in your ear, that's exactly what happens.

I shrugged. "If you want to."

It was relatively late in the season and a Friday, so the line at the lift wasn't that long. O'Connor shussed up to us.

"Good to see you two," he said loudly. "Odds we can have a race when we get to the top?"

"Damn good," Sid said.

Adrienne slid into place next to her husband. "He's so competitive."

Sid couldn't help laughing. As if he wasn't.

Sure enough, when we got to the top of the run, Sid held me back and winked. Dale and Adrienne arrived a minute later.

"Well, Sid," Dale said. "What about that race? Maybe add a little financial challenge?"

Sid snorted. "O'Connor, I'd just be taking your money. Lisa could beat you."

Dale looked at me, then looked at Sid. "Nice try, Corporal. Now, seriously. What do you want to put up?"

Sid grinned. "I'm serious. How about five hundred bucks that Lisa kicks your backside?"

"Against Lisa?" Figures Dale would fall for it. "You're on."

I sighed and looked at Adrienne. She rolled her eyes. The only thing saving me was that I knew I could outrun O'Connor.

We let Adrienne tell us when to go. I was off like a flash. The problem was that we were doing some relatively late season skiing, which meant icy moguls, which are difficult to see when you're rushing down a slope. I almost lost my balance a couple times. The weird thing is, so did O'Connor, who had presumably been down that run at least once already. Still, I'd been on skis since I was four (maybe three), and late season skiing? I'd been doing that as long as I'd been skiing. Those two times I didn't see the mogul ahead of time didn't really matter because I instinctively knew how to right myself. O'Connor had more trouble. At least, that's what Sid told me later. I didn't really know because I was focused on doing the run.

It was glorious. There is something about rushing down a slope, with the wind in your face, that is... Well, addicting. It's as though I'm flying. I love the feeling of it. I wasn't sure where Dale O'Connor was, and frankly, didn't care except that he was behind me. I tried not to think about the five hundred bucks Sid had bet on me, even though I knew it had been a sucker bet.

As I finished the run, I went into a side stop that just happened to spray snow all over. I wished I could have hit O'Connor, but he was too far behind me.

He slid up a couple of minutes later. "Good run. Seems you got lucky."

I shrugged. "If that's what you want to think."

Sid and Adrienne slid up next to us.

"Hey, Dale," Sid called. "Want to go double or nothing?"

O'Connor glared at him briefly, then shook his head.

"We'll catch up later," he said, pushing himself toward another lift and run.

I looked at Sid. "There was a second run up there. You want to do it?"

"I always want to do it." His grin got really hot, and I could see that he was thinking about the two of us making love. "But, yes, we can do that second run."

"At least you've started smiling at me again." I said, shifting with the thought.

Sid looked at me. "I smile at you a lot."

"It's that one smile you get," I said, flushing again. "I can tell you're thinking about doing it with me. I just haven't seen much of it since last summer and I thought maybe you weren't thinking about us making love that much."

"Oh, I have been and am," he said, the smile getting even hotter. "And trust me, it's more fun to think about now than ever."

My breath caught. "Good."

It was a perfectly lovely afternoon. We stopped skiing just long enough to call Nick at four that afternoon (we'd moved into another time zone). Sid and I were late for dinner with the rest of the group, although not for the reason most of them thought. It was just a little too cold for that.

"Lisa talked the lift operator into one more run," Sid told Marian as we gathered around a fondue pot in the hotel's bar area.

Gwen Flowers had arrived with Mark and Beatrice in tow. Lillian had declined to join us for that part of our trip since she did not care for skiing. Dale and Adrienne joined us at the fondue pot, cocktails in hand.

"Well, Dale," Andrew said. "We heard Sid and Lisa set you up this afternoon."

"I didn't set anything up," I said, dipping chunks of bread into the rich, cheesy sauce in the pot.

Dale glared at Sid.

"I don't understand," Sid said. "I thought that since you knew Lisa grew up in your district, you'd figure she could ski pretty well."

"That may have slipped my mind," Dale grumbled.

"You're spending too much time in Washington." Sid laughed.

"I don't understand," Gwen said.

I shrugged. "Dale is the congressional representative for South Lake Tahoe, where I grew up. It's a mountain resort area in California. I've been skiing as long as I can remember."

I could see that Dale was looking the two of us over. Adrienne hinted somewhere along the line that Dale didn't dare challenge Sid to a race. After all, if I could beat Dale that easily, then Sid must be even faster. I didn't say anything. Sid gave up racing me years ago, largely because he can't beat me.

Dinner was quite leisurely, but I could see that Sid wanted to get back to the chalet. He kept looking at the firepit in the restaurant, then looking at me. As his smile grew hotter and hotter, I blushed and caught my breath. Finally, the dinner dishes were cleared, and Sid got up.

"Honey, you want to make it an early evening?" he asked me.

"Of course."

I knew darned well it wasn't going to be an early evening, though. When we got back to the chalet, Sid and I built the fire in the fireplace. As it got going, Sid went upstairs and brought down a sheet. As he explained, he wanted to protect the Persian carpet and, well, rug burns are no fun.

He let me sleep in the next morning, but not that long. The slopes were waiting. As Sid and I rode up the lift together, my mind wandered.

(February 24, 1973)

It being the middle of the skiing high season, Daddy didn't get too many chances to go skiing with me, especially on a weekend, but he must have seen something going on. I wasn't quite fifteen, and it had been a really lousy week.

"You seem pretty down," he said as the lift chair took off.

I made a face. "Danny stopped calling last weekend. I finally got him to talk to me and he broke up with me."

"He did? I'm so sorry, honey." Daddy may not have liked Danny much, but he was sympathetic when I got dumped, as I usually did.

"He got fresh, and I had to tell him no."

"As you should."

"Daddy, what's wrong with me? Tammy Winters said that the boys don't want to go with me because I act too smart. She says I should play dumb. Danny was smart, but he didn't care about me being smart. He just wanted to feel me up."

"Honey, not all boys are like that. You did pretty well last summer."

"That's because they only have a week with me. They see me as cute, but that's it." I blinked as I tried not to cry. "And it doesn't matter if they want to mess around because they're only here for a week and then they're gone before that can get started. I just want a guy to like me for me. Why is that so hard?"

Daddy sighed. "Sweetheart, you are a very special young lady. If boys now can't see that, it's probably because they're too young. But you will meet a man someday who will appreciate your brain. You may have to wait until you get to college, because that's where the smart boys go, but you will meet someone."

It had taken getting beyond college for me to meet that someone. As I had told Sid, dating non-Christians was a pain because all they wanted from me was sex. Then dating Christians was a pain because all they wanted was to get married and I did not want to get married.

"What are you thinking about?" Sid asked.

I shrugged and told him.

"And then you went and fell for the horniest of them all," Sid chuckled.

"Well, yeah, but it wasn't about you being that horny," I said. "We got on because we weren't having sex. And I knew you weren't going to marry me. It was always about the friendship. The falling for each other just happened in spite of ourselves."

"I suppose you could say that." He looked at me. "But you still don't get how attractive you are."

"Attractive for what? Somebody's plaything? Or devoted servant? Believe me, they aren't coming around because I have a brain."

"Well, I am." He nudged me with his shoulder. "Trust me. Your brain is possibly the sexiest thing about you, and I've always thought that."

I smiled. "You always know what to say."

"Not always, but often enough."

We hopped off the chair and made our way to the start of one of the runs. Mark Flowers greeted us as he and Beatrice shoved off. Sid and I made our way down the slope in a leisurely fashion. We stopped about midway down because Beatrice had fallen next to some trees.

"Are you alright?" I asked, sliding up to her.

"Quite fine, thank you." She smiled weakly. "Mark was ahead of me, then I hit an icy spot."

Sid reached over and between the two of us, we got Beatrice upright, although in the process, I dropped one of my poles.

"There's a lot of ice out here," I agreed, then bent to get my pole back.

"Thank you." She slid off.

I looked at Sid. "But there isn't any right here."

"Maybe this is where she landed." Sid looked back up at the run.

Four men scrambled out of the trees and came right at us. I tried to push off, but one of the men was already standing on my skis. I wrenched the boots from the bindings while trying to elbow him in the ribs, screaming for all I was worth. I heard another scream echo a little below me. Sid had gotten free of his skis, as well, and began punching, only to dance back when one of the men came at him with a knife. Sid swung his pole at the man and fended him off that way.

I wasn't so lucky. Even as I reached for the man in front of me, another got behind me and I felt the icy sting of a blade at my neck. I released my one pole as the man pulled me backward. He said something to his fellows and two of them went back into the trees, I could only guess to get something.

Breathing heavily, Sid dropped his ski pole. There was more screaming from around the slope as other people noticed what was going on. Sid was about to back up when

I jammed my knuckles hard into the sweater-clad arm that was holding the knife to my neck. The man dropped the knife and ran, as did his partner. Sid and I didn't waste any time. We got our skis back on, grabbed our poles and pushed off and away.

Beatrice met us at the end of the run, her face creased with terror.

"Oh, my god!" she gasped. "Are you alright?"

Sid cursed. "Lisa, you're cut."

I touched my neck where it stung. "It doesn't feel serious."

Sid slid over next to me, glaring at the cut. "Okay. Doesn't look that deep, either, but we'd better get something on it."

I was almost more annoyed that blood had stained my lovely new sweater. After Sid had gotten my cut covered with a couple of bandages, I rinsed the sweater out with cold water. I had a t-shirt on underneath, so taking the sweater off was no big deal. The rinse job meant I wasn't going to be wearing the sweater outside until it dried. I put the sweater next to the dining room fire pit. It wasn't quite lunchtime, but I figured if I ate lunch then, the sweater would dry. I could always catch a snack around two or three, and possibly again at four, when Sid and I called Nick. Sid joined me, as did Marian and Dale O'Connor.

"Well, this is simply beyond annoying," Marian said. "Whoever attacked you got clean away, no thanks to Beatrice's caterwauling."

"I started it," I said, feeling guilty. "I was trying to look like a civilian."

"Now, are you three still so certain that Sid and Lisa aren't our targets?" Dale snarled.

Marian rolled her eyes. "No one said that they positively weren't. Only that it seemed unlikely, and it still does."

Sid frowned. "I also got a strange vibe from those guys. It was as though they wanted to take us out rather than take us hostage. And it was strange that Beatrice just happened to land right there."

I sighed. "She said she slipped on some ice, but there wasn't any nearby."

"She was calling for help," said Marian.

"So did I." I bit my lip. "How much of that was cover and how much was real?"

Sid shook his head. "She also could have slid further than we realized. On the other hand, why would she set us up? It's possible she figured out that I'm an operative when she stayed at my place, but I don't see how. I was watching her pretty closely."

"Unless Mark set her up," said Marian. "And why he would do that, I have no idea. The problem is we don't have a lot of evidence either way, and, unfortunately, we still don't know what the actual objective of the Croatian plot is beyond getting the American government to negotiate with them."

Dale shook his head. "Okay. You're right. There's a lot we don't know about what's going on. But I say we need to keep a solid eye on Sid and Lisa."

Marian nodded. "I'm afraid so."

I sighed. "Maybe we should go back up to where we were attacked and see if we can find something, like maybe that icy spot Beatrice supposedly slipped on."

Dale, Marian, and I ended up going down that run. My sweater had dried nicely by the time we finished lunch.

Sid decided to hang around with Mark and Beatrice in the hopes of getting something, anything, from them.

I was right. There wasn't even the least bit of ice or bumpiness in that immediate area. In fact, there wasn't any ice anywhere near there, nor were there the tracks that would have been visible if Beatrice had slid a significant distance. In fact, nothing had disturbed the snow around where Sid and I had been attacked, except for that immediate area. I got my skis off and planted them, then walked back into the trees, with Dale close behind me. The men had clearly run, and I suppose we could have tracked them, but Dale decided that we didn't need to. I had to give him credit. Tracking them probably wouldn't have revealed that much.

That evening, Marian, Andrew, and Dale decided that they would stay as close to Sid and me as possible. Except for when we were in the safe house, which was fine with Sid and me. That part of our adventure was working out remarkably well.

We spent another day, Sunday, in Gstaad. Gwen asked Marian over fondue that evening if Marian and Andrew were headed for home, and Marian told her that the two of them would be following Sid and me to Venice. I suppose I should have been paying more attention. Except that Sid was distracting me by nibbling on the back of my neck.

There is something incredibly special about Venice. The ancient buildings, the smelly canals. Art is everywhere. And there aren't any cars, although the motorboats make up for it.

We took the water taxi in from the airport, then ate lunch at a small trattoria just off the Piazza San Marco. The next stop was the drop-off station. It was at the top of a small apartment complex not far from the piazza. We had to walk up three floors, then cross an enclosed bridge over a canal to get to the apartment in question.

The decor had a very Eighteenth-Century look, with ornate woodwork on the sofa and chairs in the front room. Everything was white and gilt gold, with dark burgundy velvet upholstery. A dark gilt frame on the side wall surrounded an oil still life painting of fruit and a gold pitcher, with the light purple forget-me-nots strewn around.

We found the hiding places quickly. An ornate clock on a what not table under the front window had a back that opened. The table lamp was crystal and split apart at the side. The inside panel on the chair hid that hiding spot. The back panel of a painting of Venice at sunrise came apart. The waste can had big knobs on the side that twisted off.

We'd barely found everything when the knock on the door came, and our luggage was brought in by a young woman who promptly took it to the back bedroom.

Marian checked her watch. "We need to get back to the plaza. Lillian is going to meet us there at St. Mark's so that we can spend the afternoon touring the cathedral. Then we'll have tea with Dale and Adrienne and meet another of our club members."

I looked at Sid.

"Sounds good," he said.

Lillian was happy to see us, and the tour was fascinating, even the relics, which Sid thought were pretty strange. The thing was, as we left the cathedral for one of the many little trattorias surrounding the Piazza, I got the feeling that we were being followed. I glanced at Sid, who nodded.

Lillian, Marian, and Andrew sent the two of us off on a gondola tour of the canals and were waiting for us when we got back. Covert glances behind them told Sid and me that someone was, indeed, following them, but had not followed us.

The man sitting with Dale at the trattoria was not whoever had been following us. That person was still somewhere behind. I was not happy to see Dale's companion, though. Neither was Sid. The man was average-sized, balding, with his remaining hair neatly clipped and brown. He did not look happy to see us.

"Hello again," he grumbled as we walked up.

"It's a pleasure to see you, too," Sid said, a fake smile on his lips.

Dale stood. "Sid, Lisa, this is Clint Foster, Central Intelligence Agency, and our South America liaison. Clint, Sid and Lisa Hackbirn."

I glared at Dale but decided not to say anything, then shook Clint's hand.

Lillian pushed Dale on the shoulder. "Dale, can't you keep it straight? Lisa's name is Wycherly. She's not changing it."

Adrienne wandered up carrying a large shopping bag with several boxes in it.

Dale laughed and shook his head. "And how big a dent have you put in my bank balance?"

She smiled and kissed the top of his head. "The shoes here are divine."

I couldn't help grinning. I love shoes.

We ate pastries and drank coffee. Well, I did heavily doctor mine, but I was getting used to it. Sid really enjoyed the coffee, although he only had one cup. He hadn't been getting any headaches, but if he drank more than one cup at a time, it would upset his stomach a little. Clint and Dale were having quite a good time, with Sid on the edge of the conversation. I chatted with Lillian about what we were going to do the next day, then saw Dale glare at Sid, who shrugged. Clint, for his part, looked at me funny.

Adrienne convinced Lillian and Marian that we women should go shopping. I agreed to meet them because it was getting close to four and Sid and I needed to call Nick before he went to school. Marian arranged with the cafe's owner to let us use his telephone.

It was a quick conversation. Nick was annoyed that he'd forgotten to do several math problems over the weekend.

"They're easy ones, but I gotta get them done before school," he complained to me.

I handed him over to his father, who knew immediately what was going on and asked Nick what he'd done to get assigned math homework over the weekend. Sid took a couple more minutes to talk to Stella, then hung up.

"So, what did Nick do?" I asked.

"He was bored in math again and got caught reading a Spiderman comic book under his desk." Sid shook his head, then smiled and pushed a roll of money into my hand.

"What?" I asked.

Sid grinned. "I finally collected on that bet from Friday. That's five hundred bucks in lira. Go buy some shoes on Dale."

"Why?"

Sid folded my hand over the cash. "You won the race. You get the whole thing."

"Okay." I smiled weakly.

Sid smiled, then sighed. "I gotta get back and listen to the macho men. Believe me, I'd rather be shoe shopping."

"Maybe tomorrow." I looked around. "Marian said they'd be next door, so…"

"I'll see you at dinner." He gave me a warm kiss and sent me on my way.

The shoes were nice. But I didn't find anything that really got me excited, so I passed. We moved on to a dress shop. Adrienne was quite happy, but either I didn't like what I saw, or I knew I could make it for cheaper and so it would better fit me. In fact, I didn't buy anything at all.

Sid was a little surprised when we met the men for dinner. I handed him the money he'd given me.

"What's going on?" he asked, pulling me aside in the foyer of the restaurant.

I shrugged. "I just didn't find anything I liked."

"We're in Italy. Home of Ferragamo. You not finding anything you like is like you turning down food."

"I just didn't want to buy anything. Okay?"

Sid looked at me and I squirmed.

"It's a couple of things," I finally said. "I really, really don't want to play into O'Connor's stupid comments about Adrienne spending all his money."

Sid sighed. "I get that. But we are equal partners. It is, technically, our money."

We had set up a business partnership and mingled our assets over a year before.

"I know. Still. I'm not really feeling good about the money you gave me."

"Why?" he asked. "You earned it."

"You set him up."

"Big deal." Okay, he added an obscene epithet in the middle.

"That wasn't right."

"He deserved it. Lisa, I am up to my eyebrows with his sexist nonsense and his B.S. about not remembering that you're keeping your name. And I'm guessing you are, too."

"Yeah."

"So? Normally, you'd be looking to show him up faster than me."

"Possibly. Probably. And there's Clint, too. He keeps looking at me like I'm about to come unglued."

Sid laughed. "We scared him last year, didn't we? Good." He patted my shoulder. "You'll be fine, Lisa. Clint will get over you or he'll get clobbered. Just like you took on Dale and won us some money."

"I don't know. I just don't feel right keeping it."

Sid smiled and shook his head. "Lisapet, you would find a way to forgive Hitler. Alright. I'll take custody of the cash for the time being. But in the next day or two, we are going shoe shopping. For both of us. I could use a pair or two of nice Italian loafers."

I giggled. "Or a nice Italian cut suit. We just have to figure out how we're going to get the alterations done."

"You know. We could get them done after we get home." He grinned. Sid has an exceptionally good tailor.

"As long as I don't have to do them. I hate alterations. All that unsewing." I shuddered.

Sid laughed, and we returned to the others. Although Lillian and Marian pulled me aside while we were having an aperitivo in the bar before going to our table.

"Are you and Sid okay?" Lillian asked. "It looked like you two were not happy a few minutes ago."

I flushed. "Yeah. We were having a disagreement." I shrugged. "We settled it." I looked at the two of them. "Look, Sid and I disagree all the time, and sometimes it gets a little heated. But we always settle it."

Marian's eyebrows rose. "Indeed. Well, I suppose that's all to the better."

I shrugged again. "It always is."

Dinner that night was a complete feast, and then some. It certainly rivaled the amazing meal we'd had at Marian and Andrew's townhouse on our first night in London. Okay, it surpassed it. We had perfectly chilled prawns, a gorgeous creamy mushroom soup, sole that had been poached in fish broth, veal cutlets breaded with ham and cheese then covered in buttery tarragon sauce, a salad of bitter greens, then four different and utterly delicious cheeses with dried figs. Not to mention a different fabulous wine to go with each course.

During the middle of the meal, I saw Sid and Marian talking seriously and softly about something, but since they were at the other end of the table from where I was sitting with Adrienne, Clint, Lillian, and Andrew, I had no idea what they were saying.

Dinner was followed by delicate pastry filled with cream and bits of perfectly candied citrus rinds, and coffee. Then grappa, an Italian brandy made from the leftovers of the wine-making process. The potent brew pretty much blew my stabilizers out of whack.

Sid was, no surprise, in quite a mood by the time we got back to the drop-off station. Still, I was curious about that conversation he'd had with Marian over dinner.

"What about it?" he asked, nuzzling my ear.

I turned and faced him. "It looked pretty serious, and you both looked my way a couple times."

"She and Andrew just don't know you all that well yet." Sid winced. "And you have been a little off since we caught up with them."

"I'm sorry," I said.

"For what?" Sid lifted my chin and looked me in the eye. "It has been overwhelming, and you are not in your usual element."

"You can say that again." I blinked my eyes. "Remember last year when we were feeling so off? It's beginning to feel a little like that."

"That actually makes sense. No matter how married we've been over the past year, doing it formally has got to be having some effect on us." He smiled and stroked my face.

"And having to be social on top of it is not helping."

"No, it's not." Sid chuckled. "But we have to remember that the only times we've had contact with most of the others, we've been working. You're a lot more confident then, because you do know how good you are. Even I forget sometimes how shy you get around new people." He cupped my face and kissed me, oh, so softly. "Now. I propose that we forget about Marian and indulge ourselves in a little connubial bliss."

"But are you up for anything?" I asked, smiling. "We've had an awful lot to drink tonight."

Sid laughed and pressed himself up against me. "I don't think I'm having a problem with that."

"I don't know." I grinned, even though it was more than obvious he was not having any problems. "Drink 'provokes the desire but takes away the performance.'"

"As long as I have my tongue and my fingers, performance will never be an issue." Sid still groaned happily. "However, tonight, I think the traditional performance will win out."

It did.

We spent most of the next day on a bus tour of the immediate region, with the O'Connors and Lillian alongside. It was fun, but not terribly exciting, although we found a painting we really liked. Sid got a little wistful on the bus as we watched the surrounding landscapes pass by late that afternoon, after we'd called Nick and Stella.

"What are you thinking about?" I asked as we headed back toward Venice itself.

"Something Stella just told me. Her father's family was supposedly from this region before they came to the United States." Sid shrugged. "Might be interesting to do some research along those lines."

"You're interested in your own genealogy?" I grinned.

"I wasn't before, but now I am."

I chuckled. "That could be fun. I suppose I should do some research on my side of the family, too."

"We'll see. It's not as though we don't have other things to keep us busy."

The five of us met up with Marian and Andrew in time to do a little shopping and enjoy an aperitivo at a trattoria before yet another feast that started with artichoke hearts stuffed with crabmeat, through a salad, then a timbalo, or drum, of pasta with layers of rice, vegetables, and salamis. Shrimp steamed in vermouth, followed, and after that veal in lemon sauce, more cheeses, then spumoni ice cream for dessert. Clint Foster joined us. Adrienne demurred and went back to hers and Dale's hotel room. Given the risk to her figure, I almost understood. I was a little surprised to see Sid eating, but he'd picked up on how best to pace himself during these monster meals. However, as we ate, Marian and Andrew had some news that cast a bit of a pall on the proceedings.

"Mark Flowers is not only here in Venice, he's been talking to some of the Croatians," Andrew told us.

Sid sighed. "It might help if we set up an opportunity for an attack."

"I can't say I like that idea," I grumbled.

"Still," Lillian said. "It would be one way of ferreting out what Flowers and the Croatians are up to. Marian, can you call Gwen tonight and let her know when Sid and Lisa are going to be someplace that we set up?"

"Quite easily," Marian said. "I'm just not entirely sure we should assume that Sid and Lisa are the targets. I grant you, there's a fair amount that suggests they are. But I get the odd feeling we shouldn't assume that."

"Then let's split them up," Dale said. "I'll take Sid and Clint with me, and we'll set up a sniper vantage point."

Sid snorted. "If you want a sniper, take Lisa. She's the dead-eye in our operation."

He grinned with pride, and I flushed. Dale and Clint did not look happy, but had to concede lacking other opposition.

The plan was relatively simple. There was an area of exclusive shops that was also surrounded by a variety of apartments. I'm still not sure how Marian and Andrew set it up, but by one o'clock that afternoon, after Sid and I had done a walking tour of Venice and eaten lunch, I found myself assembling a high-powered rifle as Dale and I looked over the piazza, I mean, plaza, surrounded by high-end shops, from an apartment overlooking the area. Clint had taken another lookout position on the plaza itself.

Sid, Marian, and Andrew wandered in and out of the stores. I had a feeling that Sid had made more than one purchase but didn't know. I was too busy looking for Croatians or other thugs getting ready to jump my beloved.

I must concede I was a little startled when the Croatians finally did show, even though I should have probably figured they'd do it next to an alley where they could get away. When the men jumped, they seemed intent on dragging Marian and Andrew off. They mostly ignored Sid. Andrew went into action, as he'd done in London, but there were six men, and that was a bit much even for Andrew. I squeezed off a few shots just close enough to the attackers' feet to get them worried. They backed off, then ran.

Then Mark Flowers wandered into the plaza.

"Take him out," O'Connor growled.

"Who?" I asked.

"Flowers."

"No."

"That's a direct order, Hackbirn."

I glared at him. "In the first place, my name is not Hackbirn. That's Sid's name. In the second, I do not kill people on purpose."

"He's an enemy."

"I don't care. I don't kill people."

"He's out to get us."

I pressed my lips together. "We don't know that for certain and even if we did, that is not who I am or what I do. You want an assassin, pay for one."

I began disassembling the rifle. Frankly, I wanted out of that apartment as fast as I could. I didn't know Italian gun laws, but I was willing to bet they were a lot stricter than they were in the U.S.

"What the hell do you think you're doing?" O'Connor yelled at me.

"I'm getting out of here. You want to get caught in a European nation with a gun, that's up to you. Me? I don't want to."

O'Connor cursed. "What is it with you two? Do you get off on insubordination?"

"What?" I yelped. "Are you out of your freaking sexist mind? We are undercover. I do not want my cover blown. I'm leaving. See you around."

I left the rifle, too. Somehow, O'Connor got out of there without problem. I didn't want to know. Sid, on the other hand, did want to know what had happened. I told him over an afternoon snack that Marian called tea, never mind that we were drinking coffee. Then Marian and Andrew followed Sid and me as we went shoe shopping. Okay. The shoes were pretty awesome, and I found several pairs that I really liked and bought a few. Sid also got several pairs of shoes himself. I'd been right that he'd been actively shopping earlier. There were several Italian cut suits that arrived at our house in Beverly Hills after we got back.

The big problem was when we made our daily call to Nick. Drat that kid. He always knew when we were doing something dangerous, and it worried him to no end. I always felt guilty about worrying him, too.

"Honey," Sid said after we'd hung up. "It's part of who we are, right?"

"Yeah. I know." I sighed. "I just hate getting him upset."

"I do, too, but it's part of our lives." Sid sighed. "He's surrounded by people who love him. He'll be okay."

"I sure hope so."

I felt a little guilty going back to buying shoes and other goodies for Nick and my nieces and nephews. But they were what was important, not sexist operatives asking me to kill people for no good reason. Heck, even Marian and Andrew had told me that Flowers was worth more alive than dead, and I knew they had no problem with killing people.

G iven that Sy Flournoy had studied in Vienna, it would have made sense that Sid and I would have mentioned that we were there to Stella that first afternoon after we arrived. I don't know how much of the fact that we didn't had to do with me knowing that Vienna had been kind of a sore point with them way back when or Sid's and my general reluctance to let anyone know where we were. We told her eventually. We kind of had to. We did some shopping and had our purchases shipped, as we'd been doing, and she would have noticed the return addresses.

But that was after we'd arrived at the drop-off station, checked out each of the different caches, then found ourselves on a bus tour of the city. Dinner was a lot more fun, despite Dale introducing me as Lisa Hackbirn again. I looked at travel club members who had come to say hello and decided not to argue about it. Both Sid and I recognized Eduardo and Elena Montoya. Eduardo was Elena's father. Elena was my usual Orange County contact, and she'd been hanging out there for some time, compensating for the missing hub and floater on the Red Line.

Both Eduardo and Elena were the floaters for the Seattle port of entry and the Blue Line. Elena would be headed back up that way once she and Eduardo got home, since Sid and I were now floaters for the Los Angeles port of entry and had a hub team.

The next morning Sid and I went running, then got ready for yet another bus tour, this time of the surrounding area. Marian, Andrew, Lillian, and the Montoyas joined us for that one. Marian and Andrew still weren't too sure about leaving Sid and me alone after all the attacks we'd been subject to. That wasn't such a bad thing. We were getting to know them and Lillian better and realizing that we really liked all three of them. After Sid and I had settled into our seats on the bus, I felt my mind wander again. I don't know why I went back to the worst year of my life thus far.

(May, 1968)

Grandma Wycherly was tall and forbidding. I had always been a little scared of her. But when she'd come to stay with us when I was ten, there was a part of me that was grateful. After all, Mama, Daddy, and Grandma Caulfield had all gone to San Francisco that spring. I didn't entirely understand what Mama was up against, just that it was really, really bad. She had breast cancer, and all I understood about it was that she could die. I don't think it registered. The tension and the fear did, though, and me being who I was, well, I acted out.

Grandma Wycherly, who was German by birth, was not pleased when she pulled me out of the horse barn that afternoon.

"Why are you doing this?" she demanded.

"Doing what?" I asked.

"Jumping out of the hayloft onto the floor. Do you want to hurt yourself?"

"There's lots of hay on the floor."

"Lisa Jane, why can't you be more like your sister? She is good and ladylike. She gets good grades. Why can't you do that?"

"I don't know."

"You will never get a husband this way."

"I don't want a husband."

"What are you saying? Of course, you do. And if you are going to get one, you need to be a good young woman. A quiet young woman. You need to be ladylike."

"Yes, ma'am."

I wasn't entirely a troublemaker, and I knew what I was supposed to do. But being ladylike was a total bore.

"You're looking pensive again," Sid said with a playful nudge.

I grimaced. "Just thinking about my inglorious past."

"What?" Sid laughed.

I shrugged. "I got into a fair amount of trouble for not being a nice little Kate, conformable with other household Kates."

Sid nuzzled my ear. "And I'm glad you're not. You wouldn't be nearly as much fun."

"I'm glad you think so." I smiled, even though I didn't entirely feel it.

The reality was Sid understood me better than any other man I'd ever known. But that didn't mean he entirely understood the pressure I felt. Why would he? There was how he'd been raised, which was darned unconventional, and why he understood that the conventional social mores often bothered me.

I'm not saying he didn't try to understand the rest. He most certainly did. He simply had no way of understanding what I had been taught. He hadn't been taught the same things. Nor had he been subject to the same messages that I had because he was a man, and I wasn't.

We got to see a concert that night, and it was a lovely one, too. Sid was so happy he got even more frisky than usual on the way back to the drop-off station. The other really nice thing about Vienna was that we were not attacked or even followed. Sid and I weren't sure, but thought we had an idea why.

The next morning, we were on another flight, this time to Brussels.

"What was the name of that movie from the late sixties?" I asked Sid. "If it's Tuesday, it's Belgium?"

"I have no idea." Sid blinked. The flight was too short for him to take out his lenses.

"It was about a bunch of American tourists on a bus tour of Europe."

"You know. I think I did see that one. The tour guide had a different girlfriend in each city." Sid chuckled. "I used to think that would be a fun way to see Europe. And please note, I said used to."

"I know." I smiled. "I think the idea behind the title is that the group was going so fast through so many countries, they couldn't remember where they were. I'm almost feeling the same way."

Sid laughed a little. "You could almost say that. We certainly got more than we bargained on."

Brussels was gorgeous, filled with medieval buildings standing next to more modern ones. The drop-off station, though, was in a modern high-rise building, and it didn't take Sid and me long to find all the hiding spots among the blue Danish modern furniture. Marian and Andrew, who were with us, rushed us out of the apartment to go have lunch with Lillian, Dale, and Adrienne, and yet another two travel club members.

The members turned out to be Marge Benson and Hattie Mitchell. Marge was a crusty old lady who lived in her RV in several different spots, but mostly in South Lake Tahoe. As in, she knew my parents, and I always got the weird feeling that she wanted to rat me out to them, never mind that she needed to keep her cover as much as Sid and I did. The weird thing was that I really liked her, even though she and Dale O'Connor were buddies. Sid agreed that wasn't exactly a selling point on her behalf.

On the other hand, Hattie was a very dear friend. Sid and I had been writing for her magazine almost since I'd first come to work for Sid. Hattie has her fingers in a lot of different pies, but her primary work is with the defense industry. She owns a major defense electronics contractor and was probably involved in intelligence work in the early Sixties. We're not sure, and Hattie has never said.

Both Hattie and Marge took us around Brussels and were exceedingly well-informed when it came to being tour guides.

"I've just traveled a lot," Marge said, as we relaxed at a cafe on the Grande Place with Dale, Lillian, Marian, and Andrew.

Sid and I had called Nick. He was going to his friend Josh Sandoval's place for a sleepover that night. Adrienne had gone shopping. Marge kept referring to everything in Brussels by the French names (except for Manneken Pis, the iconic statue of the little boy peeing). Hattie explained that she'd worked in Belgium for several years before getting married. That's where she'd met Marge shortly after SHAPE (some sort of military alliance) had moved there and they had even worked at an air command facility in the French part of Belgium called Glons.

I plowed through a huge pile of frites, or French fries. Marge had recommended getting them with a tarragon mayonnaise on the side, and she was right. That mayonnaise was amazing. Sid got several fries, even though he usually avoids potatoes.

"Those are good," he said, going after another fry.

He also enjoyed the Belgian beer. I preferred the wine. We were both pleasantly tiddly by the time we wandered over to the restaurant Marian had selected. Which may have been why things erupted as they did over dinner.

Marge made several suggestions for a day trip the next day. I wanted to go to Bruges. Sid wanted to see Antwerp and the diamond center there. We couldn't really do both.

"We'll go to Antwerp," I said, finally.

"You don't care about diamonds," Sid retorted.

"I do." I looked at him a little frantically.

Sid looked at the rest of the group, then got up from his chair. "Excuse us. Lisa and I need to settle something."

He pulled me away to the plaza in front of the cafe.

"You didn't need to do that," I complained.

"Yeah, I did. Why are you caving in?"

"Why not? You want to see diamonds, we'll see diamonds."

"But you don't want to." He looked at me, a little worried.

"So what? I want you to have a good time. It's your honeymoon, too."

"It's our honeymoon. Lisa, what's going on?"

I looked at him, bewildered. "Nothing. I just want you to have what you want."

"Bull puckey." [That's not what I said. - SEH]

"I can't concede to your preference sometimes?"

"If that's what I thought you were doing, I'd probably be fine with that."

"Then what am I doing?" I glared at him.

"I have no idea. Normally, you'd be trying to find a way to do both. Or something. You wouldn't just roll over."

I glared. "Well, maybe I'm trying to be nice to you. Did that ever occur to you?"

"Except that's not how you are nice to me."

"Since when?"

"Like never."

"Maybe I'm trying something new." I snorted. "Why can't I defer to you sometimes? I love you. I want you to be happy."

"We both agreed a long time ago that being martyrs doesn't work for us."

"So, if I defer to you, that automatically makes me a martyr?"

Sid glared at me. "No. What makes you a martyr is that you're not happy about it."

"I'm happy enough."

"No, you're not."

"And you get to decide whether I'm happy or not."

"No." Sid rolled his eyes. "I can tell when you're happy or not. And you're not happy this time."

I winced. The problem was, I wasn't happy about going to Antwerp. It just felt so selfish to want what I wanted. And, yet, I couldn't say that. I wasn't sure why, but I couldn't.

"I want you to be happy," I said finally. "That's all."

He looked at me and sighed. "And I want the same thing for you. Look. Antwerp. Bruges. Neither really makes that big a difference to me. On the other hand, I know how much you love lace. It's not like we'll never get back here. Why don't we do Bruges? We'll do diamonds some other time."

"Sure. If that's what you want."

He shook his head. "What about what you want?"

"That's what I want."

His eyes narrowed, and I squirmed, not entirely comfortable with the way he was looking at me. Still, we went back to the others at the cafe and announced that we would spend the day in Bruges.

I'm sure Antwerp would have been lovely, but Bruges was incredible. Our entire group went, including Dale and Adrienne. The city was easily one of the most picturesque places I'd ever been. I took tons of photos. Hattie lectured on the differences between the different Gothic styles of architecture. Marian and Andrew watched passively. Lillian got into a debate with Marge and Hattie about whether it was worth ordering mussels at that time of year. We ate chocolate and pastries. We did the canal tour. We drank wine, beer, and coffee. We bought a series of pen and ink lithographs and some more watercolors. Sid bought me a bobbin lace making kit, as if I needed another needle craft hobby. But I had to admit, seeing the beautiful laces and the women making them, I was hooked.

Later that night, as we got ready for bed, I finally had to ask him.

"Sid, my darling, I'm curious. You're usually so strict about your diet. Yet since we've been in Europe, you've been eating almost like I do."

Sid chuckled. "Not in the same amounts, but yeah."

"Why? Given how many lectures I've gotten on how our health is the only thing we have, I have to wonder."

"Well." He shrugged and winced a little. "It's actually something you said a few years ago. Remember when you ate your way through lower Manhattan?"

I giggled. "You were disgusted."

"Not quite. Yeah, the sheer amount of food you consumed that day was pretty frightening. But it was something else. You got mad at me and told me that you experience the world with all five of your senses." He smiled softly and looked at me. "That's when I began to realize just how passionate you really are. It's like I've been telling you all along. You are a very passionate woman. Just because you said no to sex didn't change that. You were simply just as passionate about your convictions was all. Anyway, I was thinking about that, and it occurred to me that maybe I should try living with all of my five senses, too. We can't eat like this all the time. But this is a special occasion." He reached over and kissed me, then softly moaned. "Oh, yeah. I do like living this passionately."

I smiled back. "So do I."

Of course, the downside of all that was that we'd gotten back quite late and had to be up early the next morning to catch a train to Wiesbaden, West Germany. I was feeling pretty dopey as Sid and I sat in the train compartment with Lillian next to us and Marian and Andrew in the seat facing us. Marian and Andrew were traveling forward, but I didn't mind. It was kind of fun seeing where we'd been as things flashed past.

(March 18, 1974)

It was three days before my sixteenth birthday. All my friends were determined to get our driver's licenses on the day of our birthday. I was the first of that group to turn sixteen that year. Only it didn't look like I was going to get my trip to the DMV.

"Why not?" I practically screamed at Mama. "We've been planning this. You said I could."

"I said I thought you could. But your father has decided differently, and that's that."

"But, Mama, I was the best in my driver's training class. I passed the written test without one mistake."

"I know. Your father is just a little worried about you driving by yourself until the ground's a little more thawed out."

"That's ridiculous. I managed it when I hit that patch of black ice the other day. Daddy said he couldn't have done any better."

"And that's with us in the car. By yourself is a different issue."

"It's not fair. Mae got her license on her birthday."

"Perhaps Mae was just a little bit more mature than you are right now."

I made a face. "What? I'm not immature!"

"Well, huffing around like you are right now isn't help-ing."

"But Daddy's wrong. I'm a good driver."

"That doesn't make any difference. He's the one who gets to decide."

"Why?"

"Because he's your father. His mind is made up, and that's all there is to it."

"Why can't you talk to him?" I began to suspect Mama agreed more with Daddy than disagreed. She certainly knew how to get around him.

"Maybe you ought to try sweet-talking him yourself. You catch a lot more flies with sugar than vinegar."

It took a day or so, but I did eventually convince my father that I was mature enough to get my driver's license on my birthday. Still, it had been like that my entire life. We always deferred to Daddy. If Mama wanted her own way on something, she usually found a way around him. But more often than not, Daddy had the final word, and that was it.

I looked over at Sid. He'd been right those two nights before. Martyrdom had never worked for us, and we could always tell when the other was trying to make it work. Still, I wanted to please Sid. That was so important to me. I mean, I loved him. Why wouldn't I want him to be happy?

After we'd crossed the border into West Germany and the conductor had stamped our passports, Sid glanced at me, then looked at Marian and Andrew.

"Does Gwen Flowers know we're going to be Wiesbaden?" Sid asked them.

Marian made a face. "Not yet."

Sid nodded. "Mrs. Flowers did not know we were in Vienna or Brussels, did she?"

"No, she did not," Marian said.

Sid looked at her. "So, given that Gwen Flowers reportedly likes to talk, and that her son, Mark Flowers, appears to be up to his hips in whatever this plot is, then it is reasonably safe to say that when Gwen knows where we are, Mark does, and that he is taking an interest in that bit of news."

Marian rolled her eyes. "We do not, in fact, know that to be the case. However, it seems likely. I will be calling Gwen this afternoon so that we might test that hypothesis."

"Nice to know," said Sid, glancing at me.

Lillian chuckled. "The good news is that we'll have the ever-formidable Barb and Lita with us."

"Oh, good," said Marian. "They're worth five of Dale."

"And we won't have to deal with covering for their children," Lillian said. "Lita's oldest is down with the chicken pox, which means odds are good the rest of them will be getting it, too, so Moishe – he's Barb's husband - said he and Pedro had better stay home just in case."

"I don't understand," I said.

"Barbara Wasserman and Carlita Delgado are the Yellow floater team," Lillian explained. "They took their training trip just a little over a year ago. They've been best friends since they were girls. I think Lita started out in intelligence in the late Seventies. Either way, we got her as a mover in Seventy-Nine. A year later, we realized that we were going to need a second mover in Miami, so she recruited her best friend, Barb. I'm not sure how they survived the attack on their line three years ago."

"They probably were not recognized as the threats they are," grumbled Andrew.

Lillian laughed. "Probably not. Both were married by the time Barb was recruited, and Lita was pregnant with her first. They have five children between them. Their husbands used to have only the vaguest idea that they don't just have a chain of children's clothing stores, but Barb and Lita recruited them and they're the Miami Yellow hub team. The men also stay at home to raise the babies." She smiled at me. "In a different way, they remind me a little of you, Lisa, in that no one would ever guess what they really do."

"I assure you," Marian said, her smile just a touch evil. "You do not wish to cross either of them. Not that I think you will."

"They're why Dale and Adrienne will not be joining us," Lillian said, mischief in her eyes. "I believe I told you that some of us are an acquired taste. Well, let's just say that Dale O'Connor is not going to acquire a taste for Lita and Barb any too soon."

"What happened?" Sid asked.

"Do any of us actually know what it was that Dale said?" Marian asked.

Both Andrew and Lillian shook their heads.

Andrew cleared his throat. "It was, apparently, grossly offensive to Lita, who smashed his face into the table.

When he came after her, Barb stopped him with a frightfully fast kick to his family jewels."

I laughed. "I think I like these women already."

Sid sighed. I was rather good at finding where it hurts on guys, too, much to his dismay.

When I finally got to meet the ladies over lunch in a little restaurant near the famous baths, I did sort of like them. I just was not in good shape to deal with them. They reminded me an awful lot of the women I knew at church, except that there was an edge to their chatter that was utterly absent from my friends.

"Oh, this is so exciting!" said Barb, who had blond curly hair and a full figure on a not very tall frame.

Lita was also short, with black hair and dark eyes, and a few curves. If she smashed Dale's face into a table, then she had a lot more speed and reach than you would have thought to look at her.

"And congratulations!" Lita squealed. "You are so lucky your husband is your partner. My poor Pedro had the worst time until we recruited him and Moishe."

"We have been wanting to meet the two of you since forever," said Barb. "Well, since we heard you are the two who got those schmucks trying to take out our line three years ago. Why would somebody do such a thing?"

Lita rolled her eyes. "It doesn't make any sense, does it? But we're so glad you got them."

"We were so scared we'd be next."

"It was terrifying."

"You did some other takedowns, too. We've heard you're awesome investigators."

"And now you're part of our club!"

"This is, like, terrific!"

Had I been in any other circumstances, it would have been a lot easier to just let their chatter wash over me. I smiled, though, and only Sid really saw how much of a toll it was taking.

I got up from the table. "You know what? I really need a nap." I looked at Marian. "Is there any reason I need to be available?"

She looked at me, clearly wondering. "Shall we see you two at dinner?"

"Yeah. Sounds great."

Sid and I found our car just outside the restaurant and the driver, whose name we didn't know, took us to the drop-off station, a small house on the outskirts of the city.

"What's going on?" Sid asked softly as the car pulled away.

"I need quiet," I said. "I'm sorry. I don't know why. But I feel like if anyone else talks to me, I'm going to smash her face into a table."

Sid nodded.

I suddenly quailed. "I'm not being selfish, am I?"

"Not in the least. In fact, I think I know what's going on."

He didn't say anything more. We spent the rest of the afternoon at the drop-off station. Sid silently brought me my knitting. I went to work on the sweater and felt the knots in my shoulders slowly unwind. There was a phone in the station, and we called Nick at four, but held off leaving until Marian called around six to let us know where everyone was eating dinner.

"She's fine," Sid told Marian because he'd taken the call. "We both just needed a little quiet time." He put his hand over the mouthpiece and looked at me. "You up for dinner, even with Barb and Lita?"

I nodded. "I'll be fine."

"We'll be there…" He listened for Marian's response. "No. Tell them they're okay. Lisa just got a little overwhelmed is all… It's exactly like what I was telling you before. Too many strangers and not enough butts to kick…" He laughed. "Right. We'll see you in an hour."

He hung up. I sniffed.

"She thinks I'm a basket case, doesn't she?"

Sid slid up next to me on the couch where I was sitting. "She's concerned, yes. But more that you're not having a good time."

I winced. "I'm sorry, Sid. I'm just not good at this social thing."

"You're good enough. Let's face it, we've been doing parties and dinners and what not since the middle of last month. It's no wonder you're getting tired of it. I know I am."

"Then why aren't you freaking out?"

Sid laughed. "Because you're beating me to it, and not by that much." He shook his head. "I was ready to smash both Barb and Lita's faces into the table."

"The sad thing is, they are kind of nice."

Sid chuckled. "They are who they are."

I can't say Barb and Lita had completely toned down their chatter, but they were more subdued over dinner. There was a lot about them that I found familiar and comfortable. They talked about their kids. They talked about their business. They talked about their husbands. Then I found something I could talk about, and it was really nice. I could brag about Nick in a way that I couldn't with anybody else.

"He is amazing at tailing people," I said. "Of course, he'll get made doing a solo tail, but it takes the subject a lot longer to spot him."

"How old is he?" Lita asked, sipping on a cola. Or what I'd thought was a cola.

"Thirteen."

Barb's eyes grew wide. "And you're training him?"

"Sure," I said. "He was bound to find out about us when we took custody a year and a half ago, and he did pretty quickly. So, the safest thing to do was teach him how to handle himself."

"Thirteen." Lita shuddered. "That's right on top of the teen years. I am not looking forward to that."

"I like teens." I laughed. "They're way better than toddlers. I remember when my nephew Darby was two. He was horrible."

Sid laughed. "Worse that the twins?"

"My sister's youngest two," I told Barb and Lita. "They were two when I met Sid and he met them. And, yeah, the only reason their terrible twos were worse than Darby's was because there were two of them. Janey wasn't as mouthy, but she was three times as stubborn. Trust me, I am so glad we missed Nick as a toddler." I shuddered. "He is such a handful now, and that's just because he's so curious and hyper. At least we can reason with him. You cannot reason with a toddler."

"But you can contain them," Barb said. "And they're so cute at that age." She sighed. "I wish we could carry pictures."

I snickered. "I don't have to. Nick looks just like his dad, only with glasses and longer hair."

"He is a little charmer," Lillian said. "During the wedding reception, he asked me to dance with him after the little dust up I had with that fellow."

I rolled my eyes. "My Uncle Leonard. He needed that one."

Lillian laughed. "Anyway, your son wanted to know how to do what I'd done. We went out to the garden, and he had me in a headlock in record time."

"That's my boy," I said with a grin. "He learns fast."

"A perfect gentleman about it, too." Lillian sighed. "And yes, I'm glad you are training him. He guessed that I was connected to our espionage operation. He didn't say anything, but I saw the look in his eyes."

Sid and I grinned at each other.

"I am so proud of him," I said, sighing. "I miss my sweet guy."

Lita looked at Sid and me. "Okay, I'm a little confused. The boy is your son, Sid, right? But not Lisa's?"

I glared at her. "He's my son."

"Lisa adopted him," Sid said quickly.

"Oh, duh." Lita hit her forehead with the heel of her hand. "I'm so sorry. Of course, he's your son. It's just how he got that way that had me confused."

I noticed Marian looking at me in speculation. I suspect I had her confused for some reason, but then Sid says I do that to people. [You, my dearest, are a fascinating study in contradictions to those who don't know you. - SEH]

The only trouble was, Sid and I got back to the drop-off station quite late.

"How are you feeling, sweetie?" Sid asked as we got ready for bed.

"Tired, but okay. You?"

"Okay." He looked at me. "How are you feeling about making love?"

"Um. Sure. If you want."

He sighed. "Which means what?"

"I don't know."

"Lisa, you can say no."

"I know. I just don't necessarily want to."

He shook his head. "Are you trying to keep up with me or something?"

"What do you mean, keep up with you?"

"I don't want you to think you have to be some sort of sex goddess for me."

I looked at him with a frown. "You weren't worried about that before."

"No." He frowned. "Things were different. It wasn't about you having to satiate me because we were working around the jeans and the no bodily fluids. Now..." He sighed. "You said you were worried about being enough for me. Honey, I gotta tell you, not only are you enough, you're more than enough. If anything, you're wearing me out."

I blinked. "I'm sorry!"

"No. Don't be. It's been great. It's just that we haven't missed a night since the wedding, and sometimes twice. That's a lot more sex than I've ever gotten."

"But you were out four to six times a week."

"And I struck out a lot. Usually, I only had sex two to three times a week. Yeah, there'd be times when I was going at it pretty heavily. But not like we've been going at it."

He gently ran his fingers through my hair. "Don't get me wrong. I've been loving it. But if you've been going along because you think you need to satisfy my appetite, trust me, it's been satisfied and then some."

"Oh." I winced. "That's good to know." I shrugged. "I guess we can get some sleep then."

We finished undressing, got into bed, and kissed each other goodnight. There was only one problem.

"Sid?" I asked softly. "This doesn't feel right."

"What do you mean?" He lay on his back, staring at the ceiling.

"I want to make love. I mean, I'm tired and if you're too pooped, that's fine, too. It's like I said. I don't need Superman."

"I'm glad. But you know what?" He chuckled. "I was thinking I want to make love, too." He rolled over onto his side and looked at me. "I don't believe it. You are every teen boy's wet dream."

I flushed. "That sounds gross, but what?"

"You're a nymphomaniac."

"I'm not that bad."

Sid laughed and pulled me close to him. "No. You're worse. You're the first person I've ever met who loves sex as much as I do."

"Well, you are really good at it."

"So, are you." He kissed me hard, then looked down at me. "We're not going to say no to each other, are we?"

"I don't think so."

"Oh, well. Who needs sleep anyway?"

Actually, we both did. That next morning, we got a message to Marian that we were going to stay in until lunchtime, then meet everybody to go over whatever plans would be made. Marian had told Gwen exactly where she was going to be shopping, even asking Gwen if she wanted anything from the shop in question, so we had a decent idea of when the attack would come. If it did.

I have to admit, I was in a better frame of mind when we met Barb, Lita, Lillian, Andrew, and Marian at another little restaurant for lunch. Fortunately, Dale wasn't around to try and bully us into seeing things his way. Although the one time his name came up, I got the feeling from Lita that she would have loved another chance to smash his face into a table. The big problem we all had was that we weren't entirely sure who the specific target for the attack was. Sid watched as I took a final pull on my beer (which I enjoyed even though I don't usually like beer), then he sighed.

"As much as I don't like the idea of being set up for target practice," Sid said. "The only people in this group that have been attacked have been Marian, Andrew, Lisa, and me. And Lisa and I are the only people who were attacked independently of anyone else. Why don't we assume all four of us are the targets?"

Marian sighed. "That does make sense."

He shrugged. "Then the next question is, do we want these guys to think we're civilians or do we care?"

"Oh, that opens up quite the can of worms, doesn't it?" Marian groaned.

We went back and forth for some time. After all, Andrew's black belt was well-known, and as Barb and Lita pointed out, self-defense classes were all the rage in the U.S., so there was no reason not to believe that I could handle myself.

"You know," I said slowly. "If we're going to operate on the theory that civilians can do hand-to-hand, then why don't we do the whole scream for help thing? That's what all the experts kept saying to do when I did that article on self-defense for women a couple of years ago."

"It does work." Sid grinned proudly at me. "People almost always underestimate Lisa."

Marian glanced at Lillian, who smiled and nodded. "So, we've been told."

"It works for us, too," Barb said. "You would not believe some of the situations we've gotten out of because somebody thought they'd gotten a civilian by mistake."

"It seems like a rather novel approach," Andrew said. He looked at Marian thoughtfully. "Although perhaps that's why no one seems to suspect us of covert activity. We are, to all appearances, the worst of the rotting aristocracy, slothful and hedonistic."

"That's not how I care to think of us." Marian snorted, then ate a bit of pastry and sighed happily. "We are known for our diplomatic work, as well, I should hope. Well, in certain circles, we are." She sighed. "But Andrew is right. Most people don't know we serve on the diplomatic corps, and that work is primarily entertaining foreign visitors before Mrs. Thatcher gets a hold of them." She sighed. "It is an image which serves us well, I suppose. Now, shall we go on to the shops?"

I must give the attackers credit. They took their time to attack. There were three shops in a row along the tiny side street. Apartment buildings surrounded the shops and filled in the block across the street.

The first shop featured pens and fine writing paper. Our friends didn't quite have to drag Sid and me out of there, but as Marian put it, it was a near thing. Sid got

Lita hooked on fountain pens when he invited her to try a lovely Pelikan with a gray pearlescent barrel.

"Oh my god!" Lita squealed. "Barb, you have got to try this!"

Barb did and squealed, too. Sid bought them each a basic model. Then we added several more pens to our collection, including the one with the gray barrel, and bought several bottles of ink. I also bought a couple more brightly colored fountain pens for Nick, along with the converters that sucked the ink into the barrel rather than using cartridges.

We were expecting the attack to come as we headed for the second shop, which sold wines from the local wine region known as the Rheingau. Marian had asked Gwen Flowers if she'd wanted any of the wines there, so we were expecting something. Nothing happened except that Barb and Lita got Sid back for the fountain pens by introducing us to dry rieslings. Sid and I like riesling, only these were a whole new type of wine. Several bottles got shipped home. There was a touch of reluctance to leave, as we fully expected the attack to occur after we left. Nothing happened.

I tried to go into the third shop, which was a delicatessen, but the others dragged me away, promising more delicious sausages and other meats at a nearby cafe. Barb, Lita, and Lillian took the lead toward the main street ahead. Marian and Andrew walked behind Sid and me. They were the first to be pulled away after we'd crossed an alley. Marian got enough of a chirp out to alert Sid and me.

We turned, and I yelped loudly. Andrew was on the ground, with one man standing over him and holding Marian in a headlock. The other four had knives and ran at Sid and me. We didn't have time to run, so we went into basic defensive postures. Barb and Lita, screaming like banshees, ran up and pounced on two of the men. Sid dodged as his opponent feinted. I twisted, slamming back first into mine, and grabbed his knife hand, bending back his wrist so that he dropped the knife. I elbowed him in the ribs. He backed off a little, and I whipped around. He clocked me in the side of the head, but I bounced back, then whacked him in the nose with the heel of my hand. He dove at me, only to land with my knee hard into his privates. Groaning, he slumped. I turned.

Sid rabbit punched his guy, then looked at me and sighed. Lillian scooped up the knife that my guy had dropped and slowly approached the man holding Marian. This was going to be tricky. The man holding Marian could very easily have snapped her neck, given the hold he had on her. Lita danced around her opponent. How she'd turned up a knife, I'll never know. Barb disarmed her opponent and whacked his head up against the wall. He slid downward. Andrew suddenly kicked the man holding Marian, and she stumbled forward as he let go.

From down the main street, the alternating wail of police sirens approached. The men who could, bolted. Andrew got groggily to his feet.

"We'd best leave, as well," he said, pointing to an alley across the street.

We hurried across and down the dark space. I'm guessing Andrew radioed ahead for our cars because they were there waiting for us. We didn't worry about whose of the two cars was whose. We just got in. I landed with Barb, Lita, and Andrew. Andrew told the driver to go to the drop-off station. That driver radioed the second car, and we were soon sprawled around the living room of the station, comparing notes on our various aches, pains, and cuts. Marian and Lillian were relatively untouched and together assessed who was dealing with what.

Andrew had taken a good knock and had a goose egg forming under his ear. Sid had a small cut on his ribs and bruised hands. Barb's hands weren't in much better shape, and she had a skinned knee. Lita had gotten three cuts, one on her left arm and two more on her ribs, all more scrapes than anything. My head was achy, and my lower back was tight. It hadn't exploded into the bad pain, but it felt like it could at any second.

I stretched and asked if there was an ice pack, then went over to Sid and helped him out of his sweater and shirt.

"Well, this one's ruined," I grumbled, looking at the blood-soaked tear in the white dress shirt. "I just hope I can save the sweater."

"Damn. I hope so. I liked that one." Sid frowned.

It was a blue argyle that I'd made for him, and he had really liked it.

"I'll have to stitch it together right now before I lose any stitches, then see if I can re-weave it when we get home. At least I still have some yarn left from that project."

"Did you knit that?" Barb asked.

"Yeah."

"That is amazing."

I shrugged, rolled my shoulders, then went upstairs to the bedroom where we were sleeping to see what I could use to stabilize the tear before it got any worse. Fortunately, I had my other knitting, and I pulled some yarn from one of the balls and went downstairs.

Not surprisingly, there was a complete first aid kit in the station. I helped Marian and Lillian bandage cuts, then settled onto the couch next to Sid, with the ice pack firmly against my lower back, and went to work on the sweater.

Marian sent the drivers to fetch dinner and drinks for us all - food being the one thing the stations were rather short on. There were several canned dinners and the like for emergencies, but an emergency would be the only reason to eat any of it.

Lillian waved a penlight in front of Andrew's eyes. "Well, they're dilating okay. Any nausea?"

"None," he grumbled, adjusting the ice pack on the place he'd been hit. "Just a miserable headache."

Once the food had arrived, we all staggered into the small dining area and passed plates around, poured shots of icy cold vodka and started eating. Well, Lita pulled a bottle from her purse and doctored some cola.

"Cuban rum," she explained. "It's the best there is."

"Any impressions?" Sid asked, sipping from his shot.

Barb got an evil glint in her eyes, and her voice got low and growly. "Make him an offer he can't refuse."

That's it. I lost it. Even Sid and Lillian laughed, and Lita shrieked hysterically.

"That is positively the worst Godfather impression I have ever seen," said Marian, trying to keep a straight face.

"Alright," said Lillian, getting control of herself. "Some analysis might help right now. How did this go down?"

"Andrew was attacked first," Marian said. "From behind, and the intent certainly seemed to be to immobilize him."

"Our crew is getting smarter about that black belt," Sid said.

"The one just held me," Marian continued, then looked at Sid and me. "However, they went after you two with knives. They didn't really pay attention to the others."

"Which makes no sense," I said. "If they were trying to get rid of Sid and me and took you two down to get at us, why didn't they go after Barb, Lita, and Lillian?"

"I think you just hit on something," Sid said. "They were trying to get rid of us, as in kill us." He looked at Marian and Andrew. "You two, they just knocked out or held."

My mouth fell open. "Which could mean you two are the target of the plot and they think Sid and I are your protection."

"That doesn't make any sense," Marian said. "How would capturing Andrew and me force your government to negotiate?"

Lillian sighed. "That's a good question. Your government isn't any more likely to negotiate with terrorists than ours is."

"Nor has anyone tried to drag us off anywhere," Andrew pointed out. "Although they may not have had much opportunity."

Marian sighed. "At least we have established that Mark Flowers is involved in all of this."

Sid shrugged. "He's obviously letting the terrorists know where you guys are. That Lisa and I've been there each time probably has more to do with you two following us around so closely."

"Hm." Marian glared at a spot across the room. "I'm afraid you're probably right on that one. The question is, how do we separate ourselves?" She sighed. "We leave for Paris tomorrow."

"Mierda," Lita said. "Barb and I have meetings in Milan through Friday."

"That's when we go to Copenhagen." Marian turned thoughtful. "Lillian, would you be willing to take Sid and Lisa through? Andrew and I could certainly find a way to stay in Paris a few more days."

"What about protection?" Lillian asked. "If you two are the target of the plot, no matter how little sense it makes, it might not be a bad thing to have."

Marian sighed. "We'll simply have to draw upon the resources of our extended staff, I suppose. That might throw Flowers off regarding Sid and Lisa. We'd beg off Paris, but we've already committed to meeting Gwen and family tomorrow for dinner, and I'm afraid Gwen is expecting Sid and Lisa to join us."

Sid shook his head. "I'm guessing it's safe to assume that if we're not there, that might be suspicious."

"I fear so," Marian replied.

Sid and I both rolled our eyes.

The others did eventually leave for their hotel, although Barb and Lita wanted to stay at the drop-off station. There was a second bedroom. I think Marian convinced the two that even they would find Sid and me carrying on more embarrassing than they wanted. Okay, Sid and I try to keep it down when necessary. It just doesn't always work.

H onestly? I don't get Paris. I'm not saying there aren't a lot of interesting and cool things there. But there are a lot of similarly cool things in a lot of other places, including several of the cities that Sid and I had just been in. Maybe it's because the first time Sid and I had been there, things were a lot more tense. That had been the summer of 1983, when (assuming we're being honest about it) Sid and I fell in love with each other, but realized we had a major problem with our respective values not meshing. Oh, and we were facing probably having to take on new permanent identities as a married couple when we were nowhere near up for anything close to that.

We took the train from Wiesbaden at a ridiculously early hour. The only good thing was that Sid and I had a compartment to ourselves, and, no surprise, took advantage of it. We really tried to keep the noise down and we didn't get any complaints, so I guess we were okay.

We found the drop-off station on our own and were pleasantly surprised to realize we'd already been there back in '83. Our driver had let us know when and where Marian and the rest of the group would meet us for dinner, but that left us with a few hours of free time, which really wasn't enough to see anything, then get back to the drop-off station in an apartment on the Rue St. Denis in time to change for dinner. Only the driver came back without our luggage and with a message to call Marian at her hotel.

I made the call.

"I'm afraid you'll have to come stay here," Marian said. "Mark Flowers is not only here, the first thing he asked is where you two are staying. So, I told him you're staying here at the hotel. I don't want him anywhere near that station right now, nor do I want you two to ditch a tail in case he's still wondering about you."

"Okay. What did you say about us not arriving at the same time?"

"That you went off to see some sights. Why don't you spend an hour or two running through Montmartre? That's longer than the tour bus will give you and should get you back here soon enough to check in and dress for dinner."

"Okay," I said.

I told Sid what Marian had said, and he shrugged.

"That sounds reasonable enough." He put his tan sport coat back on over his dress shirt and jeans. We made our afternoon call to Nick, then took off.

I had a feeling Sid wasn't that excited about going to see another church, including the gorgeous Sacre Coeur, but he insisted. On the other hand, the surrounding neighborhood with its artists was very interesting. In fact, by the time we got to the hotel and checked in, we had a couple of oil paintings with us. Sid looked at them and shook his head as he put on a suit, and I got out my cocktail dress.

"I hate to say it, Lisa, but I think this art collecting thing may be getting more out of hand than our sex life."

"But they're so gorgeous!"

The two paintings were in fact one landscape split in the middle in a cross between abstract and Impressionism, with lovely purples and pinks on a mottled green background.

"I know. That's why we bought them. The question is, where are we going to hang them? We have a fair amount of wall space, but it's not unlimited."

I sighed. "I know."

Sid kissed my forehead. "We'll figure something out."

Dinner was another extended affair in a private room off the hotel's restaurant. We started in the restaurant's foyer with cocktails and a particularly good pate served canape-style on rounds of good baguette. It turned out there was a bit more of a crowd than I expected. Clint Foster had re-joined us, this time with his wife, Dierdre, in tow. Marge Benson and Hattie Mitchell arrived right after Sid and I did. Dale and Adrienne O'Connor stood talking with another couple that I didn't recognize, while Lillian chatted with Gwen and Mark Flowers. Lady Beatrice watched the room anxiously. Marian and Andrew moved around the room, saying hello to everyone. Dale spotted Sid and me and waved us over. I went reluctantly, expecting yet another round of explaining to Dale that my name was not Hackbirn. Fortunately, Sid found a way around that.

"Well, hello, you two." Dale grinned at Sid and me, then looked at the couple. "Danielle, Liam, our newest members—"

"Sid Hackbirn and Lisa Wycherly," Sid said quickly, offering his hand. "Nice to meet you folks."

Dale looked a little nonplussed. I murmured my hello and shook hands. It turned out Danielle and Liam Connelly were a cover couple who lived in Paris. Danielle was French and Liam was Irish. They joined the travel club through Steve and Ray.

"Have you met them yet?" Danielle asked.

"Not yet," said Sid. "Will they be here tonight?"

Danielle shook her head. "No. They are going to Copenhagen on Friday. I believe they have some business there."

"Are you going to Copenhagen, too?" Sid asked.

"I'm afraid not," Liam said. "We already promised the Flowers we would meet them in Athens this weekend."

We chatted for a couple minutes more, then moved on. Lady Beatrice pulled us aside.

"I need help," she told Sid softly. "I need to get away from Mark."

"I don't understand." Sid glanced at me, puzzled.

"He's a terrible person." Her eyes blinked rapidly. "Worse yet, he's up to something that's going to get both of us in a great deal of trouble, and I don't want any part of that."

Sid smiled reassuringly. "It's not that I don't want to help, Beatrice, but why are you asking us?"

"Oh." She sighed. "I was hoping... I guess not. I'm so sorry to have troubled you."

I put my hand on her arm. "Wait, Beatrice. I don't know what we can do, but maybe we could put you in touch with the American embassy. I mean, if you need asylum or something like that. I'm not sure how it's done, though, and I don't know anybody over there."

"That's quite kind of you. But no." She smiled weakly. "I need other help. Thank you."

She moved away. At that moment, we were shuffled into the private dining room, where two tables were set with the full array of flatware. We had scallops, sizzling in shell plates, chicken bouillon, sole meuniere, filets of beef wrapped in mushrooms and puff pastry, an endive salad, three amazing cheeses, followed by a divine bit of pastry and insanely good coffee. The wines were beyond amazing, including a pink Champagne that made me cry, not to mention what Sid said was a premier cru Bordeaux, which, apparently, was one of the best such wines made.

After dinner, Marian whispered to us that we'd meet for breakfast around eight that morning. Sid whispered back that we had something for her as well. We managed to get to sleep at a reasonable hour and Sid nudged me out of bed around six.

"Why?" I groaned.

"We need to go running," he said.

"Yes, sir."

"Lisa," Sid groaned.

"Sorry."

There was a park across from the hotel and Sid and I were able to do several laps. However, during that first lap, as we came around the bend to the opening to the hotel, I saw someone near a tree who startled me. Sid saw the man with clipped blond hair and ramrod erect posture. We ran past, ignoring him, and he didn't appear to notice us at all. I even looked back, just in case.

"I thought he was dead," Sid gasped softly as we started the next lap.

I shook my head. "It's not quite the same guy. But still..." I stole another look at where the man was leaning against the tree, watching the hotel. "He looks an awful lot like him. I suppose we'll need to talk to Dale about it."

"I suppose so."

We got our full hour of running in, then walked the last half lap to cool down. Somewhat later, dressed in jeans, sweaters, and shirts, we got to the hotel dining room to find Marian already there, eating croissants and drinking coffee at a round table set for four. I asked the waiter for some whole wheat toast and fruit for Sid, then went to the buffet that had been set out and filled my plate with four traditional croissants and a couple chocolate ones.

"The strawberry jam is quite nice," Marian said as I put my plate at a place setting next to her. Sid ambled up with a croissant on a plate and sat on my other side.

"It does look nice." I cut a chunk of butter from the block in front of me and spooned some jam onto my plate.

The waiter came and offered Sid and me coffee and we both said yes. I found some cream and roughly lumped sugar on the table and doctored my cup.

"Where's Andrew?" Sid asked.

"Talking with the police in Wiesbaden," Marian said, lightly buttering a bit of croissant. "Oh, these are divine."

"About the other day?" Sid placed a tiny bit of butter on his croissant and nibbled. "Oh my god. These are good."

"I got your toast and fruit," I told him, then buttered and jammed one of my plain croissants. It was heavenly.

He smiled at me. "Thanks." Then he turned to Marian. "Won't the police be suspicious if Andrew talks to them?"

"Well, he is speaking with whomever is the head of that department." Marian chuckled. "Thanks to our diplomatic immunity, there isn't much they could charge us with, even if we had been the attackers. But it would have taken forever for them to figure it out and probably gotten quite nasty in the process. It may be a bit of a cliche, but if one must deal with the police in Germany, it's easier to do it from a distance."

"So, what did you want to talk to us about?" Sid looked at her.

"Actually, I wanted to find out why Lady Beatrice was talking to you last evening. She looked quite unhappy."

"That." Sid looked at me and shook his head as I started in on my second croissant. "She told us she needed help. That she wanted to leave Mark. Apparently, he's up to something."

"Well, we know that much." Marian looked at us. "But why would she ask you two for help?"

Sid shrugged, then looked at me. "That's what we asked her. She said something about hoping, then Lisa said we could help her get in touch with the American embassy, while pointing out that we don't know anybody there."

"Which we don't," I said.

"Anyway," said Sid. "She said thanks, but she needed some other kind of help."

"I wonder if she was testing you to see if you're operatives." Marian glared at the rest of her croissant.

"Possibly," said Sid. "But there's no way of knowing."

Marian sighed. "I'm afraid not."

"We also have something for Dale." Sid looked around the dining room. The waiter came by with a bowl of fruit and some wheat toast. I pointed at Sid.

"He should be here any minute, and without Adrienne. She seldom eats in the morning."

I had eaten one of the chocolate croissants and was buttering the third plain one when Dale ambled up to the table with two hunks of baguette on his plate. He saw the fruit in front of Sid.

"Where'd you get that?" Dale demanded.

"Apparently, all you have to do is ask." Sid ate a bite of whole wheat toast.

Dale waved down a waiter, demanded some fruit, then Sid asked politely for a glass of prune juice.

"There's somebody out in that park across the street watching the hotel." Sid looked at Dale. "Somebody who looks an awful lot like a friend of yours."

Dale cursed. "I thought I saw him yesterday."

"Oh?" Marian asked, her eyebrows lifted.

Lillian came up, her plate filled with croissants. "Is there room for me?"

"Of course," I said. I got up and fetched another place setting from a table behind us and placed a chair between myself and Marian. Sid shifted over to make room for me. Dale stayed put.

Marian glared at Dale. "Dale was just about to tell us that he saw someone yesterday."

"I said I thought I saw someone." Dale paused as the waiter returned with his fruit and the prune juice for Sid. "Turns out these two also saw him. When, I don't know."

"When we were out running this morning," said Sid. "For a minute there, I thought we were looking at Karl Mittman."

"Mittman?" Lillian's eyebrows rose. "Wasn't he your aide?"

"Yeah." Dale shoveled fruit into his mouth and talked around it. "Mittman died when his plane blew up in

Catalina last summer. The man you saw was Rudy Meisner, his older half-brother. He seems to have popped up on the fringes of this plot, which was why I was so sure Sid and Lisa were the targets."

"Does he blame us for his brother dying?" I asked.

"As far as I know, he's never heard of you two," Dale said. "Mittman hadn't had any contact with him, probably because Rudy was in the wind again. They didn't particularly like each other, although Rudy set Karl up for that weapons plot."

"How do you mean?" Sid asked.

"It's Rudy's style. He foments trouble, but rarely causes it directly." Dale shook his head. "He's had it in for my butt for a long time." Dale glared at Marian. "And, no, I am not being paranoid, and this isn't just about me." Dale chewed thoughtfully for a moment. "Meisner got his nose bent out of shape when I first ran for congress. He offered me a sizable donation from the American Nazi Party, which, no surprise, I turned down flat."

"How badly did you need the money?" Lillian asked.

"It doesn't matter." Dale shook his head. "It was a public donation. If people had found out I was taking money from that group, my goose would have been cooked. Meisner promised to hide the source, but truth be told, I didn't want their money, anyway. Give me all the crap you want. I do have my ethics." Dale sighed. "I'm not sure how Meisner did it, but he set up his half-brother Karl to apply as an aide in my district office, then later, set him up for that weapons deal. You all know that I was one of the suspects in that case. That was Meisner's work."

"So, you've made your point," Marian said. "But that still does not explain why or how he is involved in this current plot with the Croatians. Or why he would be after Sid and Lisa."

Dale shuddered. "The guy is a classic psychotic narcissist. As in, he has a god complex a mile wide. According to our best intel, in the past year alone, he has been talking with the Irish Republican Army, the Palestinians and the Egyptians, several of the Soviet republics, Afghanis, North Koreans, the Saudis, Iranians, Iraqis, and all the different Yugoslavian ethnic groups. Anywhere he thinks U.S. interests are at stake, he's there trying to stir up trouble. I also know that he's talked with Mark Flowers on any number of occasions. So, my guess is that he's the mastermind behind the plot and far enough away from it to come out smelling like a rose."

Marian glared at him. "And when, exactly, were you going to share this critical little tidbit with the rest of us?"

"When I got confirmation on it." Dale snarled. "Which I got this morning when Sid and Lisa also spotted him."

"That still doesn't explain why Lisa and I would be the targets of this plot." Sid glared at Dale.

Dale rolled his eyes. "Lisa's parents? My constituents? If I fail to negotiate with the Croatians that makes me look really bad back at home. Meisner wants me out of office and in the worst possible light. Believe me, that arms thing last summer was hardly the first time he's tried to make me look bad."

"The problem is," said Marian. "The plot has been in the works since early January."

"Exactly," said Sid. "We didn't know we were coming here for sure until the middle of that month. Also, how would this Meisner have known we were coming?"

"He wouldn't have." Dale rolled his eyes again. "But he would have been watching me, seen me get friendly with two people he doesn't know, then do some checking. It's not that hard to find these things out, especially if you're friends with, say, Mark Flowers."

Marian frowned. "Gwen knew fairly early on that we had two new club members, and she did have your names. It seems a bit of a stretch, but it is possible."

"Nonetheless," Lillian said. "When that attack occurred in Wiesbaden, it seemed pretty clear that the attackers wanted to do away with Sid and Lisa."

"And there was that attack in Gstaad, too," I pointed out, then flushed as the others looked at me. Okay, it was the first time I'd said anything since the discussion started. "Both Sid and I thought the men were trying to take us out rather than capture us."

"Bugger!" Marian's eyes flashed with annoyance. "She's absolutely right."

"On the other hand," said Sid. "If you and Andrew are the actual targets and Lisa and I are viewed as potential protection, then the attacks make sense."

Marian rolled her eyes. "Which is what we determined the other night. But what could they hope to achieve by capturing us?"

Dale slapped the table. "Embarrassing the U.S. by not negotiating on their friend's behalf."

"You know," Lillian said. "That makes sense. Whether or not those negotiations would really happen is another issue."

Marian sighed. "So, now what do we do? Is it worth letting it happen? And how do we protect Sid and Lisa's cover in the meantime?"

"Splitting up would probably help," Sid said. "Maybe not while we're in Paris."

"You could do the usual bus tour," Lillian said. "That would be expected of a pair of tourists and it's early enough we can get you on a decent one."

Marian groaned. "We'll have to get you back in time to change for dinner. Alas, Gwen has scheduled yet another one tonight."

Lillian nodded. "I think we can set up the tour." Her eyes lit up. "In fact, I'll go with you two. There's a tour that hits most of the major sites and allows some time for shopping. They should be meeting..." She checked her watch. "In another half hour. Are you two ready?"

I sighed. "Do I have time to go upstairs and get my purse and the camera?"

"Just barely." Lillian grinned. "Go."

I ran. As to whether Marian and Andrew were going to let themselves be captured by the Croatians, Sid and I were not part of that discussion, and frankly, I was glad we weren't.

The tour, on the other hand, was a blast. Sid and I had been on a similar tour when we'd been in Paris in 1983, but there was something about this one. We saw all the major sites, including Notre Dame and the Louvre. The tour guide ran us through the Louvre so fast Sid didn't have time to count a single brushstroke, although it lasted long enough for me to fall in love with the huge painting of the crowning of Josephine by Napoleon, by somebody David, I think. We saw the Mona Lisa behind glass and from afar. We also saw Venus de Milo and Winged Victory. Sid was glad that we didn't have time to go up to the top of the Eiffel tower.

We got back to the hotel just as the sun was beginning to set. Sid hurried to our private bath to do his second shave. I went to the armoire in the room to get my cocktail dress. I opened the double doors to the dress section and a pair of sightless eyes appeared to look straight at me. A moment later, cold, dead flesh fell on top of me.

I know I screamed. It was generally remarked upon how loudly I had screamed. I don't remember much past that. Just coming to consciousness in another room - Marian and Andrew's it turned out - sitting on the edge of a bed with Sid's arms around me. My stomach heaved - I somehow knew it was not for the first time that afternoon - and I spilled what was left of my guts into a waste can that Sid put in front of my face.

"Oh, lord," I groaned.

"It's okay, lover." Sid's voice was soft and calming. "I'm right here."

"It was a stiff."

"Yes." He handed me a glass of water.

I sipped gingerly. "I thought I was getting better about those."

"Seeing them, yeah. This was full body contact with one."

My stomach turned, and I reached for the waste can again. Too bad there was nothing to bring up. I gagged for several minutes, then my throat loosened up.

"Whose body?" I finally asked.

"Lady Beatrice."

"What? Why?"

"That we do not know yet, but there are several theories floating around." Sid began rubbing my back, starting in a circular pattern, and working his way out.

"Marian hates me, doesn't she?"

"She's a little worried. But she knows what you can do. She has no reason to be. The good news is that no one, but no one, is going to think we're operatives."

I whimpered. "I'm sorry."

"It's all to the better, lover."

Marian and Lillian were both surprised that I had reacted so badly to Lady Beatrice's body falling on me. I winced as Sid explained that I had a little phobia of stiffs.

"It was the business that did it to her," Sid growled at them. "Lisa's been working through it and doing reasonably well. This was the first actual body contact we've had since she started the work."

"Still..." Lillian began.

"Look," Sid snarled. "She has managed when I haven't been around. Or have you forgotten the Wisconsin case?"

Lillian looked at Marian and shrugged. Frankly, I hadn't handled the Wisconsin stiff all that well, but since I was supposed to be a civilian, it had worked out. This time it seemed to have worked out, too. Sid was right. Nobody was going to think I was a hardened operative after upchucking multiple times while crying hysterically. Since Sid had been focused on taking care of me, he'd gotten cover as well. I could only thank God for that.

That night's dinner was canceled, no surprise there. I got a perfectly lovely tray in our room, then had to call for a second one an hour later. Sid smiled, both appalled by my appetite and glad to see it returning.

As if having a stiff fall on me wasn't bad enough. Or maybe it was why. It was a really bad night, thanks to having my blood-stained nightmare multiple times. Then the next morning, as I got dressed, a heavy wool blanket of depression enveloped me. Yes, I should have recognized it. It's not like I don't get these moods every so often. But it's the perverse nature of the mood that I never really see it for what it is.

The other weird part of it is that I make an extra special effort to hide what I'm feeling. So, it was not surprising that Sid didn't really see what was going on as we got on the plane for Copenhagen that morning. It was also early and I'm not a morning person. Nevertheless, once we were in the air, I found it hard to sleep. Sid snoozed away. My mind flashed back to a summer right before my sophomore year of college.

(July, 1977)

"Mae, this film is amazing!" I grinned.

Mae rolled her eyes. "I know. I've heard. Big deal."

"Oh, come on. We haven't gone to a movie together in forever."

"Yeah, well, I have other things to worry about than movies."

"But it's Star Wars. I swear you have never seen anything like it. It is so awesome."

"I understand, Lisa."

"But you want to see this in a theater. It's mind-blowing."

"I don't have time."

"I'll go get the tickets and stand in line all afternoon. You just have to show up around six or so."

"And who's going to watch Darby and Janey?"

"Maybe Neil? You know, their father? He'll be home by five. He always is."

"And Neil is tired after working all day. It's not fair to dump the kids on him."

"How much you want to bet he wants to spend some time with them?"

Mae sighed deeply. "Lisa, one of these days, you are going to have to realize that I have to put my husband and children first."

"But it's just going out to a movie and a pretty awesome one at that!"

"It's only a movie. Neil and the kids are more important."

"One night is going to mess that up?"

"It's my family, Lisa. They are more important."

On the plane, I sighed deeply. It had always been Neil and the kids first with Mae. Mama had taught me the same thing. Now, I had Sid and Nick to think about. I hoped I wasn't being too selfish.

We got settled into the drop-off station, a nice apartment in a modern building, before noon and in plenty of time to meet Steve Parsons and Ray Spinoza at a nearby cafe for lunch. Truth be told, the guys were great. They were based in New York and had plenty to say about co-ordinating with the Company, none of it good. They'd been a couple forever, and the floater team for the Green line almost as long, and I realized I'd seen Ray a few times before.

Sid seemed up for touring with the two for the rest of the afternoon, and I agreed, even though I wasn't feeling all that excited by it. That's when Sid looked at me funny and said that we'd try to catch up with the guys for dinner. It was either that or we'd call their hotel to meet the next morning.

Steve and Ray weren't quite sure what to make of it, but they took one look at me and realized that something wasn't right. I felt horrible.

Sid took me back to the drop-off station.

"I'm sorry," I said as he shut the door on the apartment done in lovely lavenders and white.

"Why?"

"It's my fault we're here and not touring Copenhagen?"

He shut his eyes, then opened them. "Sweetie, A- I think I know a blue funk when I see one and B- you're completely deferring to me again, which is not normal even when you don't have a blue funk going on."

"I'm sorry."

"I know you are. That's the problem. Lisa, why are you acting this way?"

"What way?"

"The deference thing. You're not happy, and while I know some of that is your funk, some of it isn't. You were acting this way yesterday, even before the stiff. In fact, you've been playing the nice little wife ever since London."

The nice little wife. I almost cursed.

"I'm not playing," I said, sinking onto the purple Danish modern couch in the front room. "I'm trying to be."

"What?"

"I'm acting married," I groaned.

"I don't understand."

"Of course you don't!" I snapped. "You haven't been force-fed messages all your life about what being a good wife means. It's everything that I was afraid of."

"Huh?" Sid looked at me and then the light suddenly dawned on him. "Ah. Husband and kids first, right?"

"Yeah. I didn't even realize I was doing it."

He sighed. "We get to define what being married means to us."

"But you haven't been indoctrinated from the cradle. You haven't been taught relentlessly to defer to your spouse, to be the nice Kate, conformable with other household Kates. You don't have to deal with an entire culture out there determined to mold you into a nice little wife. I have. That's all I've heard my entire life. Be nice. Be quiet. Don't let the guys know how smart you are. Give them what they want. Submit to your husband. And you are my husband!"

"I've been your husband, more or less, for almost a year now. Maybe not officially."

"Well, now, it's official." I looked away, trying not to cry. "Seriously, Sid. I don't know what switch got flipped in my brain, but it did. I don't want to be this way. I really don't. But it's like I can't help it. And the worst of it is, I do love you. I love you so much, all I want is for you to be happy. It's just that I keep thinking that what I've been told all my life is what will make you happy, and that's what I should be doing."

"Even if it doesn't." Sid's face was a little pained.

I took a deep breath. "I've told you about primary socialization. All those early lessons. They are really, really hard to get past. It's you and believing in God. You just can't because that's what you learned as a kid."

"I also learned that marriage was a crock and got past that."

I frowned. "But when you talk about being married, for you, it's about sharing a bed, mingling our assets, raising our kid, and sharing toiletries."

"And you said the same things."

"Okay!" I yelped. "I did. But I think even then, I knew it was more than that. At least, for me, it's about being a good wife. You know. That stupid commercial from the Seventies. 'My wife, she does all these wonderful things. I think I'll keep her.' Women's Lib, my ass. I'm the one who's supposed to be taking care of you, taking care of everyone within reach. If I get to take care of myself, I'm being selfish."

"But you're not. You're taking care of yourself so you can take care of me and Nick. And I take care of myself so that I can take care of you and Nick." He pulled me close. "I think I get it. You're right. There are a lot of messages out there about what it means to be a woman in our culture. Maybe I'm not as tuned into them as you are, but I do understand that they're there. And as long as I've known you, Lisa, you've been fighting them. Why is it so hard for you to fight them now?"

"I don't know." I took a deep breath. "Maybe I didn't realize I was giving in to the messages. It was the thing about wanting to make you happy."

Sid chuckled. "You know, we've been using that as a metaphor for sexual activity."

I laughed also. "There is more to it than that."

"I got that much." He stroked my hair. "So, if I am hearing what you're saying, you've been unconsciously playing into the stereotypes and cultural expectations."

"Yeah." I could feel the tension draining from me. "That's it exactly. I didn't even realize I was doing it." I swallowed. "It's pretty hard not to."

"You've only had it drilled into your head since you were a kid. That doesn't mean you have to give in to it."

"I know."

"Then let me stand with you. You know I don't want that kind of wife. I want you. Stubborn, feisty, giving me hell you."

I looked at him. "Really?"

"Okay, giving me hell sucks, but it's better than when you defer to me. I really hate that."

"Why?"

"Because I want you to be happy, too. And when you do the deference thing, you are not happy. And that sucks worse than anything."

I laid my forehead against his. "You are an incredible man."

"And you are an incredible woman."

He kissed me so softly. I wasn't entirely sure I was over the whole deference thing, but now that I knew what was happening, it would be easier to fight it. We both knew the martyr thing was not going to work, and I had been trying to be the martyr.

"Alright," I said, finally. "So, now what?"

Sid squeezed me. "We need to re-connect with Steve and Ray."

"Yeah. We should. I don't want them to think I don't like them." I paused. "Mostly because I do like them and there's no reason to hurt their feelings."

So, Sid called their hotel, and we met up with them at a cafe near The Little Mermaid statue.

"We just had some expectations to work out," Sid explained to them. "It's the whole newly married thing."

Steve sighed loudly. "I totally get it." He was a tallish man with a bit of a gut and receding blond hair. "I only wish we could."

"We are married in spirit," said Ray. Ray was medium-sized, wore wire-rimmed glasses, and had dark hair liberally sprinkled with gray.

"I wish you could, too." I sighed looking at them.

"You okay?" Sid asked.

"Just thinking about Rick," I said. I looked at the guys. "A friend of mine who wanted to marry his boyfriend. It was just so sad because Rick got AIDS and died last year. Then Rick's family got ugly when Rick left everything to Dave. Fortunately, Rick's lawyer had made sure everything was as airtight as it could be, but if they'd been married, there wouldn't have been half the trouble defending the will."

Steve and Ray both shuddered.

"That's happened to so many friends of ours," Ray said. "It was bad before AIDS. A couple friends of ours had been together over twenty years, but when Lonny got cancer, his family swooped in and cut Dennis out completely. Dennis couldn't be there when Lonny finally died, even though Lonny wanted him there. Then Dennis went through hell during probate. It's just gotten worse since AIDS started killing everyone off."

"Thank God we've been together for the past ten years!" Steve blinked and grabbed Ray's hand. "And we've been faithful. That's the only thing that has saved our asses."

"I'm afraid so," said Ray. "We've lost so many friends. It's been hell."

"Oh. My god!" Steve yelped suddenly. "I totally forgot to tell you. Lillian said that she'd meet us for dinner. She said they got some information from the Wiesbaden police?"

"Good," said Sid.

"And Dale is not going to be here," Steve continued. "He has a little problem with us."

"Oh, I'm so shocked," I said, rolling my eyes.

"Who wouldn't be?" Steve said. "And Barb and Lita are coming, too. Love those girls!"

I laughed. "So do we. This is going to be fun."

"Really?" Sid looked at me, grinning.

I shrugged. "I've been having a little problem with group socializing. I don't do well with parties and lots of strangers."

Ray grinned. "Then I am really glad we've been able to do this just the four of us. I know exactly what you're talking about. One of the reasons Steve and I volunteered to meet you two here in Copenhagen is that most of the rest of that crew don't want to come up here. I hate crowds. I love Marian and Andrew, but some of those crowds they pull together. Oy!"

We went back to the hotel and dinner there. Lillian was there waiting for us in the dining room, where a smorgasbord had been set up. Sid sighed when he saw it and my eyes lighting up. We were just getting settled when happy cries announced that Barb and Lita had arrived.

"Happy birthday!" Lita crowed, setting a gaily wrapped box next to me.

My jaw dropped. "Is today the twenty-first?"

"Yes, dearest." Sid laughed and put another package in front of me.

Lillian pulled two other packages from the shopping bag she'd had hanging from her chair, and Steve and Ray also had a box for me.

"Thank you," I gasped. "I'd completely lost track of what day it was."

"Marian and Andrew wanted to celebrate last night in Paris," Lillian said, her eyes twinkling. "But Sid convinced them that you'd be happier with a much smaller celebration."

"Just as well, the way things turned out." I sighed.

Lillian nodded. "Let's get some food and then we'll talk about all of that after we've eaten."

Okay. The way my plate ended up piled high was a little embarrassing, but I wanted to try everything. I was halfway through when Sid looked at Lillian.

"Steve said you had something for us from the Wiesbaden police?" he asked.

"Yes." Lillian winced a little. "They had found those fellows that we'd left behind, and they were definitely Croatians. They were turned loose on the theory that someone had attacked them."

"That would make sense," I said. "What about Beatrice?"

"Lady Beatrice?" Barb asked. "What happened?"

Lillian watched me carefully. "Are you sure you're up to talking about that?"

"Of course." I shrugged and ate some salad.

"Very well." Lillian glared at her food as if her stomach wasn't doing very well, then told the others what had happened the day before.

"What did the police say?" Sid asked.

"Not much of anything." Lillian frowned. "She was strangled. Given what she told the two of you the night before, it's entirely possible Mark Flowers did it. However, he made up some cock and bull story about masked men and the gendarmes bought it. Mark couldn't say how his wife's body ended up in your hotel room. However, he wasn't as entirely distraught as one would think and seemed pretty interested in your reaction, Lisa."

I flushed and sighed. "I guess it worked out, then."

"We knew it would," said Sid, patting my hand.

"Have any of you been followed today?" Lillian asked us.

Steve and Ray looked at each other.

"Nope," said Ray. "It's been nice and quiet."

"Lita? Barb?"

They both shook their heads. Lillian went on to brief the others on Rudy Meisner as I got up to get some more food.

"We've been keeping an eye out for anything related to Meisner for a few years now," Steve was telling Lillian. "Like you asked us to."

"Rudy is one scary boy," Ray said. "He'd've overthrown the U.S. government by now if those White supremacists were better organized and less paranoid."

"Well, Dale pointed him out to me as I left just after noon." Lillian shrugged. "He was still watching the hotel from that park. Thank goodness that Marian and Andrew had left out the back."

"Left?" Sid asked. "Where are they going?"

"They have a villa near Athens," Lillian said. "They decided to retreat and regroup until we get there on Sunday."

There wasn't much more to be said after that. I had cleaned my plate a second time, and most of us got up to select desserts. Sid just had some coffee. He doesn't really like sweets that much and worries about his weight. I just ate and was glad when no one decided to sing Happy Birthday. The presents were nice. Barb and Lita had brought a small gilt and pink jewelry box that they said came from Florence (which was not that far from Milan, where they'd been). Steve and Ray got me a nice edition of fairy tales by Hans Christian Andersen. Somehow, Marian and Andrew had found a whole stash of antique rosewood knitting needles and sent them. Lillian apparently had been collecting knitting magazines from everywhere we'd gone. Those were in the original languages, but I was able to figure out at least some of the patterns. She'd also found some German sewing magazines that had sewing patterns on folded sheets in the middle, but the magazines had been translated into English.

I opened Sid's package last. It was a little music box in an Eighteenth-Century style, with polished dark blue rounded sides and gilt ornamentation. When I opened the lid, which had a little miniature of lords and ladies being pastoral, I recognized the tune and flushed. Sid smiled his hot little smile, which did not help at all. He knew I'd heard him singing in the shower or tub after all.

I laughed. "So, I get grand opera?"

"Oh, definitely." Sid purred like one of our cats.

Steve snorted. "I don't who's making me hotter. Her or him. And I don't go for her."

"I don't think we have Need to Know on the rest," Lillian said, her face getting red.

"Sorry, Lillian," Lita said, laughing. "I want to know."

Sid chuckled. "Sounds better than it is. It's just a little joke between us with several years of context behind it."

His eyes never left mine, and no one was surprised when the two of us left shortly after that. Back at the drop-off station, we entered the code into the door panel, verified that the place was empty, then hurried inside. Sid slammed the door shut. I set the packages and my purse down and then our clothes went flying all over the place.

Sometime later, I awoke on the couch. The lights were still on. Sid was still on top of me, his head laying on my shoulder. He was quiet, but not yet awake. Then I heard it again. A light beeping sound.

Sid lifted his head. "What's that?"

The door to the apartment opened.

"What the hell?" The man had olive-toned skin, dark hair, and a medium build.

"Code?" Sid got up.

I realized I was in my birthday suit in front of a total stranger and yelped. Sid tossed his shirt at me. I put it on as fast as I could.

"Zulu Whisky Alpha two four four one. You?"

"Lima Golf Romeo seven six eight two." Sid remained standing and watching the new arrival.

"Why the hell aren't you guys in the back?" the man asked, obviously annoyed.

"We got a little carried away," said Sid, glancing back at me. "Long story. We're here as couriers. Any reason you need to hide what you've got?"

"Nah. I guess not. It's going to Dragon, fifty-three-Quebec." As in Lillian. "I hear she's in town."

He held up a nine by twelve envelope. Okay, given that we were in Europe, it probably wasn't nine inches by twelve inches, but the metric equivalent. Sid walked over and took it.

"You want one of the bedrooms?" he asked the man.

"I want out of here." The man went for the door, shaking his head.

Sid shrugged, then looked at me. "You okay?"

"Yeah." I swallowed, then began picking up clothes.

"Well, the way we go at it, it's bound to happen." He bent and picked up my deck shoes. "At least we weren't still doing it."

"Oh, my god. You're not going to stop if someone does, are you?" I felt my face going hot.

"Why?" He looked at me, genuinely puzzled. "I mean, I get the privacy thing. But why ruin a perfectly good—"

"Sid! I hate it when you use that word for what we do."

He shrugged. "Fair enough. Still, you get what I'm saying, don't you? We try to see to it we don't get caught, but if we do, no point in ruining things."

I took a deep breath. "I don't know if I'm up to that."

"We'll see what happens, then." He smiled softly, rolled his shoulders and stretched his neck, then blinked. "Damn. I fell asleep with my contacts in. I'd better get them out right away."

He grabbed the bundle of our clothes, and I followed him into the bedroom. We were up again about two and a half hours later when the phone rang. Sid picked it up, then said we'd be dressed within a half hour.

"What?"

"They're coming over here with breakfast. Lillian got the call about the drop we got."

"Oh."

When the others arrived, Sid was dressed but wearing his glasses since his eyes were a little sore after sleeping in his lenses. They are the soft lenses that you're supposed to be able to sleep in, but it doesn't usually work out that way. It was weird that he was wearing his glasses, though. He hates how he looks in them, even if he still looks pretty good.

I was brushing my hair out and getting my usual light makeup on. And dealing with the aftermath of my blue mood from the day before. Cramps and a messy period.

Sid and I wore jeans and sweaters again. It had been somewhat warmer in Paris, but Copenhagen was downright chilly.

Real Danish pastries, brown bread and butter, and several coffee cups filled the table in the tiny eating area. Lita and Barb were already in the living room, sitting on the couch with their plates in their laps and cups of coffee in front of them on the light pine coffee table. Steve sat in between them, also eating, but grinning at me and Sid. Lillian sat demurely in a Fifties wingback chair that also held the hiding place. Her coffee cup was next to the table lamp that had a bottom that unscrewed. She had the envelope that we'd received and was reading the contents and shaking her head. Ray and Sid stood next to the eating table and chatted.

I filled a plate with pastries, then grabbed one of the small wooden chairs from the eating area and dragged it around to the living room. Then I went back to the table and doctored some coffee and brought the cup back to the living room. Steve got an evil glint in his eye, then started humming the tune from the music box as he held up my panties from the day before. I turned a darker purple than the couch. Lillian glared at Steve as Ray rolled his eyes. Sid laughed and grabbed the underwear and put it in his pocket.

"I'm afraid we've got some bad news," Lillian announced. She held up a sheet of paper from the envelope. "This is a dossier on Mark Flowers and his family. Now, Gwen and Mark went back to the UK with Beatrice's body yesterday. Gwen is distraught, having lost her connection to the gentry through Beatrice, who was the daughter of a duke. Mark appears to be simply doing what is expected. Nonetheless, going over their holdings, it appears that Mark owns, among other properties, an ancient monastery north of Volos, Greece."

"How close is that to Athens?" I asked, trying not to wince at the pain in my gut.

"Close enough to be of significant concern." Lillian glared at the paper. "My first task will be to contact Marian and Andrew with this bit of news. The problem is, there are several such structures in that region. The cliffs in that area made it quite attractive for the contemplative set. The trick will be finding the right one."

Sid frowned. "Is it possible that somebody else on our side checked Flowers' place out, perhaps sometime last month?"

"Why do you ask?" Lillian looked puzzled.

"Another unprocessed drop," Sid said. "Honey, do you still have those photos in your purse?"

"I'll bet I do." I found my purse next to the door. I pulled the photos out. "Here they are. And here's that code you were trying to break."

I found my roll of strapping tape, cut a bit off it, and taped the bit around the purse handle. Sid's eyebrow rose. He had probably figured what I'd be dealing with that day, but I had just confirmed it.

Lillian took the photo with the code on it. "Oh, damn. This is definitely a Company special. Those idiots. They set up a code, then can't even write it accurately."

"That does make it harder to break," said Lita.

"And impossible to understand when it needs to be." Lillian shook her head. "Well, the location is definite-ly north of Volos." She compared the code sheet to the dossier. "It makes sense. According to the dossier, the monastery had been converted to a bed-and-breakfast inn that failed spectacularly. So Mark swooped in and bought it. That's rather typical of him. He's lost untold amounts of money that way."

"Which may be why he's working with Meisner and the Croatians," Barb said. "He needs the cash."

"He may, indeed," said Lillian, frowning over the code photo and the dossier. Finally, she shook her head. "The first thing to do will be to warn Marian and Andrew. Then we should think about finding that monastery."

Barb grabbed the photos and looked at them. "Lita, you want to rent a boat and do some recon?"

"Sure." Lita giggled. "Hey, we got those monokinis. You want to freak Moishe and Pedro out with some tanned boobs?"

Barb rolled her eyes. "Since when will anything you and I do freak those two out?"

"Too true." Lita sighed. "But we have to keep trying. We don't want them getting lazy."

"No, we don't."

Lillian sighed deeply. I was beginning to think she was just a touch on the prudish side.

Steve got the photos from Barb. "How fast do you think you can get a firm location? Ray? I think we can do some work from the ground on the joint. What do you think?"

"Sounds like fun," said Ray.

I was beginning to feel a little left out. "So, what can Sid and I do?"

Lillian looked apologetically at us. "Not much right now."

We watched with Lillian as the other four went over getting to Athens, and from there, Volos, and how to communicate with each other. They, naturally, had their wireless radio equipment. I felt pretty annoyed that Sid and I didn't.

"We'll get you some equipment," Lillian said softly as the other four left the drop-off station.

"I hope so," I grumbled.

"Are you alright?" Lillian looked at me carefully.

"Cramps." I sighed. "I get them every now and then."

"Perhaps you should be lying down."

I shook my head. "It doesn't do any good. It's actually better if I have something to do." I sighed. "Now what?"

"I need to make a phone call." Lillian said.

Only she couldn't get an answer from whatever number she'd been dialing.

"It doesn't mean anything," she told Sid and me.

So, we went out and wandered the city. We ate lunch. We walked around some more. Sid and I waited until six to call Nick because it was Saturday, and we didn't want to wake him too early. He chattered on about Josh and a couple other boys and how they were going to the beach that day to practice skateboarding stunts. My heart stopped.

"Nick, when did you start skateboarding?" I asked.

"When I was a little kid. Well, Mom would never let me have one." Nick's first mom was an emergency room doctor, and I could well imagine she didn't want her child riding a skateboard. "But Josh and I have been riding and Stella bought me one."

I rolled my eyes. Stella tended to spoil Nick.

"Well, be careful, will you? Seriously. I do not want to be dealing with broken bones, or worse."

"Mom!"

"You worry about us."

Nick's groan was utterly defeated and defiant in the same breath. It only got worse for him when his father got on the line. The only thing that saved Nick was that he had been wearing a helmet and pads.

Lillian was on pins and needles as well.

"I haven't been able to get an answer all day," she complained. "I've called Quimby. He's in Athens, though not with them. He should be radioing me with an answer soon."

We went to dinner at a restaurant that simply served meals and did not have a smorgasbord set up. The food was great, but the tension made things less than enjoyable. We were finishing up when Lillian shifted and pulled a small powder compact out of her purse. She flipped it open and adjusted an unseen earpiece in her left ear.

"Yes?" She paused as whoever was contacting her spoke. "I see... Have you contacted Congressman O'Connor...? That would be the first thing. Please tell him we have recon going on Flowers' holding... We'll be in Athens tomorrow. Can you arrange for lunch for us at the drop-off station? That will make things easier... Thank you. We appreciate it."

Lillian looked almost ashen as she closed the compact.

"Well?" Sid asked.

"It appears that the Croatians have gotten Marian and Andrew. Quimby says that there are signs of a struggle at their villa and neither of them is to be found. It looks as though it just happened this morning, so that may be why there's no news of the kidnapping yet."

"So, what do we do?" he asked.

Lillian shook her head. "Go to Athens tomorrow. I'll see to contacting the other four."

Both Sid and I hate enforced inactivity, but there was no help for it. We went back to the drop-off station and tried to get some sleep.

T he news was not good when we got to Athens. We'd flown in with Lillian and were met at the airport by Dale O'Connor and Clint Foster.

"The Croatians haven't made any demands yet," Dale told us as we headed out of the airport. "But they definitely have their Lord and Ladyship."

"We're just not sure where they have them," Clint said.

"What about that monastery near Volos?" Lillian asked.

Clint snorted. "We checked that back in January. It was empty and no signs of improvements. The place was a mess."

"That doesn't mean they haven't fixed it up in the meantime," Lillian said. "Flowers does own the place. Do we have any intel on his movements?"

Clint and Dale looked at each other guiltily.

"Not yet." Dale shrugged. "He's not at his apartment, but that doesn't mean he's not staying with his mother. She's not receiving or talking to anyone, so who knows if he's there or not? No one has seen him, for what that's worth."

We went straight to the drop-off station, which was just outside of Athens, itself. It was a white-plaster villa that looked a little run down, but probably wasn't. Blue and other decorated tiles adorned the walls, and the for-get-me-nots were featured in a mosaic on the wall of the living room. Dale glared at Lillian as Clint paced.

"What assets do we have from CID or MI-6?" Lillian finally asked.

Both Dale and Clint looked at each other, and Clint rolled his eyes.

"For crying out loud, Lillian." Dale glared at her. "They have to keep the same low profile we would if Marian and Andrew were our people. No negotiation. Period."

The eight-day clock on the wall ticked loudly in the taut silence.

"Look," Clint said. "We've got to keep this as quiet as possible. Yugoslavia is a frickin' powder keg about to go off. We might prevent that if we can find a way to release tensions slowly. What these Croatians are doing will only pour gasoline on the fire. The good news is that we've got cover on the communications hub for the group's base back in Croatia. They haven't heard from the group here in Greece. Not sure why they haven't, but we should be able to crash the system if they attempt to go public with the news. We're monitoring radio traffic along the coast and have reason to believe they know we are."

"What reason?" Lillian asked.

"The team here sent out a message on Friday that they'd arrived and were told to get their part of the operation done and to stay off the radio. We're not sure how the team in Greece is going to confirm that they have their target. The hub in Croatia hasn't gotten any phone calls, either."

Lunch arrived then, but Lillian sent Sid and me to go find some other drinks besides the tea and bring it back. I felt really annoyed, but the truth of it was, Sid and I were in the junior position.

Sid and I found a taverna and bought a couple bottles of ouzo and some white wines from Santorini. If anyone else back at the drop-off station noticed that we'd gone, we couldn't tell.

Steve and Ray arrived just after three o'clock.

"Gotta love those girls," Steve crowed. He slapped the photos that Sid and I had gotten onto the table in the small dining room. "They're here, alright. Ray and I will show you the vantage points in a minute. But we have visuals on Marian and Andrew. And Mark Flowers and Rudy Meisner, no less. Rudy split pretty quickly and through the front door, which Ray and I just happened to be watching."

Ray sighed. "The tactical problem is that we have quite a few Croatians in the building. It would take days to establish how many, exactly, but there must be over ten of them. Our best shot at extraction will be through the back. Barb and Lita have radioed in that there is a back door. In fact, it's right here in the photo. They're waiting for dark to check it out."

Clint glared at the two men. "And how do you know for sure that our targets are there?"

"Our own two eyes aren't good enough for you?" Steve growled. "I think we know what Marian and Andrew look like. The Croatians brought them up to the roof of the place and we saw them."

Clint snorted, clearly defeated.

Sid looked at the photos thoughtfully. "So, we're basically talking about a break-in and extraction, right?"

Ray mused. "Basically. The only problems are we don't have a floor plan, we have an occupied building, and two people to be removed."

Sid chuckled. "A walk in the park."

"I wouldn't go that far," I grumbled.

"We need more intel," Dale insisted, getting up and pacing again.

Ray checked his watch. "We should have that in a few more hours. In the meantime, let's get some food. I am craving some dolmades right about now."

Sid and Ray went back to the taverna we'd found earlier and came back with even more food, another bottle of ouzo and two more bottles of the Santorini wine.

The alcohol didn't help. The tension remained high as the hours ticked by. Finally, just after midnight, Lita and Barb showed up.

"There's a way in," Barb announced. "The tough part will be getting out. Look, we can't even think about crashing that site until after dark tomorrow. Can we table strategy until tomorrow morning? I'm beat."

The good thing about a drop-off site is that one can accommodate a surprising number of people. Lillian dragged Clint and Dale to whatever hotel. Barb and Lita took over one bedroom. Sid and I had one. Steve and Ray made themselves comfortable in the living room. Sid and I tried to keep it down, but when we woke up the next morning, Steve was loudly singing the tune from the music box, and Barb and Lita cornered me to ask what it was that Sid did that was so amazing. I wish I could have told them. I did suggest they ask Sid, though.

Clint, Dale, and Lillian arrived before nine and came with a host of breads, fruit, and tea for breakfast. They also had the news that a squad of Special Forces soldiers were standing by to storm the monastery and hopefully capture both Meisner and Flowers.

"The one thing we don't want is a hostage stand-off," Dale said. "Which means we have to get Marian and Andrew extracted before the Special Forces guys go in."

Lillian looked at Sid and me. "You are the better break-in artists here."

Sid looked at me. "I believe that we still have some of the right clothes and other equipment with us from when we broke into the Flowers' place in London."

"True," I said, gazing at the photos on the table.

"Here's what we got on the site," Barb said.

She and Lita had done their work well. They had solid estimates on the size of the monastery, especially the distance from the roof to the rocky beach below. The big problem was the back door. Based on Ray and Steve's observations, the front of the place was closely guarded and watched. While the guards did watch the seaside facing part of the place, they didn't seem to think that it was that vulnerable. The back door, which Sid and I had seen in the photos, had a bolt drawn across it with an odd sort of padlock on it. Lita had unlocked it, nonetheless. I'm not sure how, but when she described what she'd done, it made sense to Sid, so I left it at that.

The problem with that door, however, was that it couldn't easily be opened from the inside.

"Even if the outside bolt is drawn," Barb told us. "You can't really push it. I tried. There's some sort of latch that keeps it closed, but I have no idea where the latch is. It may be an electronic one or it may be something else. But it can't be felt and if you use a flashlight, you'll be seen. It's pitch black down there."

"So, how do we get out?" Dale asked.

Lita sighed. "Sid and Lisa will just have to make it real quick. Barb and I can be outside, and we'll hear you. I heard Barb. There's also off the roof if you can figure out a way to get down."

"Getting down won't be a problem," I said, as Sid grimaced.

"The roof might be a better option than the back door, anyway," he said with a sigh. "Ostensibly, it's a dead-end. If we're spotted, they'll head right for the downstairs doors, but they won't be as quick to check the roof. We'll just need some climbing gear. Plus, weapons and transmitters and receivers. And lock picks. I gave Quimby's back to him."

Dale sighed. "We'll get it."

"Do we have any idea where they're being held?" I asked.

Barb sighed. "I saw a light at the end of the hall when I was down there." She drew a T on a piece of paper on the table. "This is the hall to the door. There are stairs up to the left, and another hall winding away to the right. I saw one door in that direction that looked pretty fresh, but then I heard someone coming and got out of there."

"If we keep it clean, we should be able to get in and out pretty quickly," Dale said.

Sid glared at him. "Who said you're coming with us? The more people we have, the better the odds we'll get spotted, and that's the last thing we want."

"He's right, Dale," Lillian said. "You and I will bring them in by boat." She looked over the photos. "Can we get some external coverage on the rooftop? I'm thinking covering the front door won't help much."

"Sure," said Ray. "We get set up here, here, and here. Steve and I can each take one. We're good at the sniper thing. Who wants the third position?"

"I'll take it," grumbled Clint.

"Barb and I will go in with Sid and Lisa to the door and then cover there," said Lita.

I was making a list of everything I would need if we had to take the rooftop.

"We'll also need flashlights," said Sid. "Or do we want to try night vision goggles?"

"Maybe, but I doubt it." Barb shook her head. "From what we saw from the outside, the place looks pretty well lit, so you'll have to be able to get them on and off really quickly."

"I'd rather stay masked, too," I said. "We don't need Meisner possibly recognizing us."

"You're right." Sid sighed. "Flashlights it is then."

There wasn't much else to do after that. Lillian took Dale to get the equipment and supplies. We all met at the taverna outside the drop-off station, with Sid and I wearing our break-in pants and carrying our sweatshirts, masks, and gloves. After eating lunch, Sid and I went with Dale, Lillian, Barb, and Lita to the boat Dale had gotten for us. Once out of the small harbor, Dale cranked up the engine and the Greek coastline sped by. I went over our equipment and got most of it packed into the black daypack I'd requested. Sid agreed to take the rope and extra gloves for Marian and Andrew should they need them.

Barb and Lita had also brought a huge picnic basket of food, not that I was in the mood to eat much. Lillian had radioed a message to Henry to call Nick and let him know we were alright but were in a place where we wouldn't be able to call home before he went to school that morning. I didn't think it would stop Nick from worrying, but it was better than no call at all.

Dale throttled the boat engine just before we got to the inlet, and we cruised past the monastery. Sid and I got some high-powered binoculars and looked at the place from where we were in the cabin. It looked as formidable as it had in the photos, but I had scaled a few cliffs that were worse. Dale stopped the boat in the next inlet just as the sun finally set. We needed to wait until after midnight to get there. The six of us played poker in the cabin. Dale didn't have much of a poker face, which surprised me, but didn't stop me from cleaning him and everyone else out.

Finally, Dale looked up. "Zero-fifteen."

I glanced at the clock on the cabin wall. Fifteen minutes after midnight. As Dale fired up the boat's engine and got us headed toward the monastery, Sid and I pulled up our shirts and put on our transmitters and receivers underneath. We made one last check on the equipment, slid on back waistband holsters, then added the magnum .45 automatics. After getting on his sweatshirt and zipping it up, Sid crossed the hank of rope across his chest. Barb and Lita had the shore boat inflated and in the water.

"Is that thing going to hold six people?" Sid asked.

"It's supposed to hold eight," Lillian said.

Sid and I helped paddle, and we were on the gravel beach in short order.

Lita and Barb took over on the door. It opened silently, which told Sid and me that it had been installed recently, although we'd all figured that out. As we shut it, Sid asked me to cover him. He went over the doorjamb with a flashlight as quickly as he could.

"There's the latch," he whispered, pointing to a small switch near the side of the door that opened. He switched the flashlight off, then felt for it. "Alright. Good."

"Green Back in position," said Ray's voice in my ear.

I looked at Sid. He'd heard them, too.

"Kelly Green in position." Steve's voice answered.

"Company One in position," Clint grumbled.

Barb chuckled. "Red team is in the building. Yellow team is in place."

"Alright, everybody," Dale said from the boat. "Hold positions. Red team, move."

We were already moving. As Barb had said, there was a lighted hallway at the end of the pitch-black hall we were in. Once there, we paused and waited for any sound of movement. There was none, so we slid toward where Barb had seen the fresh door. The room was unlocked. Sid opened the door, and I slid in first, my .45 already drawn. I usually go first since I'm the better shot. The room was dark and empty. We shut the door silently and moved around a bend in the hall. There were several rooms along the hall that had been lit by flickering bare bulbs, but the wood on those doors was crumbling. Another unlocked, fresh wood door led into another empty room. The hall emptied into a second faintly lit hall. Sid spotted the fresh wood door down the way and waved me along.

This door was locked. We heard chain clink on the inside. Sid grabbed the lock picks out of his pants and went to work, getting the lock open within a minute. He slid in first, since we doubted that there was a threat on the other side. I shut the door behind me so that Sid could use the flashlight. Marian and Andrew had been manacled to the wall with a heavy black chain. They lay in a pile of straw, asleep, curled up next to each other. As Sid went to work on the first padlock, Marian sleepily sat up and gasped. I stayed near the door, listening for movement outside. Andrew woke also, just in time for the chain to drop from Marian's waist.

"What time is it?" Marian whispered.

"Oh-one-hundred-twelve," said Dale's voice in my ear.

"Quarter after one," Sid whispered.

"They come by on the half hour," she hissed.

The chains clinked as Andrew was freed.

"Let's go, then." Sid looked up at me, then back at Marian. "What's protocol for the check?"

"This hour of the night, they just stop and wiggle the door handle."

Sid cursed softly. I nodded and opened the door and slid through.

"Clear," I hissed.

Sid pushed Marian and Andrew out, then went to work on the lock to re-lock it. A minute later, we were hurrying down the hall in the direction we'd come from, Sid in the lead, Marian and Andrew behind him, then me following. Sid and I had our guns drawn and ready. We hadn't even reached the first hall crossing when Sid pulled us up short. The man turned the corner and Sid put a bullet in his leg. The gunfire echoed so loudly it hurt my ears.

It also alerted some of the others in the monastery. We could hear steps pounding down the hall to the back door. Marian pointed down across that hall to the other side and we ran in that direction. As Barb had suggested, the place was lit up. We got up a stone stairway without being spotted, then ducked into a room just before several of the Croatians ran past.

"Roof?" Sid asked Marian and Andrew.

"Can we get down?" Andrew asked.

Sid held up the huge hank of rope. Andrew pointed to another stairway, and we ran up. Fortunately, most of the Croatians thought we were headed down to the back door, at least, the ones we saw were headed in that direction. We landed in a square stairwell and scrambled up two more stone staircases. At the top of the second one was a rickety wooden staircase with a Croatian man at the bottom looking up. Sid slid up and knocked him out and slid him under the wooden stairs. A door opened at the top of the stairs. I could see the night sky just beyond it and Mark Flowers step onto the wooden landing at the top.

He spotted us immediately and reached behind to what had to be a back holster. I put a hole in his shoulder, and he crumpled. The gunfire echoed again, and we had to assume that it would alert others. We scrambled up the stairs as fast as we could. As Sid reached the top, Flowers struggled to his feet. Sid knocked him backward and hurried to the door. I slid to the open side and Sid nodded and opened it.

Behind us, Mark dangled off the landing with one hand.

"Good riddance, you miserable wife-beater," Marian said.

She stepped on Flowers' hand, and he fell, screaming until his body bounced down the stairwell. Choking back the bile, I slid onto the roof.

"Clear," I hissed, and the others followed me outside. The moon was just short of being full and we were far enough away from any urban area that the stars crowded the night sky. I couldn't see our sniper back up, but they saw us.

"Yellow team," Ray's voice sounded in my ear. "Red team and targets are on the roof and preparing for descent."

I had the daypack off and pulled two crampons out while looking for the best place to anchor them. I found one in a seam between two squared off stones and another at the base of the wall surrounding the roof. Sid unwound the rope and gave the extra gloves to Marian and Andrew. I felt the bullet pass over me before I heard the gunfire. It had to have come from the cliffs above us.

"Damn it, that was close!" I hissed.

"Hold fire, Company One," Ray said.

More shots rang out from the cliffs and whoever had been trying to get out the roof door wisely retreated for the moment. I fed the end of the rope through the crampons, then knotted the end into a loop.

"Andrew, you're going first," I told him in a low voice. "You're the heaviest, and it will be easier with the three of us to hold you."

Andrew nodded. He hung on and was lowered in surprisingly good time. The second the rope was loose, Sid and I worked hand over hand to haul it up. I sent Sid down next, trying not to notice that more gunfire was coming from below, as well as from our snipers.

"Damn it, Company One!" Lita yelled into her transmitter. "You almost hit Andrew. Let us take them down here."

The rope loosened, and I hauled it up as fast as I could with Marian helping.

"You're next," I told her.

"How are you getting down?"

"I'll rappel. I've done it before."

Shaking her head, Marian went over to the side. The second the rope was loose, I fed the end on the roof through the crampons and got into my harness. Somehow, a Croatian had escaped the sniper fire and came at me. I whipped out the automatic and caught him in the shoulder, then slid the rope through the harness and tossed the rest over the side.

"Little Red," said Sid's voice in my ear. "I have both ends."

"Starting descent," I said. Another bullet whizzed over my head, this time from the doorway, and I went over the wall. The nice thing about rappelling is that it's really fast. I was on the ground in less than a minute and got out of my harness. Sid yanked the rope down on top of us.

The six of us scrambled for the raft as Dale's voice told the Special Forces guys that the hostages were clear and to commence entry. Our snipers kept the Croatians away from the roof edge until it became obvious that the Croatians had bigger problems down below. All six of us paddled back to the boat and got back on board safely and smoothly. There was a fair amount of cheering on the boat as Dale gunned the engine and pointed us south. The most gratifying part, however, was when I took off my mask and Marian gaped.

"What?" Sid asked, pulling off his mask and straightening his hair.

"You two?" Marian asked. "But Lisa..."

"Is only frightened by crowds of people she doesn't know and stiffs," said Sid. "We're all scared of something."

I smiled at him. He doesn't like heights and going down the side of that monastery had been hard on him.

We all met in Volos a little later at a small hotel there and had a party with plenty of ouzo and pats on the back. As Ray pointed out, since we usually worked by ourselves, it was an exceptional treat to be able to celebrate together. The only downside was the news that Meisner had apparently escaped, but then, we were not surprised by that. They did get eleven Croatians and recovered Flowers' body. We were still awake by the time dawn broke, and Marian and Andrew put Sid and me on a Lear jet at a nearby airfield.

"Enjoy your time off," Andrew said. "It will be quite private."

"What are you two going to do?"

Marian smiled. "Apparently, the Croatians made their ransom demand last evening, so we're going to back to our villa to show up and ask what are they talking about? We've been here all along." She looked at me and smiled even more deeply. "I'm not sure I understand you, dear, but I am glad that I hadn't misjudged you after all."

I shrugged. "Marian, I'm all those things you saw. Shy, afraid, and intense when I need to be."

She cocked her head. "That's what makes you interesting. Well, have a good time relaxing and a safe trip home."

Sid and I landed in Nice, in a lovely vacation home on the top of a hill overlooking the city. Andrew had explained this was one of their luxury rentals and it included a staff to clean up after us and then disappear when we wanted to be alone. We slept most of that morning and were quite happy to find that the luggage had arrived when we finally got up in time for a lovely lunch of bouillabaisse and dry pink wine from the region.

It took a little convincing from Sid, but he got me out on the private terrace for another experiment. You see, I get sunburned a lot and Sid wanted to help me get a real tan. It's just that Sid doesn't believe in tan lines. It was really relaxing, though, laying outside even in the raw, with Sid rubbing lotion all over me and then getting it all over himself as we made love.

Our second, and last night, there, we went to the casinos in Monte Carlo and gambled and stayed up pretty much all night. The staff had assured us that we could change clothes before getting on the Lear jet before dawn and that Sid's dinner jacket and pants and my cocktail dress would be sent to us.

That house in Beverly Hills had never looked so good as I pulled up in my truck. Sid and I had gone from the airport to the garage in the San Fernando Valley to get our own cars and put them back in the garage. Sid had just barely beaten me there and had the garage door open. Stella's rental car was gone, however, and that was fine with me. We'd told Nick the day before that we'd be home that Thursday, but didn't know when.

I checked my watch. Nick wouldn't be home for another hour or so. Sid and I brought our luggage upstairs to our room to find a note from Stella that she had something she was looking into but would be back at the house by dinnertime. Downstairs, Conchetta pulled together a nice chicken salad for our lunch and said that she'd have dinner ready at the usual time.

Motley was ecstatic and a little whiny. Long John Silver glared at Sid as if she had felt deprived by the lack of his lap those few weeks. Fritz was outside and probably wouldn't come in until dinnertime. I went to unpack, and Blueberry opened one eye from where she was curled up on the dresser, then went back to sleep.

I had just gone downstairs when I heard the shout from outside the front and a minute later, Nick bounded into the house and into my arms. Laughing, Sid came out of the office and got tackled next.

I do not know how Sid found the energy to play the organ at Holy Thursday mass that night, but he did. Although, when we weren't at church doing the Good Friday and the Easter Vigil services, we pretty much laid around the house, writing thank-you notes for the wedding presents, sorting out packages from Europe, and telling Nick and Stella a little about what we'd been doing and had seen.

Sy showed up Friday afternoon. Stella got him from the airport and the two went off on several errands. Stella wasn't saying what, though. Sid and I were too tired to care. Easter Sunday, the O'Malleys came to celebrate. My parents called from Tahoe, too. Presents were distributed and Sid and I had to talk a little about the Travel Club and how nice it had been.

It was fairly late when the O'Malleys left and Sy and Stella decided to spend the night at a hotel before flying out to New York the next morning. Finally, we had the house to ourselves. As Sid and I tucked Nick into bed that night, I told him the plan Sid and I had come up with on the plane home.

"You're off school this week, so your dad and I want to take advantage of that and have a little family honeymoon," I said.

"Cool," said Nick.

"Yeah," said Sid. "As Lisa and I traveled these past few weeks, we discovered that we needed to spend some time together figuring out who we were as a legally married couple. Now that we three are legally a family, we want to spend some time with you to figure that out as well."

So, we did. We went skiing, biking along the beach, hiking in the Santa Monica mountains, playing board games. We went out to Pasadena to celebrate Ellen's eighth birthday on April first, but other than that, it was just the three of us. Which got me into trouble Thursday night.

Nick got an invite to go to the movies with Josh the next afternoon and I said absolutely not. Sid pulled me away into the office before Nick and I could start yelling at each other.

"Why not?" Sid asked.

"You know why not. This week is important for us."

"I know." Sid glared at me. "But did you have to unilaterally say no? You couldn't have at least asked me?"

"I thought we'd agreed, just us."

"Yes, we did, but that doesn't mean you had to go and make the decision all by yourself. We could have conferenced on it."

"We didn't need to."

"Maybe we did!" Sid's eyes flashed. "I thought the idea of this family thing was that we work as a unit."

"But this isn't the sort of thing that Nick gets to make a choice on. It was something we decided because it's important."

"It's one afternoon, and the issue is that we discuss these things, not just make decisions."

"But I thought we had discussed this." I blinked back tears. "I didn't think there were going to be exceptions."

Sid rolled his eyes. "Okay. You're right about that part, but it would have been nice to be consulted."

"I'm sorry. I should have." I sighed. "It's just that this time is the most important thing in the world to me right now." I looked at him. "Sid, I wouldn't have believed that my commitment to you and to Nick could have gotten any stronger, but it has."

"Yeah." Sid looked thoughtful. "It has for me, too. Which is why you said no, and why I wanted to be consulted."

"And I guess that's what being married really is. At least, for us." I leaned my backside on my desk.

Sid took a deep breath. "And it's going to take time for us to figure it out."

"And when we do, it will change." I looked at him. "But that's the commitment, right?"

"Right." He gathered me into his arms and leaned his forehead against mine. "So this is going to be our life now."

"Yeah. I'm really looking forward to it." I smiled, then kissed him softly. "Let's go get Nick."

Topic of the Day: What Else???, cont.

That family honeymoon we did was so great. Yeah, we were doing a lot of fun things, but it wasn't about what we were doing, but being together that was so important. I remember Mom and Dad getting into a fight that Thursday night. Funny thing is, I don't remember what it was about. We talked a lot about being a family that week, and what that meant, and how it might be something different for us, as opposed to other families. It wasn't just the side business, although that did make things really different. It was also who we were as people.

And now, it's yours and my turn to do the same, to build our little family, then figure it out again when and if a kid comes, then figure it out again as the kid grows up and moves away. I'm so excited and I can't wait.

With all my love, Nick.

Coming Soon

Book eleven in the Operation Quickline series, **Silence in the Tortured Soul**.

When no one can see the cry for help

Undercover operatives Sid Hackbirn and Lisa Wycherly face many of the usual problems of newlywed parents, including raising their son, Nick, a pre-teen dealing with a pack of girls chasing him and an exploding appetite. But they also get a more ticklish job than usual - protecting one of the engineers working on a satellite with some new capabilities. What makes it ticklish is that the engineer is Sid and Lisa's good friend Esther Nguyen, and not only do they need to protect her from anti-nuke protesters and even the KGB, Sid and Lisa need to draft Esther and her almost husband Frank into the ultra top-secret Operation Quickline, and then train them.

Add Sid's aunt suddenly moving to Los Angeles, that their good friend's wife is dying, and a host of parents who can't deal with Sid, Lisa, and Nick all having different last names, and it's no wonder Lisa finds adjusting to being a wife and mother harder than she imagined. No matter how much she loves the two guys in her life.

Thank You for Reading

I do hope you enjoyed the book.

If you can do me one small favor, please. Can you go to one of the social media/retail profiles below and leave a short review? It doesn't need to be a lot, just honest.

amazon.com/This-Forward-Operation-Quickline-Book-ebook/dp/B0CLSY3N98

facebook.com/RobinGoodfellowEnt

pinterest.com/AnneLouiseBannon/

bookbub.com/books/from-this-day-forward-by-anne-louise-bannon

goodreads.com/book/show/200690348-from-this-day-forward?from_search=true&from_srp=true&qid=DE3OcjAuIz&rank=1

Other books by Anne Louise Bannon

I'm so glad you liked this book! Check out my other novels, available in print or ebook at your favorite retailer:

Old Los Angeles Series:

Death of the Zanjero

Death of the City Marshal

Death of the Chinese Field Hands

Death of an Heiress

Death of the Drunkard

Operation Quickline Series:

That Old Cloak and Dagger Routine

Stopleak

Deceptive Appearances

Fugue in a Minor Key

Sad Lisa

These Hallowed Halls

My Sweet Lisa

A Little Family Business

Just Because You're Paranoid

From This Day Forward

Freddie and Kathy Series:

Fascinating Rhythm

Bring Into Bondage

The Last Witnesses

Blood Red

Daria Barnes:

Rage Issues

Mrs. Sperling:

A Nose for a Niedeman

Brenda Finnegan:

Tyger, Tyger

Romantic Fiction:

White House Rhapsody, Book One and Two

Fantasy and Science Fiction:

A Ring for a Second Chance

But World Enough and Time

Time Enough
And I would be honored if you left a review for this and
any of my books on the below sites. It really helps.

BB bookbub.com/profile/anne-louise-bannon

g goodreads.com/author/show/513383.Anne_Louise
_Bannon

f facebook.com/RobinGoodfellowEnt/

amazon.com/stores/author/B00JCRXST2?ingress
a =0&visitId=bfadb491-d1ac-4575-84da-bb4f7d325a
d9&store_ref=ap_rdr&ref_=ap_rdr

pinterest.com/AnneLouiseBannon

Connect with Anne Louise Bannon

Thank you for sticking it out this long! Please join my newsletter. It's the best way to stay up-to-date on my upcoming projects, blog posts and even the occasional game and giveaway.

You can sign up for the Robin Goodfellow Newsletter here: http://eepurl.com/zH0Ab or by visiting my website, annelouisebannon.com

And don't forget to connect with me on your favorite social media platforms:

BB bookbub.com/profile/anne-louise-bannon

g goodreads.com/author/show/513383.Anne_Louise_Bannon

f facebook.com/RobinGoodfellowEnt/

a amazon.com/stores/author/B00JCRXST2?ingress=0&visitId=bfadb491-d1ac-4575-84da-bb4f7d325ad9&store_ref=ap_rdr&ref_=ap_rdr

P pinterest.com/AnneLouiseBannon

About Anne Louise Bannon

Anne Louise Bannon is an author and journalist who wrote her first novel at age 15. Her journalistic work has appeared in Ladies' Home Journal, the Los Angeles Times, Wines and Vines, and in newspapers across the country. She was a TV critic for over 10 years, founded the YourFamilyViewer blog, and created the OddBallGrape.com wine education blog with her husband, Michael Holland. She is the co-author of Howdunit: Book of Poisons, with Serita Stevens, as well as author of the Freddie and Kathy mystery series, set in the 1920s, the Old Los Angeles series, set in 1870, and the Operation Quickline series, plus several stand alones. She and her husband live in Southern California with an assortment of critters.

www.ingramcontent.com/pod-product-compliance
Lightning Source LLC
Chambersburg PA
CBHW071210210726